Desert Rose

Carol Hill

CHill Publications 2014

Published by
CHill Publications

DESERT ROSE
© 2014 by Carol Hill.

Printed in the United States of America.
Library Info

ISBN: 0615948642
ISBN 13: 9780615948645
Library of Congress Control Number: 2014900436
CHill Publications, Yazoo City, MS

*"… so that they may take hold of
the life that is truly life."*

(1 Timothy 6:19b)

For Scott, who listened to countless versions of this story
and provided excellent commentary and ideas.
You are truly my partner in so many ways.

And for my three dear friends,
Kathryn, Wendy and Marie,
who read and offered wise counsel and
priceless editing to this work. Thank you;
your encouragement and insights
enabled me to see this through.

. . . Let the one who hears say, "Come!"
Let the one who is thirsty come;
and let the one who wishes take
the free gift of the water of life.

(Revelation 22:17b)

Introduction

My COUNTRY IS *being torn apart by war. For several nights now, the countryside has been lit up like a fireworks display, and the sound of heavy artillery is getting closer. I sit in my window and watch, wondering how much longer we can stay here before the fighting consumes our city, our neighborhood, and then our home. We ran once before—when I was eight years old. An entire decade has passed, but the fighting continues, fueled by anger and hate, eating everything in its path like a giant monster that chews up buildings and spits them out. Piles of rubble have replaced the beautiful buildings of Al Cazar—my country, my home.*

The sun faded into darkness and a smoky haze settled over the city. The distant blasts grew further and further apart until the sounds subsided altogether. The eerie mist of heavy gun-smoke hung in the air, muffling any sound. The exhausted city fell asleep, wrapped in its heavy, gray cloak.

Somewhere in the heart of Anazir, a single truck roared to life and slowly made its way through the deserted streets. Curfew had been instituted with a deadly force several years ago; the people knew better than to venture into the dark. But tonight, soldiers—worn down by the fierce battles of the past few months—dozed at their posts, lulled to sleep by the calm that had finally claimed the night.

Rolling at a steady pace now, the truck passed several guard posts unnoticed. An earth-shattering event was unfolding without even a hint

Carol Hill

of resistance. Rebel forces had planned for at least one glitch, °but they never would have hoped for the success their mission seemed to be having tonight. Along the route several resistance workers made their call, whispering enthusiastically that the truck had indeed passed their marker. With every call, they were 5 kilometers closer to *the target.*

⊷⊨◉ ◉⊨⊶

Sitting in the dark cellar, Dahlia closed her journal and leaned her head against the cool, damp wall. The nights this time of year were unbearable—with dry, hot winds blowing in from the Sahara. Scorching during the day, it became impossible to breath at night in the suffocating heat. Even the desert night air couldn't beat off the heavy, hot winds out of north Africa.

Her mind traveled back ten years to a happier place—their summer home overlooking the Amerian Sea. Waves shimmered in the fading light, crashing on the rocks far below their house. The terrace jutted out over the water, and it seemed like she could walk straight out the double French doors and into the ocean. As a little girl, she would play along the shore in the sandy cove that was their private beach. Each afternoon, extravagant meals were laid out on the terrace, and all the important dignitaries vacationing there would settle around the table amidst luxurious linens and fresh-cut flowers. Dahlia would sit upon her father's knee in her pretty little sundress until one of the men said something that sounded like serious business. With a kiss and a pat, her father would send her down to the beach to play with the women and children who were their guests. She always longed to sit and listen to what the men talked about in hushed, deep tones, but over the years, they became more and more secretive in their discussions. When the city of Lamirya—their beautiful coastal retreat—was destroyed under rebel fire, her family had fled back to Anazir, the capital city, for good. No more were the afternoons collecting shells on the beach or the long, lazy meals around the big table on the terrace. The men she had known all her life now met in her father's study behind closed doors, and only late at night when the rest of the city's people were locked inside their homes, forbidden to go out into the streets.

Dahlia opened her eyes and looked over the bottles of olive oil that lined the cellar walls. She remembered walking hand-in-hand with her father through their olive grove the day he told her he was going to become the leader of their country. He had been so happy, and there was a gleam in his eye that had been contagious. Strong men were drawn to him, and they had become her father's loyal supporters over the years.

Proud of the powerful position he held, Dahlia was saddened nonetheless by the violence that had come with her father's reign. There hadn't been a peaceful year in the decade and a half that he had held his position as leader of their country. Her mother, once a strong and influential woman, had become a fragile shell—weakened by the stress of living under a hostile public eye. It had been hard on all of them, and Dahlia sometimes hated the weakness she saw growing in her mother. She didn't stand up for anything anymore; she had faded into the shadow of her husband. Dahlia wondered if her father preferred it so.

Dahlia herself had been exposed to the best instruction available, sitting under the private tutelage of several prominent professors. She had a growing desire to follow in her father's footsteps, to eventually take a position of leadership and do what she could to make their volatile world a better place, but her professors gently guided her away from her political studies with a firmness that she was growing impatient with. Their country was being brought to its knees with insurgence, and time was running out if there was to be any hope for Al Cazar.

Opening her journal again, Dahlia began to outline a plan for reconstructing control of the nation. There had to be a way to bring the people to reason. Wasn't everyone ready for peace?

A blinding light exploded above her; the ground quaked and for one long moment, Dahlia wondered if the world was coming to an end. In the darkness that followed, she found herself lying on the floor under the heavy oak table with a warm, thick fluid gushing down her face. She lay still, afraid to move, unsure of how badly she was hurt. When there was no pain in the moments that followed, she sat up and listened for any sign of life around her. The night was as quiet and still as it had been a moment before the explosion. She crawled up the steps, afraid she might faint if she stood. A soft light shone through several cracks in the door. Terrified of what she might find, she gripped the doorknob with trembling hands and leaned against the frame for a minute. Turning the knob slowly, she pushed, then leaned the entire weight of her body against the door. Unable to open it, she slid down onto the doorstep and began to cry. Hours passed, in which she faintly recalled thinking that she must be trapped behind fallen debris. Other thoughts fought to enter her mind in hazy moments of consciousness, but she didn't seem to have the strength to face the one foreboding idea that lurked in the recesses of her mind.

⇥◉ ◉⇤

When she finally heard footsteps crunching across the kitchen floor, she called out in a desperate whisper, "Momma!" The steps quickened, scuffled at the door and she cried out again in a breathless sob. There was no response, but the weight that held her prisoner was pulled away from the door and she suddenly found herself looking up at a man she had never seen before. He had a salt and pepper beard and reminded her of Gustavo—the old gardener her father employed to manage the palace grounds. Reaching out her hand to him, she found the strength to rise. He guided her into the maid's quarters and helped her onto the bed.

"Rest here," he said, then left the room. For what seemed like an eternity, she heard loud scuffling and hushed whispers that sounded urgent and upset. Then, she awoke to another new face—a handsome one, one that seemed concerned and a little confused.

"Who are you?" the young man asked.

"I live here... My name is Dahlia," she said. Feeling much better now, she sat up and saw that the sun was beginning to make its colorful ascent. Her thoughts began to clear in the cool morning air, and she began to realize that something was terribly, terribly wrong. With the shock of the explosion now worn away, the one screaming thought that surfaced was for the well-being of her parents.

As he watched her eyes grow wide in realization, he looked away and drew in a deep breath.

"They're gone," he said. They were simple words, easy to understand, but she stared at him in terrified confusion. "They were killed in the blast." He stood and backed away; he hadn't come here to comfort a mourning child.

A fresh wave of shock laid Dahlia flat on her back and she squeezed her burning eyes tightly shut. Hot tears found their way out and silently poured down her temples. When she was sure she was alone again, she curled up into a tight ball on the bed.

Hours passed, and the heat of another scorching afternoon forced her to stretch out for some relief. She stood and opened the window; even the hot winds would feel better than the stifling heat in the room. Looking down at the garden, she saw that rubble had crushed most of the beautiful plants; the concrete-eating monster had finally found her home, had chewed it up and spit it out.

The mirror behind the dresser caught her eye and Dahlia remembered the gushing blood she had felt the night before. Pulling back her long brown hair, she found no trace of a scratch or even dried blood; only olive oil that matted her hair in stringy dreads down her back. Was she the sole survivor of the blast? Who were the men who had found her?

Opening the door slowly, she gasped when she saw the damage to the house. Nothing was left of the main part of her home; all had been taken out in a giant explosion that was meant to demolish every room. The maid's quarters off the back of the kitchen was all that remained standing amidst the ruins.

Two men sat in the now "open-air" kitchen, guns across their laps, sunlight streaming down around them. Shielding her eyes, she looked at them cautiously.

"Ibrahim will be back later," the elderly gentleman said. His thoughtful eyes studied her as if to assess how she was handling all of this.

"You were supposed to be on a college tour this week with your mother," added the other in an accusing tone. He was a young man, strong and muscular with long black hair. He didn't look kind.

Dahlia slowly looked from one to the other. "How did you know that?"

The words had no sooner escaped from her lips and she knew. She sank to the floor and stared at them in realization. These were her parents' killers, sent by the rebel forces to assassinate her father.

She wanted to cry and scream, to throw things at them in her rage, but she couldn't find the strength to lift the broken mortar in her fists. Turning away, she cried quietly to herself.

⋅→⧉ ⧉←⋅

Ibrahim returned after dark with fresh pita bread wrapped around warm slices of spiced lamb and vegetables. Starving, and too exhausted to resist, Dahlia sat at the table with her captors and ate. Ibrahim was clearly in charge, she noted, although he seemed an unlikely terrorist with his clean-cut look and starched white shirt.

"You'll stay here with Hasan and Artashir," he told her quietly. "Don't use any lights at night, and don't go any further than the garden.

It's for your own protection; the people don't know you're here, and as long as they think you're dead, you should be safe."

"Safe from *who*? You're already here! You've already killed my family! Who is there to hide from?!!" Her chest heaved in uncontrollable rage. How could he sit here and threaten her in her own home after all they'd done?

Ibrahim glanced around the table as if weighing his next words carefully. "You have a lot to learn about the country you live in," he said; and that was all.

Offended by his comment, but unsure of what he meant, she remained quiet. It was an odd statement, to be sure. She wanted to retort with a comment about how her father had *created* "the country they lived in," but at the thought of her father, she suddenly felt a strong urge to vomit. Pushing away from the table, she fled to the garden below and knelt in the bushes. Over and over again, she whispered the words, "My parents are dead, my parents are dead."

After throwing up, she lay down in the grass and slept.

Chapter 1

Troubled dreams disrupted her sleep throughout the night. Bombs on the hillside rode towards her house on crashing waves. She stepped out onto the terrace of their beach house and waved to her father and his friends. Looking to the beach, she saw her mother, whose eyes locked into hers and held them while the water slowly rose around her. As her mother began to drown, Dahlia cried out to her father, but he was in the study now with his advisors. A loud explosion sent Dahlia falling into the sea. The cold water gently washed over her…

Ibrahim was pressing a cool cloth against her forehead when she awoke with a start. Dahlia pulled away as he stood and left the room. The men exchanged quiet words and Ibrahim returned to her bedside.

She rolled over and faced the opposite wall.

"I'm leaving for a while," he said to her back. His voice was gentle but firm. "Remember what I said about the lights at night."

She didn't respond.

"I'll return on Friday. I'd like you to cook a meal for me and the men. We'll bring news from the frontline. Is there anyone you'd like me to inquire about? An uncle, a friend…?"

Too shocked to speak, too angry to turn around and face him, Dahlia lay in quiet outrage.

"Well then," he said and cleared his throat, "I'll see you Friday."

Grabbing the closest chunk of rubble she could find, Dahlia sat up and hurled it at his back. It smashed into a gazillion pieces on the doorframe above his head. Pausing for just a moment to brush the debris off of his shoulders, Ibrahim left the room without turning around.

⭢⊫◉ ◉⊪⭠

The days passed slowly, and her life took on a rhythm ruled by the light of the sun. Hasan and Artashir took turns clearing around the pile of rubble that was once her home. They created a path that led around the demolished house from the front gate to the kitchen—which was now open on two sides. They watched her every move, from sun-up to sundown, then locked her in the cellar at night. On the third day, with a few candles and a broom, she went down and cleaned up the dark cell that had once been her personal sanctuary.

Many jars of olive oil had broken in the blast, and the walls and floor were slick with a heavy, familiar scent that reminded her of the olive-press season. It had been a favorite time of year—the harvest complete and all the hired-hands gathered around to sample the fruits of their labor. Freshly pressed oil was poured into large platters, then seasoned with herbs and sea salt. Loaves of warm, crusty bread were ready for the dipping. With the baskets of bread and glasses of wine, all would gather and sample the oil, gorging themselves on a feast of bread, oil, olives and goat cheese. At the close of each taste-test ceremony, her father would give a powerful speech about the rewards of hard work combined with the joy of sharing the fruit of their labor. Tears would shimmer in the eyes of the simple men and women who had gathered for the season of the harvest. With their wages in their hands, and their bellies full from the ceremonial feasting, each worker would vow to be back the following year, ready to serve again.

Dahlia's family hadn't had an olive harvest in over 12 years. The fighting that consumed their country kept her father far too busy to manage the groves at their summer home. They now stood overgrown and unkempt—another reminder of the chaos harbored by war.

⊶⊷ ⊷⊶

When all the broken bottles were picked up and the splattered walls wiped down, Dahlia created a simple bed in one corner and placed candles in bottles all around the room. With most of the power-lines severed in the blast that destroyed her home and Ibrahim's bizarre rule about using lights, she was learning to live creatively.

Each day, after they had spent hours cleaning up the property, Hasan would go into town and purchase a warm evening meal and bread for the following day. Huddled in the kitchen, eating by the light of a single candle so as not to draw attention, the men would discuss the news gleaned from informants in the city. Fighting had rapidly been pushed to the east where news of her father's death seemed to weaken the efforts of the military.

Thousands of soldiers had deserted or surrendered to the rebel forces. Disheartened by the news, Dahlia ate in silence. The men didn't seem to gloat it over her, though there was no effort to hide the victories of her father's enemies. The men seemed more relieved than enthusiastic; they would often pause to reflect on the news they had received, quietly eating until Artashir would prompt for more information with questions about a mutual friend or a strategic line of battle.

The majority of Dahlia's energy had been spent on cleaning up the kitchen—a place that had become her only comfort in the midst of tragedy and isolation. The roof over the main part of the house had collapsed, crushing the rooms beneath it. It stood as a memorial to her parents—a giant mausoleum of crumbled mortar and stone. Once a beautiful mansion, all that remained was the modern kitchen (and the small apartment for the maid/cook) that had been added to the back of the structure when her father had taken leadership over the country. A long, marble terrace off the back overlooked the city, which stood quietly shimmering below her in the gathering twilight. Tomorrow, Ibrahim would return with more news from the frontline, and she was expected to cook for him.

When the light was gone from the sky, Artashir came out to go over the next day's schedule with her. Apparently, several men would be coming with Ibrahim, and after they had met and discussed their business, he wanted her to serve a simple meal. She was to act as though she were the cook, and would not speak to the men unless spoken to.

"And if I don't?" she asked defiantly.

"Then you can stay in the cellar all day!" he responded matter-of-factly. His angry, dark eyes challenged her, "Suit yourself."

Lying in bed that night, Dahlia wondered about this strange situation. Why must she pretend to be someone else? Why would Ibrahim ask her to cook for them? He didn't have to let her out. Was it true that the people would kill her if they found out who she was? She'd never cooked much before, and she didn't really want to cook for her captors—for the men who had overthrown her father's rule. They were her enemies!

An idea began to form as a simple phrase slowly emerged from the recesses of her mind. In her studies, she remembered reading about a young woman in a similar position. A rebellious country had risen up against her and in defiance of their impossible requests, the young woman responded, "Let them eat cake!"

Why not?!! She didn't support their cause, whatever it was, and she certainly wouldn't make a meal for them to enjoy. But she could make a cake—a large, hideous, obnoxious cake that expressed the contempt she felt for these men, *these murderous rebels!*

⇥⊨◉ ◉⊨⇤

At dawn, Dahlia was waiting on the top step of the cellar stairs, ready to begin her task. All night long, she had schemed, imagining the gaudy cake she would prepare: a huge representation of the nation's flag, tattered and covered in blood. Next to it would be a clump of cake that resembled mounds of mortar and brick, broken and crumbled like the neighborhoods of her city. She wanted to confront the men, to challenge them with the ugly truth of what this war had done to their country.

Hasan showed her how to create a fire in the outdoor oven, and he agreed to gather up wood for fuel while she prepared to bake. Never having cooked much before, she dumped loads of flour, sugar, eggs and salt into a bowl, not bothering to measure. When the mixture had formed a gooey consistency, she poured it into several large pans. Shoving them into the oven, she decided to let them burn just for good measure.

When the men arrived that night, there was cheering in the streets outside her home. "War heroes, returning home to the castle," she seethed to herself. How could her own people support these rebellious traitors? The cheering crowds followed them up the street, all the way to the outer gates. Once the vehicle was safely inside, the gate was securely closed and guarded. The home of their ex-leader was still off limits to the people. It had become the headquarters of "the enemy," at least in Dahlia's opinion.

Ibrahim and his men got out of their battered SUV and quietly made their way inside; they did not look like men returning home from a victorious battle. Dahlia stared at their tired faces and almost had mercy on them. Silent and sullen, the men sat at the large, oak kitchen table and held small cups of thick, black coffee in their hands.

When she was finally given the cue that it was time to eat, Dahlia went to retrieve her cake. Sitting around the table in the open-air kitchen, the men leaned back in their chairs and listened to the singing in the streets. Something big had happened, but Dahlia wasn't privy to the news. As she carried out the gruesome cake, she overheard the men discussing their families; it was apparent they hadn't been home to see their wives or children in many, many months. They were all from the province of Lamirya—near her family's beach home—and as they discussed the success of the crops there, she realized that they were farmers, men of the fields. Since none of them had been back to see their homes in quite a while, Hasan was updating them on the situation there—the harvest and various rebuilding projects that the people were communally working on. The men spoke of their land and families with such a longing that Dahlia wondered why they continued to fight. It was obvious they didn't want to be here, so far from the things they held dear.

As she placed her "masterpiece" on the table before them, the men exchanged bewildered glances. Ibrahim caught her eye long enough to raise an eyebrow and cast a sideways scowl. She glared back at him in response.

"What a nice surprise! I haven't had cake in quite a long time," one of the men said graciously.

"In honor of your victory," Dahlia replied blandly. With an air of indifference, she cut through the crusty layer of icing and blackened cake, only to discover that the fire had been too hot and the inside of the charred cake was still gooey. Trying to hide a smile, she placed huge slices of the terrible concoction on each man's plate and retreated to a chair near the sink.

Talk around the table returned to reminiscence of birthdays they had missed, children they hadn't seen in months, special occasions that had been forgotten in the strife. Ibrahim remained strangely quiet, and Dahlia wondered if he were furious with her and if there would be consequences for her dramatic act.

Finally, talk turned to the war, and she listened with curiosity as the men spoke openly of the battle strategy. It was apparent that the fighting had been pushed far east, and that her father's leading advisors were on the run from the rebel forces. Dahlia became lost in a cloud of memories that now, with the tragic loss of her family, caused her more pain than she had ever felt in her life.

When the men had gone, Ibrahim remained in his chair at the head of the table. Avoiding eye contact, Dahlia began to wash the dishes.

"The cake was … interesting," he said, pausing for emphasis. She didn't respond. She had absolutely nothing to say to him.

As the water poured over her hands in icy torrents, she began to sob uncontrollably.

"Why did you come back here?!!" she shouted, her dark eyes flashing, and with all of the pent up anger she had harbored all day, she began to throw the plates at the wall behind him, watching them smash and shatter—like all of her dreams and hopes for the future—for an education, for her country… *She was an orphan now!*

When Dahlia's tantrum had ended, Ibrahim rose. "I think you should take a look at this flyer," he said emotionlessly. He placed a pamphlet printed by the resistance on the table, then turned to leave. "By the way, it seems I remember another spoiled princess who was blamed for a bad cake joke. You and Marie Antoinette have a lot in common; you're both completely oblivious to the pain of your people. And I'm not surprised at all by your childish little display this evening, which—by the way—could have cost you your life. Don't forget that my men are protecting you here; if the citizens of this country knew you had survived the blast, there's not much Hasan and Artashir could do to keep them from storming the gates."

"And they would see what you have done to their leader! You have killed him and are now holding his daughter in this…" she looked wildly around and flung her hands out in a gesture of contempt for the disaster of a home she now lived in, "… *this hell-hole!*"

Ibrahim looked at her in wide-eyed disbelief for several moments. In a quiet, low voice, he told her the ugly truth. "This 'hell-hole' is a sanctuary compared to the warzone your father's people live in." He turned and walked across the kitchen and out into the yard. "We'll be back in a week. See if you can think up something a little less fancy next time."

Chapter 2

Tonight I read the most awful thing. I no longer know what to accept as true. Is everything I've ever believed in a lie? In the pages of the pamphlet Ibrahim left me, a gruesome picture of madness unfolded —the likes of which I've never seen or imagined. Mass graves were discovered outside of Anazir, and the atrocities were described as the cruel power-struggle of a merciless leader and his heartless cronies. How could the people have such a harsh view of my father? Who were the people in the mass graves? Could my father have been framed? There is no one to answer these questions for me. I'm surrounded by the men who rose up against my father, destroying my family and my home! Are these lies—created to destroy me, or could there be truth in this? My father's legacy is being shattered by the people he gave his life to lead.

Unable to stay in bed after a restless night with little sleep, Dahlia climbed the cellar steps and found the door already unlocked. Outside, a rosy dawn made promise of a beautiful day. Artashir sat at the table cleaning his weapon, a cup of black tea on the table beside him. He offered a grunt in response to her cheerless greeting. Outside in the garden Hasan was kneeling on a prayer carpet, quietly reciting his prayers in the direction of Mecca. All was calm and quiet, and for the first time since the explosion turned her world upside down, Dahlia felt strangely at peace.

She busied herself in the kitchen, preparing a plate of bread and goat cheese. After a quick trip into the garden, she sliced up a large tomato and cucumber, sprinkled them with a dash of salt, then garnished the platter with olives and a bowl of rosehip jam.

When she set the food on the table between them, Artashir gave her a bewildered look. Dahlia said nothing, but quietly took her place next to him and spread a piece of bread with the crumbly, strong white cheese.

Artashir slurped his tea loudly, then cursed under his breath when the hot liquid burned his lips. Hasan, meandering in from the garden, gave Artashir a slap on the back.

"Slow down, son!" he laughed and gave Dahlia a sly wink. "Leave the strong drink to the real men."

"It's not too strong," snarled Artashir. "It's just way too hot! I don't know why you have to make your tea boiling hot!"

Dahlia smirked at the men's banter. For such a big, strong guy, Artashir didn't seem all that tough at the moment.

"I wanted to make sure it was still hot enough for when our 'sleeping beauty' here finally woke up," Hasan said good-naturedly.

Refusing to smile back, Dahlia replied, "You don't need to worry about me. I can fix my own tea."

"Well," Hasan said smugly, "I wasn't so sure after last night's botched cake job. I was concerned that such a task as boiling water might be a bit complicated for our aspiring, young chef."

With a loud guffaw as proof that he found that statement to be absolutely hilarious, Artashir spewed hot tea halfway across the table and even snorted some out of his nose.

"You're disgusting," Dahlia said, curling her lips up at him. Pushing back from the table, she left the two men to their laughter. Feeling perturbed at having become the brunt of the joke, Dahlia walked outside to cool off. It seemed that everything was at her expense—even their humor.

The yard was looking somewhat cleaner; Hasan had helped her clear a lot of the rubble out of the flower beds. Outside her father's study, or what was left of it, Dahlia knelt beside the fountain that trickled into a small pond filled with brightly colored fish. Her father had loved to open his window and listen to the sound the water made as it splashed into the pond. He said it calmed his soul and helped him think. Now, Dahlia sat and watched the water's steady flow, wondering what her father had spent so many evenings thinking about. What troublesome issues had plagued him, tormenting his soul and robbing him of his peace? Maybe there were things he had done that weighed heavily upon him—perhaps he *was* guilty of crimes his family knew nothing about.

In her musings, Dahlia absent-mindedly reached over and uncovered a dusty book that lay half-buried in the rubble. Cleaning off its cover, she observed that it was a book about philosophy and political theory written by an Irish statesman named Edmund Burke. Thinking that rather odd, Dahlia was even more surprised when, allowing the book to fall open in her hands to a marked page, she found a passage underlined in bold, red ink ... by her father? It read:

"All that is necessary for the triumph of evil is that good men do nothing."

Rolling the words slowly around her mind, Dahlia began to wonder what evils her father had faced in leadership. Had he been corrupted by power? Was he the monster the people believed he was? She *had* to know, yet there was no one she could trust to give her the answers she needed. Slowly standing, Dahlia made her way towards the avalanche of mortar. The answers lay inside that room—the study from which her father had run this country. She knew she had to find the truth, and it was buried somewhere inside.

Chapter 3

By EVENING, DAHLIA had barely made a dent in the landslide of rubble. Artashir rounded the corner and found her lying in a dusty cloud, covered in sweat and grime. Wanting to give her room to pout after last night's drama, they'd left her to her digging and sorting all day.

"Find anything interesting?" he called out.

Not responding, she rolled over on her side and rinsed her hands in the pond, scaring the fish away with her splashing.

It had been an exceptionally hot day, and the heat made the men lazy. Not that they had any real work to do anyway, in Artashir's opinion. He made it well know that guarding a little spoiled brat didn't exactly feel significant in the grander scheme of things. After all, he was a soldier—one of the best trained men the rebel forces had, and here he sat next to an imploded palace, watching their ex-ruler's daughter dig amongst the rubble for her beloved family's secrets. He stood and watched her for a moment before adding, "It's time for supper."

⤙⊙ ⊙⤚

Over the following days of late summer, mealtime became an odd comfort to them all. Huddled around the oak table in the airy kitchen, Hasan and Artashir discussed—in a strangely simple fashion—their families and work back home. Hasan, a farmer from the province near the sea that Dahlia loved, missed working the land and often became emotional when talking about his grandchildren. Dahlia especially loved hearing about Timon, the inquisitive, chatty child who was obviously Hasan's favorite. Hasan was full of stories from the hours he spent working the fields with his beloved grandson by his side, and Timon's humorous actions and youthful perspectives on life provided plenty of entertaining and endearing stories.

Artashir was more of a mystery to Dahlia. His people were of a Bedouin tribe, in an area of Al Cazar that she had never visited or known much about. They had always been a somewhat obscure and restless people, moving when they wanted and settling in the most remote regions of the desert. Although Dahlia's mother had often discussed the need to educate the young Bedouin people, her father seemed to dislike talking about them.

One of the habits that Dahlia found most interesting about Artashir was his love of sitting around the table telling stories that she had never heard growing up. The Bedouin culture was rich in folklore and historical retellings that absolutely fascinated her. Sitting around the table at night, she became lost in a world that took her away from the reality of her current life. The pain and loss she felt would almost disappear as Artashir recounted horrible and wonderful myths, one after another. Sometimes, during a long evening, and drained by the heat of the day, Hasan would doze off, his head resting in his hands while Artashir droned on, his deep voice fading to a whisper. Then, with a loud boom, he would deliver the climax of the story with wide eyes and wild gestures, and Hasan would nearly fall out of his chair, causing Artashir and Dahlia to laugh until they were in tears. Suddenly awake and irritated that the young people had disturbed his nap, he would grumpily punch Artashir in the arm and send Dahlia to bed.

⊷⊶⊷ ⊶⊷⊶

When word came that Ibrahim would indeed return the following Friday, Dahlia became withdrawn and pensive. She had spent her days in a fruitless hunt for evidence to defend her father's honor; furthermore, all her digging and moving brick and tile had made her sore and tired. The last thing she wanted to do was prepare a meal for the man she had come to know as her father's executioner.

On Thursday, Artashir sat by the pond and asked her what she planned to prepare for supper.

"You know he'll expect a meal," he said, "and I doubt he'll be as understanding as he was last week with a half-cooked cake."

Dahlia continued to work, removing tile after tile and stacking them by the garden wall. She no longer really looked for anything interesting; she simply found the work to be therapeutic, mind-numbing and exhausting so that when she found herself alone in the cellar at night she simply fell onto her mattress and slept.

"Maybe I could help this time." Long pause. "Maybe I could teach you how to make something from my people." He knew that would interest her; she loved to hear about them, and he wouldn't mind savoring a favorite home-cooked meal he had grown up on.

Dahlia leaned against a stack of tiles and pushed a sweaty strand of hair from her face. "I don't get it. Why must he come *here*? Aren't there other meeting places for *those rebels*? After all, he's brought enough pain to this home. How dare he sit in *my* kitchen and plan more destruction!"

Artashir crossed his arms in front of his chest and leaned back against a pile of brick. Letting out a long, deep breath, he bit his lip and scowled.

"Oh, why am I talking to you?!!" Dahlia shouted. "How can I expect you to understand? You're one of them. You're one... *of them*!" Setting down the tile she had been dusting off, she straightened a tall pillar of only slightly broken tiles that she had salvaged from the rest. Then, in a fit of rage, she gave it a hard shove, screaming as the tower came crashing down into the pond, frightening the fish and nearly knocking the fountain over. "You're one of them," she said again quietly before turning to walk away.

Hasan was in the kitchen making tea when she entered. "I want yogurt for tomorrow. And a large, crusty loaf of bread. Can you get that for me in the market tomorrow morning?" she asked.

Surprised, he nodded "yes" and watched as she set about cleaning up the kitchen. As she calmly washed the dishes, he pulled out a hand-carved recorder and played a few airy tunes he and Timon liked to sing together in the fields. They were simple and upbeat, and Dahlia found herself working to the rhythm of the music, too numb to think or feel anything else.

Chapter 4

THE CROWDS OUTSIDE the gate announced the arrival of Ibrahim's party with joyful shouts and singing. Patriotic tunes Dahlia had once loved rang through the night, and she stood by the sink waiting for her guests to arrive. Artashir locked the gate behind the SUV and Hasan waited at the door to lead them in. Again, Ibrahim and his men entered quietly, unenthusiastically seating themselves at the table and waiting while Hasan poured their tea before beginning any dialogue. They looked tired and thin, and even in the heat of the summer evening, they each held the hot glasses of tea in their hands as if they were seated around a campfire on a cold, winter's night.

Mosul began first, explaining the positions of the troops in the northern province. Little was said of victories or losses; it seemed that the battling there was over and reconstruction had become the focus of the people.

A second man named Salim waited a moment before beginning his account. He exchanged a long glance with Artashir before turning to Ibrahim and telling him that the people in the southern desert region were doing well, and returning to their normal way of life. Artashir closed his eyes and leaned back in his chair; there seemed to be a great deal of pain associated with his people, and Dahlia was curious as to how the rebellion had affected them in such a remote place. A long moment of silence passed before anyone acknowledged the good news.

The other men gave brief reports before Hasan motioned for Dahlia to serve the food.

She placed a deep dish of olive oil seasoned with cracked pepper and spices before them and passed a tray of bread to Hasan. Giving thanks--as was his custom--he broke the crusty loaves and passed chunks of bread to each of the men. In silence, the men dipped the bread in the oil and ate. Working quietly, Dahlia ladled the chilled, yogurt soup into bowls. The scent of fresh garlic and cucumbers from the garden filled the room, and the men ate as if they hadn't seen food in weeks. It was a simple meal, one she remembered from her youth because it was what the migrant workers ate to refresh themselves after a long, hot day working the land.

With talk turning to families and news from home, Dahlia busied herself with cleaning up, trying to block out the discussion that caused her such pain. She didn't want to hear about their families; she didn't want to be reminded of her own.

When the men got up to leave, Ibrahim thanked her for the meal, and each man smiled kindly at her. They didn't know *who* she was, came the thought. They didn't know she was Seljuk's daughter.

⇥⇥⊜ ⊜⇤⇤

"Ibrahim," she said when all other men had left, "it's time for you and your men to leave the house. I don't want you here anymore." She calmly dried each dish and placed it carefully in the cabinet. This was her home, not theirs.

"You don't understand…" Hasan said sadly, but Ibrahim cut in.

"We will not leave. There's no choice for you in this matter."

With hands on her hips, Dahlia turned to face them all. "You've said yourself that no one knows I'm here. Leave and let me be!"

"This home no longer belongs to *you*! It was bought and paid for with the blood of the Alcazaran people!" Ibrahim sternly responded. A tense silence sat between them as she tried to comprehend what he was saying. It didn't seem like he was trying to justify the assassination of her father; instead, he always tried to turn it around, placing the blame for the bloodshed on her father.

"Show her the papers!" Artashir snarled. "Show her what her father's men will be tried for when they're caught!"

"NO!" All of them turned and looked as Hasan rose from his chair, a look of horror on his face. "No! Artashir, we talked about this!"

Dahlia was becoming upset; she could hardly keep up with the dialogue going on around her. "Show me what?!" she demanded.

"Hasan's right," Ibrahim said, trying to regain his composure. "We're all upset right now; this is not the way it will be done."

"What? What won't you tell me?! What are you afraid to admit in front of me? You *murderers!*"

Stunned, all three men sat back in silence and refused to look at her. Hasan looked hurt, but Artashir was hardly able to contain his fury. "You should tell her, Ibrahim. I don't care how!" He got up and stomped out onto the terrace, grumbling to himself.

"We're not leaving, Dahlia. There's more you need to know later, but you can trust me when I say that you are not safe here alone. And you're not safe out in the city. People are still angry; it may take years before they will be able to forgive and forget all that has happened."

"I don't understand," she cried. Yet again, her anger came out in pitiful tears. *How weak am I?,* she thought to herself. She wanted to be strong, to be angry at these men, but she was so confused and hurt!

"Go to bed," Hasan told her gently. "We'll talk more tomorrow over a hot cup of tea."

She looked at him with wide, tear-filled eyes and wondered at the pity she heard in his voice. Why did Hasan fear for her? Stumbling toward the cellar, she caught herself against the doorframe and rested her head against it for a moment. The air from below cooled her face, and she wiped the tears from her cheeks. With a glance at Ibrahim, she knew from his stony stare that the discussion was over. "Goodbye," she said to him with a finality that meant she never wanted to see him again.

When she had closed the cellar door behind her, Hasan went to lock it for the night.

"Don't," Ibrahim said. "She's free to do as she pleases. I've told her the truth, and if she wants to face the citizens on her own, she can leave."

Chapter 5

THE NIGHTS BEGAN to grow cooler, signaling the commencement of Fall. Hasan liked to build a fire at night, just off the back terrace in the garden. High above the city lights, they would sit around the small blaze dipping chunks of bread into spiced vegetable stew or curried lentils.

Artashir spent hours each day chopping wood in the hills above the house while Hasan shopped in the market and gathered news from the front. Dahlia found her purpose in preparing meals and gardening, but the highlight of her day was sitting around the fire with the men, listening to Artashir and Hasan share stories and memories of their families.

One evening, Artashir taught Dahlia how to make a special meal reserved for celebrations and weddings. He seasoned the lamb and showed Dahlia how to form small, oval meatballs. It was a glorious evening, the sunset colors glowing from the rocky hills that loomed behind them. A gentle breeze swirled through the kitchen and a mama-bird flew in and out of the open-air room, carrying dinner to her babies. Their nest was in a basket on top of the now useless fridge, and Dahlia found that she had quite taken to this way of outdoor living. Hasan stoked the coals in a small fire pit he had created, then lay damp grape leaves on fresh cut cedar bricks.

"Is the *kofte* ready?" he called, then continued humming a tune he had been singing all afternoon. Artashir and Dahlia gathered up the meatballs and carried them into the yard on a colorful, mosaic platter. They settled around the fire pit and quietly watched the sky colors fade to gray. Lights began to twinkle on all over the city below them and Dahlia wondered what her friends were doing. Had some of them joined the resistance? Did their lives go on, unchanged by the civil war raging around them? Did any of them mourn her death, or were they too lost in their own troubles to even miss her? Or maybe they were glad when they heard that her family had been killed.

Artashir began to tell a story about a wild boy who lived among the desert jackals and she allowed herself to enjoy the yarn. Time stood still when he began to talk, and before she knew it, Hasan was pulling the steaming *kofte* from the pit. Stars twinkled overhead and the savory aroma of roasted meat filled the air. Breaking chunks of fresh bread from heavy, crusted loaves, they ate in silence, watching the lights of the city below. All was quiet and Dahlia was content to be in the company of the men who spent their days with her.

When they were finished eating, Dahlia leaned back against a large, overturned urn. There was a slight chill in the air, and Hasan stood and settled a blanket over her. She smiled at his kindness; he had all the gentleness of a doting grandfather. Lost in his own thoughts, Artashir quietly sang a tribal song from his youth as he stirred the fire.

As the coals died down, Artashir took the bottle he had been enjoying and stumbled to his tent at the far end of the terrace. With a clumsy dive, he settled in for the night, the tent flap closing behind him. Dahlia carried the empty dishes into the kitchen, then wandered aimlessly back to the gaping hole in the kitchen wall that led out onto the terrace. From where she stood, leaning against the broken wall, she could see the red, glowing embers of the fire. Hasan was no longer beside it. The burning radiance seemed to beckon to her, but she didn't want to give into it--this numbing, pleasant warmth that was replacing the raw pain in her heart. Standing half inside, half out, she whispered to the darkness,

"Why? Why did you do this? Why did you choose to come here and take my father's life?" She clutched at her chest and let out a heart-wrenching sob. "Do you see the pain it's caused me? How can you sit here with me each night, knowing that it was by your hand that I am now alone?" Her voice was anguished, and thinking she was alone, she rested her head against the cool, marble wall and cried over the questions that had plagued her for over three months now.

"Habibi," Hasan called to her gently, using the Arabic word that would have been reserved for someone as close to him as a daughter, "Come; sit with me." He led her out to the fire, spread out his prayer rug, then knelt and patted a spot beside him. Dahlia sat, knees pulled tightly to her chest, chin resting on her knees.

Looking into the fire, she said, *"Baba,"* meaning 'father' or 'respected one,' "How could *you* want to kill anyone?"

He poked the fire and sighed. "It's too much for you to understand, little one. But one day, I will take you to my town, and I will show you." Weighing his words carefully, he added, "Your father was a good man, but he lost his way. He listened to men whose hearts were evil, who craved power more than the well-being of their people." After a long pause, he continued, "Sometimes, to kill the snake, you have to chop off its head."

Dahlia flinched at his words; she wanted to lash out, to hurt those who had hurt her, but she couldn't. "And Artashir? Why is he here? Surely the Bedouin people have no interest in all of this—the war between the rebels and the government!"

Hasan gazed into the fire. "Artashir is a lion, prowling to protect his people. I hope you never know the evil that was done to them. He would have done much more than this, but—as an outsider—he must first prove himself to the cause."

"The cause?"

"The movement to regain a peaceful country and uncorrupted leadership."

Dahlia was afraid that Hasan was seeking an ideal too perfect for this world, but she quietly respected his principles. Turning her anger to the one in charge of the whole, bloody mess, she asked, "And what about Ibrahim? Was this his plan—his perfect strategy for a unified country?"

Hasan thoughtfully cocked his head to one side. "I thought you might get that idea. Ibrahim is not in charge; he is only a capable foot soldier, willing to risk his life to do the tasks that the rest of us untrained volunteers are too afraid to do. No one thought *this,*" he made a sweeping motion towards the demolished mansion, "could ever be done."

"*THIS?* This is murder, cold-blooded murder! Assassinating a man while he lies in his own bed at night, in his own home!" Dahlia's eyes were like two tiny burning orbs.

Hasan held up a hand, gesturing toward the city lights below. "Cold-blooded murder is killing innocent women and children for no reason, in their own homes." There was an edge in his voice that she had never heard before. "Cold-blooded murder is killing thousands of peace-loving people because their customs are different than your own, and because they don't want to play the foolish, political, power-driven games that cold-hearted men try to force upon them."

Stunned by his hard words, Dahlia gasped, the air catching in her throat for a moment. "I don't know what you're talking about!" she shouted through hot, angry tears.

Hasan looked away. "You'll know soon enough. Why does Artashir have so much hate? Why was Ibrahim driven to do this when no one else dared?" He looked out at the city and pointed a quivering, crooked finger at a dark spot on the hillside across the valley. "When the rebels began to move into Anazir from the west, they camped behind that hill. Having taken all the major cities up to that point, they waited outside the capital, hoping your father would grant them an audience, the opportunity to negotiate, to bring an end to the revolt. For weeks they camped there, waiting for a response. More and more rebels from villages all around gathered, ready to fight, ready to end the injustices they had endured for so long. With years of enmity rising up inside of them, they grew impatient with your father's refusal to hear them out. Many hot-headed men demanded that the rebellion continue—insisting that they would take the capital by force. But Ibrahim's father, he had known Seljuk--your *baba*--in earlier years, and Ibrahim believed that if he could only find a way to reach your father, a violent battle would be avoided."

At the mention of Ibrahim's father, Dahlia sat forward in interest. "When did he know my father? Was he one of my father's early advisors?"

Hasan shook his head.

"I'm sure he would have listened; father always listened to his friends!" The desperation in her voice seemed hopeful, as if anything she said now could have changed the circumstances of her father's untimely death.

Hasan remained silent for a long time. "Ibrahim is from a neighborhood not far from here; in fact, you've probably driven through it many times. I wonder if you haven't seen him before on the streets or shopping in the stores nearby." Hasan stared into the fire, lost for a moment in the glowing embers.

"Does he have a family there? Is that why he comes back here for meetings?" Dahlia watched as Hasan's face softened, as if he were listening to a sad song. It had been two months since Ibrahim's last visit, and Dahlia was beginning to wonder if he would return at all. Maybe he had decided to respect her wishes. Hasan turned away and let out a loud sigh.

"Dahlia, the pains of people are so deep. I wonder sometimes if it will help you to know… or if I should keep such things from you." He looked directly at her then, and the look was hard, pointed.

"I want to know," she said, steadily. "I have a right to know why Ibrahim planned the attack on my family."

"Ibrahim," Hasan started, then cleared his throat, his eyes growing moist. "Ibrahim was studying in the university when civil war broke out. Fresh out of the school and full of new ideas, Ibrahim became a successful architect, designing reconstruction plans for neighboring cities that had been destroyed in battle. His specialty was taking broken buildings and recycling the parts to make modest dwellings and schools. Nothing was wasted; cost was minimal. Communities devastated by the war sought him out and pulled together whatever resources they could to hire his company to come in and rebuild whole neighborhoods. He was brilliant, wise beyond his years; he would have made a fortune if only people could afford to pay him."

"Then he should have been glad for this war; it gave him a name and a future! Why did he throw it all away to help destroy the very cities he was trying to rebuild?"

"Ibrahim's family…. His young wife had just had a baby." Hasan's eyes welled with tears. Dahlia shuddered and hid her face between her knees. Clouds had moved in and covered the stars overhead; the fire flickered in the soft breeze.

"Ibrahim was new to the resistance when plans to assassinate your father became our focus." He paused to look at her; when she didn't appear to be angry with what he'd said, he continued. "Up until recently, people living in Anazir mostly ignored the efforts of the resistance, quietly suffering under the inconveniences of a curfew, etc. They were oblivious to the suffering of their countrymen, caught up in the busyness of their jobs and raising families. I can't blame them, really; but my province was one of the first to suffer at the hand of your father's regime, and so I have spent much of the past few years watching the vortex of this ugly storm grow larger and hungrier with each demolished city. But Ibrahim was young and idealistic, unwearied yet by battle and the ugliness of it all; he felt certain that your father would listen to reason.

"The explosion a year ago, it was the first time this city had felt what the rest of us had—the fear of not knowing what was happening, the pain of seeing a part of your surroundings destroyed, the frustration of life disrupted as schedules were abruptly ended and workers let go. Buses stopped running; the city came to a stand-still, and then the military stepped in. Do you remember the day Anazir fell into battle?"

Dahlia remembered the day very well. It had been a sunny day, and her father had invited several of his advisors and their families over for a dinner party. It had been a strained day—the men spent most of the time in the study—scheming, as they usually did. The mothers sat in the parlor gossiping and smoking, but there was a tightness in some of their faces that concerned Dahlia. She spent the afternoon listening to music in her spacious suite with some of the older kids while the children watched a movie in a nearby room. They had wanted to play volleyball in the yard off the terrace, but her father had insisted that the noise would disturb his meeting with the men in his study. It had seemed a selfish request and Dahlia and the others sulked in her room, complaining about the war and the ridiculous people who stirred up the violence that made life so difficult for them all.

"It's like they don't even see us anymore," Nadim growled, referring to their fathers who spent the majority of their time locked away in meetings. Throwing a ball of wadded up paper through a small basket above the trash can, he continued, "All they talk about is how to control the resistance, but I don't even know why the rebels resist! Can anyone explain that? Is there a reason for this bloody war?!!"

"Of course there is," Sanshan retorted. She was the oldest of the advisor's children, and having grown up together, the majority of them felt that she was bossy and overbearing, but any explanation was welcome at the moment. "The people want more freedoms, less taxes. They feel the government has lost touch with what its people need, and without choosing who represents them, they feel as if their voice doesn't count. Many are embracing that western idea—the philosophy that people can best govern themselves by electing their own leaders."

"But that's crazy!" Reshona responded. "Suppose the Bedouin candidate won the election, or a planter from Lamirya. What would they know of the people's needs in the provinces of the north, for example? How can they any better represent the people than our fathers do now?"

"Um, Father is a planter from Lamirya,'" Dahlia interjected quickly.

"The point is that they want the right to *choose* the leaders of their country. It's called *'freedom.'*" Sanshan was a voice of reason, albeit a sarcastic one.

"How would the people even know *what* they needed?" Reshona cried. "People are too busy with their own lives to understand the political process—to even educate themselves on what is best for the whole of the country! How could they choose a leader any better? The military is strong, it holds our nation together—while a few selfish and violent men terrorize and destroy all that we are! We should just stomp them out once and for all—so that we can finally have peace! So we can have our fathers back!!"

Dahlia listened and wondered. For years, she had studied political theory and contemplated if perhaps the people only needed to be reassured—if a leader, taking the time out of all the other important things he did, could travel about and talk to the different provinces he governed, to somehow hear their voices and talk to them about their needs. Why couldn't a leader—by getting to know the people he governed—calm them when they felt neglected and gently lead them into necessary change. Instead, her father and his men sat behind locked doors all day scheming ways to control the uprisings and to quiet the loudest voices of unrest.

"I want to go away," Dahlia had said. "I want to live in a country where people practice elections. I want to see how they handle their freedom. Maybe then I can show my father a new way." The others had looked at her like she was crazy.

"You want to go off to college?" Daneka's wide eyes looked at Dahlia in fear and admiration. "But it's so different—so far from home!"

"Away from *this*... watching our country fall down around us?" Dahlia laughed. "Is *this* really that great?" She'd said it with tears in her eyes. She loved her country, her home, but she was tired of living in a country rocked by war. There had to be a better way.

"Who will listen to you, Dahlia? You're just a girl. You're father should have had a son!" Nadim punched his open hand with a hard fist, demonstrating the strong arm he felt their nation needed.

The statement hit her like a slap across the face. Is that what people really thought—that Seljuk needed a son, a powerful heir to carry on the legacy of force he had ruled with for fifteen years?

It wasn't who he really was, she thought. *Father knew the people, he could reason with them if he wanted. So why didn't he?* The question mocked her as Nadim had. What did she, a girl, understand about the ruling of a country? The leader had to be strong, firm, unbending. *Unloving,* she thought, but it didn't seem right.

Then, suddenly, the ground shook, and the light buzzed on and off a few times. Daneka let out a muffled scream. The small group of teens froze, staring at each other unsure of what to do.

"What was that, an earthquake?" Nadim whispered, crouching down beside the desk. For a moment, no one moved. Then they felt the floor rock beneath them, a muffled boom sounding as the house shook and a framed photo fell off the wall.

"We're being bombed! Anazir is being bombed!" Dahlia moaned. Silence followed, and they quickly made their way to the den where the women were sitting.

Hasan watched Dahlia through the swirls of smoke and sparks that the wind carried up from the fire. Her dark eyes were filled with tears as she remembered; she clutched her knees and sat for a long time staring into the flames.

"I remember," she said simply. The flood of memories had washed over her in one long, painful wave as she remembered the day their lives had changed forever. From then on, life became a blur of altered schedules, car checks for bombs, routines varied so as not to draw attention from anyone who might want to hurt Seljuk or his family.

Hasan observed her, listened to the way she described the city's transformation into a lifeless robot—doing only what the military commanded or allowed, eating when it was time to eat, working when it was time to work, and sleeping when it was time to sleep.

"It was a terrible year, worse even than it is now. I couldn't go anywhere without first clearing it with my father's staff, and no one would talk about what was happening or why. It was as if nothing had even changed, as if this was the way it had always been."

Dahlia paused for a long moment, letting the memories of that awful day fade away. Finally, she asked, "But what does any of that have to do with Ibrahim? He was doing something good; he had a plan to bring the resistance and my father into peace talks."

"He was with the resistance the day the bombings took place. Dahlia, you need to understand. The rebels aren't the ones who bombed the city."

"Well, of course they were. My father had known for weeks that they were getting pretty close. He warned me daily to stay near the house, not to go into crowded markets, not to go anywhere alone. He was afraid I'd be kidnapped, or the victim of a terrorist-bombing."

"The resistance didn't bomb the neighborhood. Think about it Dahlia. It was a Sunday afternoon. There were no soldiers out; they only go into the neighborhoods to enforce curfew at night. Who would the resistance have been targeting?"

"My father said a group of resistance fighters had stormed the streets of Anazir, and in an attempt to overtake the city, had begun bombing a path from the hills in; they destroyed Guardi to create a path into the heart of the capital." Guardi was a beautiful, hillside suburb of Anazir, not far from the area where Dahlia lived.

"The resistance was camped outside the city—that is true. And we were surveying your father's every move. We were waiting for the right time to strike, but our mission was not to take out neighborhoods. There are more direct ways to take down the leadership of a country. No, the day Guardi was bombed, our men were gathering intelligence in the marketplaces—seeking cooperators to help us gain access to your father's advisors. We planned to take out the head of the snake—to relieve the military from its chain of command. The day that Guardi was destroyed, one of our top men was meeting with one of your father's advisors in a coffeehouse in the middle of a residential block."

Gennard! Dahlia knew instantly who Hasan was referring to. He had been strangely absent the day of the bombings. His wife and children had been with them that day, unaware of the awful shock they were about to receive. Her father had been furious when he had learned of Gennard's whereabouts. Gennard had been one of his top advisors and friends, probably the most trusted man in her father's cabinet. Dahlia always thought that her father had been angry over his death at the hand of the resistance. But what if her father had learned that day of Gennard's treason? What if her father had orchestrated his death? It seemed absurd, that they could have all gathered that day, unknowingly awaiting the assassination of the one who had become known as the informant? Could her father really have known that Gennard was the one who would meet with the resistance, trading information with the enemy?

"So, the resistance blew up Guardi in order to get rid of one of my father's top advisors?" It seemed a bit overzealous, Dahlia thought, but then, the rebels were bloodthirsty and destructive. It was to be expected. They could have easily been blamed for the bombings.

"No, Dahlia, your father had General Gennard assassinated. When he realized there were leaks—and who the informant was, he had him trailed. Soldiers dressed as resistance workers came up into the hills, and with military equipment, bombed the beautiful, tree-lined streets of Guardi. They left nothing standing. It was a brilliant tactical move devised by your father's advisors—killing two birds with one stone. It took out Gennard and it turned the people of Anazir against the resistance. It made our workers look like cold-hearted terrorists seeking to be heard through violent, unnecessary crimes. Towards the end, your father was not much more than a puppet in the hands of power-hungry men who lacked compassion or the ability to see or hear the people they served."

Dahlia was stunned. How dare Hasan speak to her that way! Accusing, spreading lies, making her father out to be a monster, and a weak one at that! With her mouth open and her eyes wide, Dahlia wanted to retaliate, to speak on behalf of her father, but she couldn't find the words.

She closed her eyes and felt the ground shake beneath her again. She could feel the fear that had wrapped itself around her that day as they had all gathered in the parlor with their mothers. The children were in hysterics, but their mothers just sat in a daze, as if what had happened was a nightmare they couldn't explain. The men had come out of the study to comfort them. But the women sat stiff in their chairs, just listening to their husbands clarify what was happening. Their words made sense, the resistance must have attacked, but the emotions in the room had been off. It was as if the wives could see through a wall that had been blown wide open by the explosion, and they were shocked by what had been exposed.

"It is finished," Seljuk had said to his wife, patting her shoulder gently. Her mother's eyes had shone with tears.

Yes, it's over, It's over, Dahlia had told herself, exhausted from the emotion and fear that had overwhelmed her in the hours following the bombings. *But what if he had meant "finished"—a job well done, a mission accomplished, an enemy quieted? Had her father and his men orchestrated the attack on Guardi? Were they to blame for the scores of women and children who had needlessly died in their homes in the middle of a Sunday afternoon? No one could be that heartless!*

Heartless. The word described the man her father had become in the final year of his life. He had no desires, no appetite, no emotion. He cared not for his wife or his daughter, only nagged them to stay inside or take a guard wherever they went. Survival had become his only thought—but there was no heart in it, no real purpose. It was as if his life had become empty, meaningless; yet the habit of survival had been drilled into him by fifteen years of fighting for control—of not giving up or giving in.

Heartlessness. That was all that was left of her father's regime in the months that followed the Guardi bombings. It seemed as if all of Al Cazar had lost its will to live, destroying herself from the inside out.

"I can't believe that's how it was," Dalia said finally. Her eyes were dull as she stared into the fire—glazed over, no longer reflecting the dancing sparks of light.

"Dahlia, there was no battle, just a decision to take out two parties hoping to find a peaceful solution. Your father's advisors felt compromised; they couldn't stand the thought of control being taken from their hands, even if it was well-meaning. They commanded the military to fire on the neighborhoods that had been 'infiltrated.' No warning, no real reason, just the implied fear that a small section of the city had been compromised. Within minutes, missiles were fired, taking out whole neighborhoods. Apartment buildings crumbled, whole families were swallowed up in the explosions that rocked Guardi."

"And this is why Ibrahim decided to kill my family?" she asked quietly.

Shaking his head, Hasan clicked his tongue sternly. "First of all, Ibrahim did not plan an attack on your family. You and your mother were never intended to suffer. All intel determined that you would be together in London, looking at colleges." Hasan stirred the fire. Glowing coals rolled out and he poked at them, breaking them apart and releasing their heat. A fresh log caught, bluish-white flames licking and rolling over it until it took on an orange glow of its own. "Ibrahim's wife and child were killed in the explosion that destroyed Guardi. The buildings crumbled together, like one big stack of dominoes, collapsing on top of one another." Hasan paused. "The baby was less than a month old."

Dahlia watched the flames subside as they burned through the crusty bark and steadily ate away at the heart of the wood. "He never found them?"

Hasan continued. "He went down to look for her, but there was nothing left of the building. He wasn't even sure he found the right street. Guardi had become a mess of ground up concrete and steel. If you go there today, you'll find a few lost souls still digging in the rubble, but most of those who survived joined the resistance. What happened that day in Guardi… it broke him. He lost all desire to squelch the bloodthirsty efforts to take out your father. He was ready to fight."

Dahlia's heart was racing. She wanted to shout, to yell for Ibrahim to stop and listen, as if he could hear her, as if she could have stopped the maddening fury that broke loose inside of him that day. "But why? Why fight? Hasn't there been enough fighting? Enough death?!!"

It was odd discussing this with Hasan, one of the men who had helped kill her parents. Dahlia shuddered as she remembered the day before the explosion that took down her home. She and her mother were scheduled to fly to London for a long weekend; they had planned the trip for months, with tickets to several shows and long lists of things to shop for as she prepared to attend college in January. Her mother became suddenly ill the night before their trip. It wasn't unusual; in fact, the reason Dahlia was starting college late was due to the fact that her mother had been sick most of the previous year. Their final day together had been a quiet one, with Father locked in the study and her mother resting on the couch in the den.

"The attack was planned quickly; it was hard to find a moment when your father would be alone, at home. But Ibrahim was an architect; he designed the attack to bring down the entire house---so as to be sure your father wouldn't survive. It had to happen at home because he felt that it was the safest way to assassinate your father without hurting innocent bystanders."

Dahlia had begun to quietly cry, but she didn't interrupt. She was ready to hear the details.

Hasan sighed. It was time she heard the truth. The question was, would she receive it? "It doesn't matter now. Winter's coming, and you will have to go away somewhere while the resistance takes a break. There will be little fighting in the months ahead, and no one will come here. Why don't you go and stay with Artashir and his people in the desert?"

Dahlia looked up at him. "Won't they know who I am? Won't they want to '*kill* me?'" she retorted sarcastically.

"They don't have to know who you are. There are many people displaced by the war. They'll accept you and make you feel at home. It could be good for you. You've developed an interest in Artashir's people; you can go and see for yourself how they live."

"No! Hasan, please," she pleaded. "I want to go to Lamirya. Take me there with you. I'll stay at my father's villa on the coast."

Hasan smiled sadly. "Lamirya has changed, Dahlia, you know that. It's not the same place you left."

"But the sea hasn't changed! I can go to the sea! Let me go there with you. We have many friends in Lamirya; my father's workers will remember me—I can reopen the olive press. People need jobs, right?" She sounded so hopeful, so full of ideas and energy. Hasan was tempted to agree, but he knew the people weren't ready yet. No one had time to grow olives, let alone process them. Houses needed to be rebuilt before winter set in. It was their only chance for survival.

"You can come. I will show you my home; but then you must go to Sanzar with Artashir and stay with his people. It's best that way. No one will know you there. You'll be safe."

Chapter 6

The following morning, Dahlia awoke with a start. A chill had crept into her very bones, and she was surprised to find herself still lying beside the fire which was now just a cold heap of ash. Propping herself up on one elbow, she looked out at the city below and wondered at all she had learned from Hasan the night before. It felt like a bad dream now, the details of all they had talked about covered in the same shroud of gray that seemed to suppress the city this morning. A low blanket of clouds kept out the sun, and the frigid air was deathly still.

Glancing up at the terrace, she noticed that Artashir's tent flap remained closed, and Hasan had already left for the market. Feeling utterly alone, Dahlia sank into a familiar funk she hadn't felt since the week her parents had died. There was no hope, no honor to find for her father; if what Hasan had said was true, then all of the memories she had of her father were poisoned by an ugly reality.

Blinking back a fresh wave of hot tears, she looked up at the sky. The heaviness in her heart seemed to anchor her to the ground, but as she watched the sky, she couldn't help but notice that the thick, gray clouds seemed to glow with an eerie white light. A warm sensation spread through her body as she released the memories of her father, the hope she had held for clearing his name, the weight she had carried for finding some way to prove his innocence. He was, after all, just a man, and he had made choices that she just couldn't justify, no matter how hard she tried. It was no longer up to her; the truth was what it was, and she had a future to face, alone. But she didn't feel alone; Hasan and Artashir had become companions, even friends... but there was something more. Looking up at the sky, she felt hope for something greater... something celestial, something mysterious and unexplainable, something she didn't quite yet understand. But it was there, it was with her, and she didn't feel so alone after all.

A light breeze rustled in the cypress boughs nearby, and a piney scent wafted through the air. The ashes of the fire swirled up in a small cyclone, and she pulled the blankets more tightly around her chin. *When it snows, you will know...*

Glancing around quickly, Dahlia looked to see who had spoken, but found she was still alone. Resting her chin on her hands, she stared at the glowing embers the wind had uncovered and breathed life back into. Reaching out for a few small branches Artashir had stacked beside her, she placed them over the coals and watched as the dry leaves and bark caught fire. *When it snows, you will know....*

A twig snapped, and she turned to see Hasan approaching with a cloth bag full of warm bread from the market. "What did you say?" Dahlia asked, straining her neck to look up at him.

Settling down on the blankets next to her, he began to pull out an assortment of edible treats. "I asked how you slept, *habibi.*" He smiled down at her and handed her a jar of rosehip preserves. "I got your favorite. Are you ready for some tea?"

Smiling, she accepted the jar and stared at it for a long moment. "Hasan," she asked, "Did you just get back?"

"Yes. The market place wasn't very busy, but I took the long path home; up through the woods, you know. It just seemed like a good day for a long walk."

"Oh." She handed the jar back to him. "Tea sounds wonderful. Shall I brew...?"

She was interrupted by a loud screeching yawn from the far end of the terrace. Stretching slowly, Artashir rubbed his chest and scraped his fingers through a wild mass of tangled black hair. Laughing, Hasan called out, "Good morning, grizzly bear! Wouldn't you know, I found some honey in its comb fresh out of the forest this morning! Come join us and try a bit."

Dragging himself over to the fire, Artashir uttered a grumpy greeting before wrapping himself in a wool blanket and huddling beside the blaze. "When did it get so cold?" he mumbled.

With a twinkle in his eye, Hasan told them, "It's harvest time! It's the best time of the year. My people will be gathering to collect the fruits of the field and celebrate. Soon, we will know just how well the crops have done this season, and with all of the bounty settled up for the winter, we will enjoy the months of gathering together and relaxing."

"Are you going home?" Dahlia looked between the two men with a worried look on her face.

"Well, we've done all we can here, Dahlia. Ibrahim won't be coming back; he's helping a northern city rebuild, and," Artashir paused with a smug look on his face, "I've got to get back to my little gazelle. The nights get cold in the desert, and I wouldn't want her to face them alone."

Dahlia giggled. She had a hard time imagining the kind of woman who could put up with a head-strong man like Artashir. "She must be quite a lady," she smirked.

"What's that supposed to mean?" Artashir retorted.

"Dahlia has a lot to learn about the women of the desert," Hasan piped up quickly. "Perhaps she should go with you and find out just how tough your tribal matriarchs are."

Before Dahlia could interject, Artashir raised his hands in protest. "Wait a minute, Hasan; no one said anything about her coming to live with my people."

Dahlia, suddenly offended, gasped. "What's wrong with me coming to live with your people? You don't think I can handle it?"

Hasan sat back and watched. This was going better than he had hoped.

"Oh, I don't think they could handle you. You're just a bit spoiled."

"Spoiled?!! I am *not* spoiled! I am quite capable of sleeping on the ground and cooking over a fire. What do you think I've been doing the past three months?"

"Three months? That's nothing! The Bedouin have wilderness living down to an art. You wouldn't survive in the desert for a single night." Artashir shook his head and poked a finger at Hasan. "This was not part of our agreement."

"There was never an agreement, Artashir." Hasan smiled reassuringly at Dahlia. "We didn't know such a diamond would come from the dark mission we were assigned."

Dahlia sighed and took Hasan's hand. "I'm glad I found you, too," she said, smiling up at him.

Artashir scowled and glared at the two. "I don't know how this is going to work. How can I go home to get married and bring another girl with me? What will Endora think?"

"You mean she doesn't know about us?" Dahlia mocked.

"In your wildest dreams, Dahlia," Artashir said smugly.

"Please! In *your* wildest dreams, you ox!"

"Children, children," Hasan chuckled. "I have an idea. Dahlia, you can come to Lamirya with me—for the harvest. You will enjoy the celebrations, and Timon will love having an older sister. But when the harvest is in, perhaps it is best if you go to stay with Artashir's clan. After the work is finished, my people will have too much time to sit around and speculate about who you are, and that is a concern to me."

Artashir listened and nodded in solemn agreement. Dahlia waited for any objections on his part. The excitement of a new place, a new life, fluttered in her stomach, and she tried to imagine what it would be like to leave the home she had known for so long. Something cold touched her hand and as she glanced down at it, she heard the voice again. *When it snows, you will know...*

Looking up at the sky, she saw the large, wet flakes soaring down from the heavens. Artashir let out a loud, exuberant chortle that seemed to float on the air. "I've never seen snow before!" he cried, laughing and shouting and clapping his hands. Dahlia snickered at the sight, the huge man-child with arms the size of tree-stumps gleefully taking in the wonder of snow for the first time. The sound of clapping echoed off the hillside above the imploded house in thundering booms. Taking it all in—the joy of the moment mixed with the sadness of what this place had become, Dahlia suddenly understood what she had to do. "I will go and pack my things," she told Hasan.

"Very well, habibi. Very well." He seemed please with her decision. He squeezed her hand as she stood. Artashir was dancing around the yard, trying to catch snowflakes with his tongue.

"Artashir, get ready to go!" she called, trying not to laugh at his ridiculous antics.

"Not until I gather enough of these things to make a snowball. You'd better watch your back!"

Rolling her eyes, Dahlia turned and walked up the terrace steps. It didn't take long to pack the few things she had in the cellar. By the end of the day, they would be in the city by the sea that she loved. She and the two men that had become her friends.

Chapter 7

As they rode into town, Dahlia was astonished by the destruction that had robbed her beloved city by the sea of its beauty. Buildings with gaping holes stood beside windowless shells of structures. All around them, the streets were filled with people busily moving about their day. Hammering, painting, cleaning up. Dozens of trucks and horse-drawn wagons passed them, delivering goods--from milk jugs to cartloads of lumber. Everyone seemed busy; all were focused on recreating the city that was their home while going about the tasks of everyday life. Some buildings were finished, fresh coats of paint sealing the renovation, but alongside them were just as many buildings with blown-out windows and cracked foundations. Everywhere Dahlia looked, war was written on the broken walls of the city.

"I can't believe what I'm seeing," she whispered.

Hasan sat beside her, allowing her to take it all in, to get her mind around the tragic and needless destruction. It had been many weeks since he had been home, and his eyes were thirsty for the sites they now beheld. He was delighted at the progress he saw in his community's reconstruction efforts. His heart skipped a beat as he turned his thoughts to his wife and family. It would be good to put his arms around them, to hold his grandchildren on his knee again.

"Hasan, what are those strange little buildings?" Dahlia asked, pointing to a small, square structure in the center of a cleared lot. The walls reached about 5 feet tall, and there was no roof on it. "I've seen several now; are they public restrooms?"

Artashir laughed, and Hasan was quick to answer. "Those are voting booths, Dahlia. Our community held its first election just over a month ago, and the people were able to choose their new leaders."

"Oh, that's very nice!" Dahlia smiled, impressed that the city had handled its self-proclaimed freedom so responsibly.

Chuckling, Artashir elbowed Hasan and said, "Aren't you forgetting something? Don't you want to tell our friend here what those buildings were actually built for?"

"Well," Hasan stalled, "I don't think that's really necessary. Isn't it enough that they're being used for something good now?"

Dahlia glanced at each of the men, trying to imagine another use for the small, cinderblock booths.

"Those lovely little booths were repurposed into voting stations after the military was run out of town. Your father..."

"Artashir," Hasan warned, "Do you really think this is necessary?"

"Why, yes I do," Artashir snorted. "Dahlia, do you want to hear the truth, or are you enjoying Hasan's sugar-coated, little fairy tales of democratic practice?"

Her stomach churning, she looked out the window and tried to imagine these simple, hard-working people chasing the country's military force out of their city. It was hard to believe...

"Yes, I'm ready to hear it all," she responded emphatically.

"Good for you! Here's how it was: when things began to heat up after the last presidential 'election,' your father's hometown got a little rebellious. Keep in mind, that election was over ten years ago, and since everyone knew it was rigged in favor of your father, there was a loud outcry across Al Cazar. Whole towns rose up, rejecting the inauguration of your father for a second term, and deciding to make an example of his hometown, your father came down hard on Lamirya.

The small city suffered a great blow from the military, starting with curfews and ending with full-blown violence when the people wouldn't comply. Those cute little "voting booths" were built to house known resistance workers. Individuals found working to promote insurgence were chained inside the building, exposed to the elements, and publically shamed before all of their community. It was up to the family of the prisoner to feed them and provide any protection from sun exposure or rain."

Hasan remained quiet. "How long were they kept there?" Dahlia asked.

"Days, months, it didn't really matter to the military. Mercy wasn't high on their list. Some prisoners starved to death because their families feared what would happen if the military saw them helping a so-called 'resistance worker.'" Artashir cursed as he swerved to miss a cow roaming the village road. They were well beyond the city center now, heading out into the hilly countryside.

They bumped along the road for some time without speaking, each one lost in his own thoughts.

"*Soleado!*" Dahlia cried out as they passed the entrance to her father's estate. "Oh, we're so close! Can we go there now?"

"No, no, Habibi." Hasan patted her hand. "Let us go to my farm first. We'll come back under the cover of night. I swear it."

⋆⇒⊛ ⊛⇐⋆

The next few days were a blur, lost in a happy home-coming for Hasan, and a new way of life for Dahlia. It was a very busy time of year, and so the days were long and full with harvest-time activities. Dahlia went to the fields with the women each day, moving through the rows of wheat, binding the heavy, golden stalks and stacking them near the grain house. Thankfully, the women of Hasan's family all wore head-scarves, as was their custom, and so Dahlia was able to disguise herself. It was known to all who asked that she was a refugee from the capital city. There wasn't time to discuss the details; when the women weren't out in the fields working, they were preparing hearty meals for the workers. Evenings were spent around large bowls of rice, spiced meat stew, roasted vegetables, and baskets of freshly baked bread. Dahlia was exhausted at the end of each day, but she enjoyed the company of the other ladies, and found Hasan's family to be a delightful, hardworking bunch.

Artashir stayed on for a few days to make sure that her transition to life there went alright before heading on to his homeland. Before leaving, he promised to send for her when the harvest had been completed.

In the evenings, the women served the men first, then ate separately in a room filled with carpets and brightly woven pillows. Lounging on the floor, the ladies enjoyed their meal, and then massaged their aching feet and necks for one another. Talk usually revolved around who was interested in whom and several of the older girls asked about Artashir, wanting to know if Dahlia was promised to him in marriage. They were quite happy to learn that she was not.

Dahlia shared a room full of sleeping pallets with Hasan's granddaughters, ranging in age from 7 to 23. After a hard day's work, she fell asleep as soon as her head hit the pillow.

⊶⊷

When the harvest was finished, the rural community buzzed with an excitement that was highly contagious. Dahlia laughed and worked with the women, enjoying the festive preparations for the celebration. Much food would be prepared, and family recipes saved specifically for this time of year were discussed at great length. Everything had to be perfect and decorations, musical ensembles and special garments were custom-made for the occasion. Bela, Hasan's oldest granddaughter, helped Dahlia sew a simple dress for the week-long celebration.

"You will wear this in the evenings when the feasting and dancing begin," she said, wrinkling her nose in excitement. "It's very important that you look your best; it's during the winter months that the courting takes place, and the luckiest girls will be engaged by spring!"

"And whose eye are you hoping to catch?" Dahlia smiled, nudging her playfully.

Looking down, Bela blushed and waved her hand. "You would laugh if I told you."

Turning to look her in the eye, Dahlia waited. "Would you like me to guess?" she teased.

"No, no," Bela giggled and hid her mouth behind her hand. "It's just... He's not the handsomest man of suitable age."

"Bela! That doesn't matter. Do you care for him? And does he care for you?"

Nodding her head, Bela blushed again. "He brings me flowers every day when we're working in the field."

"Borak!" Dahlia gasped, remembering the gangly young man who often stopped to encourage them while they worked under the hot, morning sun. "Oh, Bela, he's so sweet. *Ladies, the work of your graceful hands makes my job light!*" Dahlia added in a deep voice, mocking the way he complimented the women as he passed by on his way to take a turn on the threshing floor.

"Dahlia!" Bela cried. "He means well! He has such a kind heart."

"Oh, I know." Dahlia smiled. "I did catch him looking at you the other day. He seems to be quite taken with you. I hope you enjoy getting to know each other this week. At this rate, you'll be happily married by summer!"

Bela smiled and hummed to herself as she finished the lace cuffs that fell softly around Dahlia's wrists. "We'll see what we can do to find a suitable husband for you!" she announced when the dress was finished.

⤏⤙◉ ◉⤘⤛

After several days of harried preparations, the countryside buzzed with an energy Dahlia had never felt before. Weeks of hard work and anticipation had mounted to one full week of seasonal celebration that seemed more exciting than anything Dahlia had ever experienced. It felt good to have accomplished so much and to know that the community was well-provided for during the long winter months ahead. Seeds were carefully stored for the spring planting and warehouses were bulging with the sustenance they would need until the next harvest.

The opening day of the week-long festival broke with a rosy dawn. Unable to sleep, Dahlia found herself walking the fields hours before any of the other girls stirred. Now that the harvest was finished, sleeping late was an indulgence that she should have been able to enjoy, but there was a restlessness inside of herself that she couldn't quite put her finger on. Watching the sun crest above the low horizon, she sat at the edge of the empty field and felt a great satisfaction in the work she had helped complete. It felt good to be a part of a community, a people that worked hard for their livelihood and enjoyed celebrating life together. It was a new feeling, a shadow of the memories she had of the olive harvests of her youth. Choosing not to dwell on the loss of her family, she allowed her heart to well up with thankfulness for the people she now lived among.

⤏⤙◉ ◉⤘⤛

The days of the week-long celebration ran together, each one with its unique set of meals, speeches made by the leading men of the community, and activities highlighting the success of the harvest. Historical accounts and family stories were told during mealtimes, and men and women ate together, unified by the success of their shared labor. When the evening meal was finished, the men and women took turns entertaining the crowd with singing, dancing and skits. Dahlia recognized many of the stories from similar folktales Artashir had told her during their nights in Anazir, but Hasan's people had their own versions accompanied by skilled actors and props. The children would gather in front, watching with wide eyes as the stories were acted out. Women would come around to each of the tables, pouring a milky drink into cups for the adults to enjoy. On the first night, Dahlia had tried it out of curiosity, and was surprised by the strong taste of black licorice. When the first swallow burned her throat, she learned to carefully sip it as the other girls did. After the stories were finished and the children put to bed, the dancing began, lit by the blaze of lanterns and a large bonfire.

On the third night of feasting, Dahlia sat entranced by the storyteller who unraveled a tale of a brave warrior named Magal. The fabled young soldier traveled the world undoing injustice and seeking a woman whose heart was pure. Lost in the charm of the storyteller and the magical outcomes of Magal's impossible victories, Dahlia sipped the milky drink the girls called Lion's Milk. A strange warmth spread through her limbs, and her head seemed to float as she felt each blow Magal defended himself against, and the joy he felt at finally embracing the beautiful young maiden he had rescued from a violent mob of Turks.

Startled by the applause the audience enthusiastically offered the storyteller, Dahlia tried to stand, hoping to move away from the crowd for a moment to get some fresh air and clear her head. A strong hand gripped her elbow and helped her rise. Surprised, Dahlia looked up into the eyes of a young man she recognized as one of Timon's older brothers. Smiling, Dahlia thanked him, steadying herself against him for a moment. Beaming, the young man led her onto the packed dirt floor at the center of the tables, joining other young couples who were gathering to dance.

"Oh, no," Dahlia protested, trying to break away from his grip.

"It's ok; I'll show you what to do," he encouraged her, pulling her toward the circle of women. Bela reached out her hand and grasped Dahlia's sweaty palm.

"Don't be nervous! It's easy. Just follow me!" Bela demonstrated how she would wave her scarf in her left hand, while holding onto the woman next to her with her right arm. Forming a semi-circle, the women waited for the music to start. Panicking, Dahlia held the scarf over her face. She found it difficult to stand; how would she ever manage to dance? And what would happen if she removed the scarf from her head and someone recognized her?

The music started, and the men danced around them, holding hands and circling faster and faster. The throbbing beat pulsed in Dahlia's head, and the women began to move in a circle, in the opposite direction of the men. Hopping from one foot to the other, the women pranced around, holding to one another and moving to the music inside the circle of men. Dahlia struggled to keep up, trying to find the rhythm, moving from one foot to the other. The other women moved quite gracefully, giggling and making eye contact with the men they found attractive. Dahlia tried to avoid the eyes of the young man who had led her onto the dance floor. Some of the girls batted their eyelashes at their beaus as they passed by, enjoying the freedom to flirt and make their interest known.

Hoping to find a way to escape, Dahlia searched the tables for Hasan, sure that he would rise to help her at any moment. When she didn't see him, the mounting fear began to choke her. Then, the women pulled the scarves from their heads and began to wave them with outstretched arms. Whistling, the men danced faster, their circle tightening around the women so that Dahlia could almost feel the heat of their bodies as they passed. It was dizzying, maddening, and her heart began to beat faster and faster as the men shouted for her to pull her scarf off. Reaching out as if to pluck it from her head, the men teased her as they passed by. "Secret beauty, reveal yourself! Don't be shy!" they cried.

Finally, one brazen boy snatched the scarf from her head as he passed by, and Dahlia held her breath as the dancing continued. Hoping no one would recognize who she was, she looked down at the ground as she danced. Her loose hair swung around her face, now unhindered by the scarf she had worn over it.

Then, out of the corner of her eye, she saw him. In a crisp white shirt, the sleeves unbuttoned and rolled up to his elbows, a familiar face glared at her from the end table near the bonfire. Gasping in surprise, she turned away, her hair swinging wildly. Looking back, Dahlia felt a wave of shock run through her body as she looked into Ibrahim's eyes. He seemed angry. Their eyes locked for a moment, and then she stumbled. Dahlia lurched towards Bela, trying to hold on for balance. The lights seemed to whirl around her, making her head swim.

"It's ok, I've got you!" One of the young men chuckled, holding her up from behind. Bela reached out to push Dahlia's long, dark hair out of her face.

"No, don't!" Dahlia cried, but it was too late.

An older man, who had come around one of the long tables to help her, stopped dead in his tracks. Staring at her with wild eyes, he shouted, "What is this?!!" The music stopped, no one moved and for a long moment Dahlia held her breath.

"Is this… is this… Seljuk's daughter?" the man stammered. An audible gasp arose from the audience. Dancers moved away from her as if she had an awful disease.

Bela stepped away and stared at her in astonishment. "Is it true?" she whispered, her eyes welling with tears.

Dahlia raised her hands to her mouth; her pulse was racing, her head still spinning. She was frozen to the spot.

Ibrahim rose and came towards her. His dark eyes seemed to shoot sparks at her as he spoke. "Seljuk's daughter! What would she be doing here?"

"I don't know! I don't know," the other man repeated. "She came as one of the refugees from Anazir." He paused. "She's been hiding out among our people! This, the spawn of our enemy!"

The people that Dahlia had come to know as her friends now looked at her with eyes full of hatred and fear.

Grabbing Dahlia's wrist and yanking her towards himself, Ibrahim called out, "Who is responsible for this girl?" He looked around the gathering and his eyes shown with anger.

Afraid for their father, Hasan's children remained silent. Taking another step back, Bela's eyes grew wide with fear.

"OK, if no one will speak for her, then I will take responsibility! And I will take her back to Anazir to face judgment for her father's actions!"

Bela shook her head, tears flowing down her cheeks. Dahlia's mouth fell open, shocked by Ibrahim's harsh treatment.

Pulling her behind him, Ibrahim strode away from the fire. The crowd followed them a few steps, then fell behind as they approached his battered SUV. Slamming her against the side of the vehicle, Ibrahim fumbled with the lock. "What were you thinking?" he hissed as he opened the door and started the engine.

Nausea erupted from somewhere deep inside of her and she lurched forward, falling to the ground and vomiting into the brush.

"And you're drunk! How could you expect to make rational decisions under the influence of *raki?*" he scolded her. Pulling her up, he helped her around to the passenger side and roughly buckled the seatbelt around her.

"Of what?" Dahlia whimpered.

"*Raki*, Lion's Milk. It's only the strongest alcoholic beverage you could possibly drink." Slamming her door, Ibrahim came back around to the driver's side. He quickly put the gears in reverse and made a wide turn. Trying to choke back the sobs that threatened to escape her, Dahlia put her hands over her face and cried.

"It's ok, Dahlia," Ibrahim said more softly as they sped away. "You're safe now."

"Where are you taking me?" she asked.

"To *Soleado*. Hasan has been meeting with me there the past couple of nights to discuss the recent election in Lamirya. He's there now; you'll be fine."

They rode the rest of the way in silence.

Chapter 8

ARRIVING AT *SOLEADO* was like walking into a dream. As they entered the broken gates, memories washed over Dahlia in waves of joy, sadness and fear at what she might find there. As the villa came into view, she was relieved to see that it hadn't been destroyed in the violence that had rocked the rest of Lamirya. A full moon shown over the dark sea below, beckoning to her like a long lost friend. Jumping out of the SUV, she ran to the terrace and looked down at the beach where the waves crashed into the rocks below.

She heard Ibrahim and Hasan talking quietly in the study, their voices floating out of the open window in soft tones. A few candles were lit, and a soft glow fell onto the terrace floor, illuminating the long table where she had shared so many lovely meals with her beloved family and friends.

"Habibi," Hasan called gently, as he came out to her. "You have returned to your villa by the sea at last!" Smiling down at her, he took her in his arms and held her close. "I hear you have had quite an adventure getting here." His voice was filled with amusement.

"Oh, Hasan! I fear I have made quite a mess for you! Your people will be angry with you for having brought me into your home." At the thought of the trouble she had caused him, she began to cry all over again.

"Nonsense! All is well; my people are in the middle of a festive time. All anger towards you will quickly subside, and they will think I am just a foolish, old man who didn't know any better."

"Does that mean... that I can return to stay with you again?" She looked up at him, wiping the tears from her cheeks.

Hasan shook his head sadly. "No, *habibi*, that would not be a good idea. My people are not prone to violence, but I would constantly fear for your well-being. It will be as we had planned; Ibrahim will take you into the desert and you will stay with Artashir's people there."

Dahlia looked from Hasan to Ibrahim who now stood in the doorway watching them. "Ibrahim will take good care of you, Dahlia. He will make sure you are safe. Is that not so, Ibrahim?" the older man spoke pointedly to the younger.

"Of course, Hasan," Ibrahim narrowed his eyes. "It is Dahlia who you should be lecturing. She seems determined to draw attention to herself."

Dahlia looked down, feeling the heat flood her cheeks. Remembering the ugly cake incident, she looked away, embarrassed. Ibrahim was right; the people of Al Cazar carried a deep resentment towards her father, and she would either have to face their anger or hide from it.

⤞⥈ ⥇⥠

Sitting on the terrace in the moonlight, Dahlia listened to the men as they talked in the study. Hasan was excited about the success of the community's first election; Ibrahim was concerned by the choices the people had made.

"But, Hasan," he exclaimed, "Jamal has no idea how to run a city! I know he means well, but the man is seriously lacking in leadership skills. He may have a soft heart, but kindness will not help him make the tough decisions that this job will call for."

"Ibrahim, you worry too much." Hasan clucked his tongue. The crisp strike of a match filled the silence between the two men and Dahlia smiled as the familiar scent of cigars wafted out of the open window. She closed her eyes and breathed deeply. "After all, Rome was not built in a day. Democracy is a new idea to our people; they will learn to choose men with appropriate abilities with each new election. And don't forget, a man can grow into the shoes he has been handed. I've seen it happen before!"

Ibrahim let out a low chuckle. "I still have a lot to learn, Hasan." With a deep sigh, he added, "Perhaps that's why I worry so much. I don't feel qualified to make the decisions that I am faced with. It's hard, knowing that so much rides on what I say or do."

"You've done fine, son. Your father must be very proud."

When nothing more was said, Dahlia stood and made her way to the staircase leading down to the beach. Letting her hand slide over the cool, smooth stone wall that served as the stair-railing, she felt her way along each step in the darkness, carefully counting her way down the steps. Thirty-eight in total if she remembered correctly. On thirty-nine, her toes sank into a cool, grainy surface. Raking her toes through the sand, Dahlia feasted her senses on the fresh sea-scent that swirled through her hair and playfully wrapped the long, flowing skirt around her calves. The rhythmic, crashing waves beckoned, and she made her way down to the water's edge.

The icy water sucked at her toes, eroding the sand out from under her feet. Staring into the blackness that was the water and sky, Dahlia tried to remember her mother's face. She could hear her mother laughing as they ran along the shore chasing seagulls, and even felt her mother's touch as she coaxed Dahlia out into the surf. "Don't be afraid," her mother had said, firmly holding her up as the waves splashed against their legs. "If you lose your footing, just lie back and float on the surface. Like this!" and she fell back into the water, arms outstretched, black curls spreading out around her face. Dahlia had looked down at her, amazed when her mother didn't sink beneath the water's surface. Leaning closer, Dahlia tried to figure out how she was managing to stay afloat. Opening one eye, her mother smiled and repeated, "Just float, Dahlia. Don't fight it." With a wink, she closed her eyes again and allowed herself to drift on the waves. The afternoon sun, reflecting off the choppy water like sparking diamonds, made her mother appear angelic. It had been a magical moment, one of the most vibrant early memories Dahlia had of her mother. Thinking about it now, Dahlia smiled, thankful that she could still remember the happy moments they had shared here together.

Something about the sea made Dahlia heady. Reclining on the beach, she dug her fingers into the cool sand and let her head fall back as she breathed in the salty air. The sensations were both exhilarating and soothing at the same time. "Just float," she heard her mother whisper, and Dahlia closed her eyes and imagined she was drifting on the gentle waves.

"Well you look quite relaxed!"

The voice jolted Dahlia back to the present. She could see his white shirt before she could make out his face in the moonlight. "I didn't mean for you to have to come looking for me."

"That's alright." He settled himself on the sand beside her. "I like the beach at night. There's something mysterious about it."

"Mysterious," Dahlia repeated, and in the time that lapsed, her ears were filled with the steady sound of the waves hitting the shore, accusing her of crime upon crime upon crime that her father's regime had committed against their people. "Mysterious... is that you would help me—after what happened to your family." From the corner of her eye, Dahlia saw Ibrahim flinch as if the reminder had been a blow to his gut. He slumped forward and she shuddered, curling her fingers and toes into the sand, wishing her entire being would sink beneath the surface. To be able to hide her head—like an ostrich! To not have to look and see the destruction all around her, accusing her at every turn. She was guilty! She had known; her father had done great evil, and though she hadn't known the particulars, she had felt the fear of the people in those last few years. It wasn't respect or great reverence that had shown in their eyes; she had only wanted to believe it was.

A tear slid down her cheek. She was sitting next to a broken man and she was powerless to make it right. Looking over at him, she watched him sob in silence. She wished she hadn't said anything. "Ibrahim, I'm sorry."

"It's not your fault," he said, his voice breaking. Wiping at his face, he added, "You're just a child!"

Feeling rebuked and once again dismissed by an unsympathetic authoritarian, she crawled to her feet and hurried away, wandering along the shore in the darkness. A single light shown in the distance, its steady radiance a beacon of hope and safety to those who worked on the water. She had never noticed the lighthouse before; perhaps it was too far off to be seen in the daylight. The light seemed to call to her, to pull her towards itself with an irresistible power. Curling up on an overturned fishing boat, she lay on her side facing the light.

In her dreams, Dahlia found herself in treacherous waters, a wild storm raging around her. Ibrahim was by her side, but in a moment of desperation, he turned and dove into the churning waters. She looked frantically around for a life vest to throw to him, but when he resurfaced, he simply turned and swam away, succumbing to the forces of the storm. Sucking in air hysterically, Dahlia forced herself to focus on saving herself, her freezing hands grasping the large spokes of the captain's wheel. She turned the boat, but she didn't know which way to go! Every direction seemed more treacherous than the last, and the darkness and bitter cold winds pressed in around her. Suddenly, a dim light caught her attention, blinking off the starboard side of the ship. Turning the wheel, she navigated the boat into the storm. With every minute that passed, the winds subsided until the intensity of the light overcame the darkness around her.

"Dahlia," it said, the tenor of its voice resonating in the very depths of her soul, "Come with me."

She smiled, reaching out her hand, feeling the warmth as it covered hers.

"Dahlia."

She loved how it sounded. She sighed and stretched, letting the warmth wash over her.

"Dahlia." The voice sounded impatient, as if in a hurry to show her new and mysterious things; good things, she felt certain.

"DAHLIA!" The voice had a familiar ring to it, and the urgency was annoyingly sharp. "Wake up!"

Dahlia opened one eye and saw Ibrahim standing over her, his hand shaking her shoulder. Her back ached from lying on the hard wooden keel, and her head throbbed. "What time is it?" she whispered; her throat was dry and scratchy.

"It's time to go. We need to get on the road before someone sees us here." He turned and headed up the stairs to the villa, not looking back to see if she would follow.

Dahlia sat up, remembering her dream, remembering the light that had given her hope. In the dim morning light, her eyes searched the coastline for a lighthouse, but there was none to be found. Stretching her sore limbs, she followed Ibrahim to the SUV and climbed into the passenger seat. "Where to now?" she asked.

"To the desert," he replied, rocks flying as the wheels turned hard into the gravel drive.

Chapter 9

With the bright sun high overhead, the SUV raced along a ribbon of sandy road that crossed the massive expanse of flat, dry land. They hadn't seen any sign of life for over an hour and the only break in the monotonous landscape was the jagged spine of rock rising out of the horizon ahead.

"Devil's Backbone," Ibrahim commented as the range loomed larger before them. It looked like something from another planet, Dahlia thought, curious how anyone could survive out here—let alone live on a day to day basis.

"Why do they live here?" she asked. "Artashir's people—what would bring them to call such a desolate place 'home'?"

Ibrahim shook his head. "They're an amazing group of people. Independent, strong-willed; survival is their way of life."

It seemed unnatural—to find strength in denying oneself the comforts of modern life. Civilization had so much to offer; what could people find so compelling as to live in the heart of the most barren region of their country?

A jackal crossed the road ahead of them, his mate and three small pups trotting along behind him. Undisturbed by the speeding vehicle, they continued on through the dry brush without looking back.

Beautiful, graceful creatures, Dahlia thought and remembered the campfire stories Artashir had told her. It all seemed so long ago. She felt a sudden wave of excitement at seeing him again, of meeting her friend's family and the fascinating people they lived among.

⊶⊷

Endora sat beside Artashir with the glowing radiance of a bride to be. The golden flakes in her dark eyes danced joyfully as they joked and told stories of all the adventures they had had as children. Dahlia admired her strong, confident laugh and the way her long hair was streaked with natural highlights from living out under the bright desert sun. It was clear they had been in love for a long, long time, maybe even since they were children, Dahlia mused. She wondered what it was like to know someone that well, especially someone like Artashir—who lived in such a bold and brazen manner. Endora must have feared for his life when he went off to join the resistance, and yet she didn't seem to be at all concerned for his safety or well-being from the way they talked and joked about their many childhood brushes with death.

"They are amusing, aren't they, dear?" Endora's mother leaned close and whispered to Dahlia, her warm hand gently patting her own.

Dahlia realized that she was grinning from ear to ear, almost ridiculously so, she thought self-consciously. "It's just," Dahlia shook her head slowly, "I never imagined someone so absolutely perfect for Artashir. It's remarkable—the way they embrace life with such tenacity!"

"I'm amazed they've both lived this long," Berlena chuckled. "They are two humps on a camel's back!"

Dahlia raised an eyebrow quizzically at the metaphor, but figured that she was referring to their unusual bond.

"You should have seen the cake she baked him."

"Cake?"

"It's a tradition among our people. You see, when a young woman is accepting a man's advances to court her alone, she prepares a cake that symbolized her desire to become the help-mate of that man. Typically, a girl personalizes the cake so as to identify the unique qualities she most admires in the man of her choice."

"And what kind of cake did she make him?" Dahlia grinned at the possibilities.

"A jackal." Berlena smiled as she watched her daughter's fiancé. "It was shaped like a jackal chasing the moon. A dreamer… utterly untamable."

"Of course."

"You know the story?"

"Yes, it's one of my favorites; I should have related the hero to its teller." Dahlia tilted her head toward the couple. "I can see how Endora chose that as the theme for his cake."

Berlena nodded proudly. "It is hoped that they will become the leading couple of our clan. It is qualities like those that most befit a leader—for our lifestyle."

Dahlia smiled at the young couple. They seemed to be oblivious to all around them, caught up in the joy of being together after such a long separation. So it surprised her when Artashir turned toward them and, with a sly smirk, said, "You should have seen the cake Dahlia cooked for *her* man!"

"I didn't realize you were engaged, dear," Berlena smiled while Dahlia sat in shock, mouth gaping as she stared at Artashir in disbelief.

"I'm not sure they've wrapped up all the details yet, but it was quite a cake!" Artashir grinned and gave Dahlia a light punch on the arm. "It was certainly quite memorable to all those present."

"Really?" Endora pried, an impish grin on her face. "I want *all* the details!"

"Oh no," Dahlia gasped. "It wasn't like that!"

"Is everything ok?" Ibrahim sat down next to Berlena, a warm cup of steaming tea in his hand. He looked from Dahlia's reddened face to the wide smirk Artashir wore.

"Dahlia was just telling us about…" Endora began.

"…about the time I cooked a cake for you and the men." Dahlia finished quickly.

"Ah, yes." Ibrahim cleared his throat. "That was quite a cake." He grimaced and looked away, annoyed at the remembrance.

Endora raised an eyebrow but said nothing more.

Dahlia sighed and smiled awkwardly.

Guffawing loudly, Artashir clapped his hands and went off to get a satchel of wine.

"Well," Berlena said, brushing her hands together neatly, "I'm off to get supper ready. Dahlia, would you care to help?"

Dahlia jumped at the invitation.

⇢▸═◉ ◉═◂⇠

Over dinner, Artashir and Ibrahim talked quietly while everyone else laughed and ate together. Dahlia felt immediately at home, reclining on large pillows around an enormous pot of lamb stew and roasted grain. Everyone shared, dipping their bread and fingers into the pot, eating their fill and washing it down with a warm, spiced wine.

When the meal was finished, the storytelling began. To Dahlia's delight, Endora was an even more captivating story-teller than Artashir, and they sat up into the late hours of the night listening to her tales of high-adventure and intrigue.

After the emotional strain of the past twenty-four hours, Dahlia was glad to be among a people who seemed to know or care little about what went on in Al Cazar. Though it was their home as well, the country's political strife didn't seem to have reached their quiet desert wilderness. Eyes closed, Dahlia rested her head against a mound of soft pillows and enjoyed the safe, warm tent that would be her winter home. Artashir's loud guffaws kept her from drifting off completely, but when

Endora began to play her pan-flute, Dahlia felt the heaviness of sleep pull her under.

For a moment, she was off—chasing a bright light through the desert. Was she a jackal? Was it the moon? The bright orb never seemed to move and yet it was always just out of reach. There was Endora, laughing and pulling her along, and Ibrahim stood on a low ridge, glaring at her in disapproval. Artashir danced around—at first, laughing and joking as he always did; then, his posture turned to the low, stealthy crawl of a warrior sneaking into enemy territory. "Don't go into the light," he growled. "They'll see you." But Dahlia found herself drawn to it all the more.

"What is it? Why can't I go? I want to be in the light!" She stretched out her arms and felt the earth begin to shake. Then, silence fell around her and a gentle hand on her shoulder awakened her.

"Dahlia," Endora smiled down at her. "You were dreaming. Are you ok?"

She felt the pulse racing in her throat, yet an overwhelming calmness settled over her. "I was dreaming," she echoed, and looked around her slowly. The elders had all gone to bed; Ibrahim and Artashir sat at the far side of the tent, their dark forms outlined by the red glow of the dying fire. They talked earnestly in low voices.

"Come on, we're going to go up on the mountain."

"Tonight?" Dahlia exclaimed. She swallowed hard, trying to wake herself up. "Endora, aren't there wild animals out there?"

"Maybe," Endora teased, then winked and pulled Dahlia to her feet. "I guess we'll just have to go and find out."

The frigid night air flooded her senses and puffs of breath floated before them as they laughed and stomped to get their blood flowing. Artashir and Ibrahim meandered along, in no hurry to keep up.

"Come on!" Endora snatched at Dahlia's sleeve, then raced on ahead following a worn goat trail into the nearby foothills. Dahlia stopped and looked up, amazed at the brightness of the stars. The diamond-studded canopy hung overhead, black velvet spun with millions of white, shining lights. Emotionally and physically exhausted after almost two days of no sleep, Dahlia relished the shock of chilled desert air that revived her. Life seemed intensely real again after months of numbness caused by her personal tragedy and surreal captivity. The crisp, fresh scent of desert sage and a silence as loud as the night sky was bright washed over her in profound perfection.

Endora stood on a large rock above her, head back and eyes closed, arms stretched to the heavens. The highlights in her long, flowing hair shown silvery in the moonlight. Without saying a word, Dahlia climbed onto the rocky bluff and looked out over the desert floor far below them. It stretched out for miles—a blackness like the ocean, fully alive and moving. Several campfires burned in the camp below. A distant coyote howled at the moon. A sudden breeze rattled the seed pods on the dry desert brush and it sounded like tiny raindrops hitting the hot city pavement in a sudden summer storm. Dahlia marveled at the sound.

When the men finally reached the bluff, Artashir wrapped his arms around Endora's waist and pulled her down from the rock. She was like a rag doll in his large arms, and she attempted, momentarily, to be angry at his interruption of her celestial adoration.

"Well," he bellowed, "Dahlia, what do you think of my kingdom?" He gestured toward the horizon and Dahlia once again took in the scene before her.

"It's more beautiful than I could ever have imagined," she conceded. "I love the serenity of this place. There is something so pure, so clean about the desert . . . I feel very close to nature here."

"Yes," Artashir sighed with satisfaction, "You can build the most architecturally spectacular cities imaginable, but come here and you'll never want to go back!"

"Well, I wouldn't go that far," Ibrahim contested.

"Oh, come, Ibrahim!" Artashir offered him a sip from the wineskin he carried at his side. "Mankind has spent hundreds of years trying to create the perfect dwelling—made of structurally sound materials, 'environmentally safe', you call it—trying to find a way to live in 'harmony with the earth' as if the solution wasn't staring you in the face. Live in nature; build structures and tents from materials gathered from the land. Abandon your concrete cities where people live stacked on top of one another like sardines in a can and stop building factories to create the materials needed to construct your buildings—a lot of needless time and energy spent for no reason, if you ask me!"

"Artashir, how can you . . ." Ibrahim coughed and blinked hard before handing the wineskin back to Artashir. "What is that?!!"

Snorting, Artashir slapped his knee and passed the leather jug to Dahlia. Endora pushed his hand away with a stern look, then pulled her pan-flute out and began to play softly.

"How can you expect everyone to live like this?" Ibrahim continued. "It has its advantages, but civilization moved on centuries ago! Cities are a necessary part of commerce and community strength! People coming together to—"

"Complete strangers, you mean!" Artashir snorted.

"To create products, share skill sets, pool resources. And architecture is a growing science!" His eyes gleamed as he drove his points home. "You should see the advances we've made in using reclaimed materials and recycled parts to create architectural masterpieces!"

Artashir rolled his eyes.

"In Bahgar, just recently, we discovered that by using metal that has been hardened in the same process used for making missiles, we can use one-tenth of the amount we would have used in regular rebar. The process is more complicated, but for one-half the cost, structures are more sound!" Animated by strong drink, Ibrahim gestured and carried on with Artashir as if the decision of whether to live in tents or skyscrapers was of imminent importance to the whole of society.

Dahlia wondered at their relationship. Two men so different, and yet united for a cause that she was just becoming acquainted with. These were the young, up and coming leaders of their nation. These were the ones who would decide the fate of Al Cazar and the helpless people who, broken by war and tired of needless violence and terror, were finally beginning the task of rebuilding their lives.

"Artashir, it's good to live off the land, to live as your people do. I see the benefit in creating and mending your own dwellings, but it's unreasonable to think that the majority of mankind could live this way. Be reasonable, man," he cried in a moment of heated debate. "After all, how can a people defend themselves from an enemy when the walls within which they dwell are made of cloth and wood?" Unaware of the pained look on Artashir's face, Ibrahim continued. "A single missile would take out an entire tribe, tearing through fabric and wiping out all those you hold dear—" The words caught in his throat. Slowly, the realization of his words set in, and Ibrahim's mind caught up with his mouth. "It would be a horrible, needless slaughter!"

"The way a single missile could take out a city block, crushing innocent lives in one bloody mass of mortar and steel?" Artashir spoke in a low, calculated voice. "Whether we build homes of cloth or concrete, they cannot stand in the face of violent weapons and the evil men who use them."

Ibrahim's eyes grew wide as he fought to control his breathing. Dahlia feared he was going to strike Artashir.

"No matter what we do, or how soundly we build our homes—even if we burrow into the ground like moles and live in windowless bombshelters, evil men will find a way to bring tragedy to innocent lives!"

Dahlia heard the shriek before she realized it was coming from her own mouth: a long, wailing scream that gurgled in her throat and broke through her clenched lips as she prayed for them to stop. Ibrahim looked from her to Artashir with wild eyes, his hands clenching and un-clenching as fast as his chest heaved up and down. He reminded Dahlia of a bull preparing to rush the red cape.

Artashir's eyes were sad; a broken, tired look replaced the stare of challenge he had worn during their lively debate. "You can't bring her back, Ibrahim. They came and they took your family, and there's nothing you can do." He brought his hands up in front of him as if inviting Ibrahim to throw some punches, to release the tension.

Reeling with the pain, Ibrahim looked about frantically as if searching for something, anything. Seizing a melon-sized boulder, he staggered under the weight of it as he made his way to the ledge. Dahlia's heart pounded, momentarily forgetting the freshly opened wound of her own heart. Fearing that Ibrahim was going to slip over the edge, she reached out as if to grab him.

"Aaaawwwwggggh!" The animalistic noise snarled out of Ibrahim as he hurled the boulder into the darkness. A moment passed before the distant sound of rocks crashing below them echoed up the cliff wall. Chest heaving, he rested his back against the large rock Endora had stood upon earlier.

Downing a quick swig of *raki*, Artashir threw the wineskin to the ground and grabbed a hold of a massive rock. Shifting his weight as he lifted it above his shoulder, he ran at the ledge and shot-putted the stone far into the darkness with a war cry that made the hair on the back of Dahlia's neck stand on end.

Having recovered from the initial shock of the emotionally charged moment, Endora made her way to Dahlia's side. Sitting beside her, she pulled Dahlia close and stroked her hair. Rocking back and forth, she rubbed Dahlia's back and hummed the sweet tune she had played for them earlier. "I know what happened to your family," she whispered. "I'm so glad you're here with us now. Everything is going to be ok."

Not caring how Endora knew, or what else Artashir might have told her, Dahlia allowed herself to be comforted and the tears began to flow. Rock after rock flew from the cliff, accompanied by loud grunts and sounds of rock shattering below. When the men were too exhausted to continue, they sat in sweaty heaps with their legs dangling over the ledge, their labored breathing the only sound.

⋅⊷⊶⋅

"Do you believe in God?" Dahlia whispered. The girls sat side by side, the large white moon high above them now.

Endora laughed, soft and easy, like music notes floating across a sheet of music. "Of course. How could I not?" She stretched her arms up to the night sky. "Look around you! His fingerprints are everywhere! It's magnificent, this world we live in; the world God created."

A night owl called out in question, *"Who? Who?"*

"But there's so much suffering, so much wrong." Dahlia gestured to the two men who rested in silence in the darkness. "Why would God allow that?"

Endora nodded. "I don't know. I guess…" she paused. "Dahlia, life in the desert is hard. For hundreds of years, my people have lived this way; suffering is a part of my inheritance. It's a part of our existence. We don't question it, we just live. We survive, and every day we have is an opportunity to embrace the beauty, the triumphs and the pain. We don't much question it, we just live."

Dahlia nodded. It was different than the life she knew, where everyone seemed determined to have the best life possible, relying on education, power and wealth to lift themselves up. To avoid hardship and suffering at all costs.

"And who do you think God is?" Dahlia asked.

Endora thought for a minute. "It's not so much that we have a real idea of who He is . . . we just accept that He is!"

"I don't understand."

"Well, as Bedouin tribes, we have a long tradition of trading with a variety of people and cultures, and our travels over the generations have placed us in contact with many prophets. They have stayed with my people, learning our ways and teaching their philosophies. We absorb bits of it, increasing our own treasure of knowledge and spiritual insight. My people speak of a man who lived among us for a time—who said the God he served appeared to him in a burning bush. This God was pure and righteous, and demanded His people's obedience, so He led them into the desert to purify them. He gave them laws to live by—good laws. Many prophets have lived among our people, spreading their teachings of Saviors, purity in life and a future in Heaven. There have been some that believed in achieving peace and enlightenment here by meditation and moral living." She paused as she tried to find the right words. "I guess I see God as a tree. Each religion is a branch, slightly different in size and make-up, but producing fruit of its own. When one branch dies or is cut off, another replaces it. God... is the trunk from which all the branches are born. They all belong to Him, yet each is only a living, growing part of the whole."

Dahlia thought on this for a moment, but her mind was too exhausted to absorb the depth of Endora's philosophy.

Chapter 10

THE NEXT THING she knew, Dahlia awakened to the sound of tinkling bells and speckles of light beams shining through tiny holes in the fabric of the tent. Lifting the flap, she peered out and saw that the sun was already high in the sky. A small shepherd boy wandered among his sheep as they nibbled on the brown, dry brush behind the tent. Memories from the night before shifted through her mind. Endora slept peacefully on a pallet nearby.

In her dreams, Dahlia had seen the stormy sea again, Ibrahim swimming into the blackness, Endora walking along the shore singing sweetly to herself, Artashir laughing at the moon, the light—the beam that called to her day and night. She followed it and this time it led her to a stream that flowed through a desert. Along its banks, thousands of parched, weary people stood, staring at the crystal clear water in awe as if they couldn't believe what they had found. Dahlia ran to them, gesturing for them to drink. And then she saw it. A large tree grew up over the stream, its massive, gnarly roots growing out of both banks, twisting up and meeting over the water, forming one enormous trunk. Dahlia leaned back her head, looking up, up, up…. trying to see the branches that grew out of the gigantic, old tree, but the sunlight blinded her. *"It's leaves are for the healing of the nations,"* a voice whispered.

Now, sitting in the tent, with her senses returning and the realness of the dream fading, she wondered what it would be like to move among

Endora's people. Their way of life was so different, so simple, and yet daily tasks—like cooking and bringing water to the camp—were hard work that required many hands. She wanted to be a help to those who were hosting her. She must show them how grateful she was for their kindness and generosity.

Dressing quickly (mornings in the desert were surprisingly chilly), she splashed some cold water on her face from the pail that Endora kept on a low table near the tent-opening. Sounds of activity and the smell of roasting vegetables greeted her. Families gathered around their smoky fires, enjoying a quick breakfast of mashed roots and baked bread dipped in honey before heading off to begin their chores. In the distance, she saw Ibrahim talking to a group of men. They stood around a warm fire, holding cups of tea and nodding enthusiastically as Ibrahim talked. For a moment, her mind saw her father speaking to the olive harvesters, praising them for their hard work. She rubbed her sleepy eyes with the backs of her hands. Artashir stood nearby, arms folded, head bowed. Again, she wondered at what the two men shared in common. What could Ibrahim possibly have to say to these simple people? Moving closer, she saw tears in the eyes of some of the men. Surprised and suddenly ashamed, she moved away, busying herself with trying to start a fire in the small pit near her tent.

It wasn't as easy as she had imagined it would be. After several attempts to arrange the twigs and dead wood in a manner that would encourage the embers from the night before, she sat back and wiped a soot-covered hand across her forehead.

"Need some help?"

Without looking up, she knew who the voice belonged to. How was it that he always managed to find her at the most inconvenient times? Chewing her lower lip, she tried to think of a polite way to decline.

"Here. You want to build a pyramid like this. The walls protect the fire while drawing the flames up through the center." A light gust of air came as if on cue and blew life into the glowing coals. The dead branches crackled and Ibrahim sat back on his heels. "That's nice, isn't it?" A friendly smile greeted her when she finally dared to look, but it didn't feel natural.

"Yes, nice." She smiled with her mouth.

"Oh, there you are!" Endora pushed through the flap, wrapping a colorful tunic around her slender frame. "We've got to get going! I had no idea how late it was! Can you believe we slept so long?" Endora patted Ibrahim on the shoulder, oblivious to the awkward moment she had interrupted, and held out a dark blue garment to Dahlia. "This is for you to wear while we're out today. I made it myself. Don't you love it?" she gushed, showing Dahlia how the sleeves could roll and tie up when it grew too hot. A thin hood would shade her from the sun. "Quick, put it on over your clothes; we'll eat on the way. I've packed some great snacks. Do you like date cakes? And some jerky—with my own special seasonings. Family recipe; top secret, of course. Artashir loves it. Here, Ibrahim; try some."

Ibrahim obediently put the dried meat in his mouth and chewed. "Mmmh," he nodded, lifting his eyebrows in surprise.

"Well, we're off! Good luck on the hunt! I want a big jackrabbit, so do your best, ok?"

Dahlia hurried after her, ignoring the quick wave from Ibrahim.

⤙⊙ ⊙⤚

Once the sheep had reached a grassy plateau high above the desert floor, the girls sat on a large, smooth stone to rest.

"Don't you think it's strange; the relationship between Artashir and Ibrahim, I mean? What could they possibly have in common?" Dahlia plucked the petals off a purple sage bloom. "And last night. Why on earth did Artashir encourage that dangerous display of rage? They could have both gotten themselves killed—behaving so recklessly like that!"

Endora lifted an eyebrow. "You don't know much about our people, do you?" she asked. "I mean, as far as the war is concerned, and why Artashir went off to join the resistance."

Dahlia tried to remember. It seemed she had heard something about the pain that had drawn Artashir out of the desert, but she couldn't remember now what she had heard. Had he lost family as well?

"We're not as far removed from your world as you would imagine." Endora looked away. Before Dahlia could press her more, she quickly rose, a cheerful spirit replacing the mysterious darkness that had suddenly come over her. She pulled out the small flute carved from an animal's leg-bone and played a little tune while they walked along a small, clear stream.

"That was wonderful!" Dahlia clapped when she had finished. Endora took a deep bow and they laughed as they skipped along the pebbled shore. When they reached a crystal pool where the stream backed up before cascading over several large boulders, Endora stopped and skipped a flat stone across the smooth surface of the water. "This is where we bring the animals to drink. It's the only watering hole for miles." Endora lowered her voice, as though preparing to share a deep secret. "Sometimes I like to go for a swim—it feels great after a hot day of wandering around the hillsides under the blazing sun! Care to join me?" she called over her shoulder as she waded into the stream.

"Now?" Dahlia asked, surprised. "But I don't have a swimsuit."

"A what?" Endora crinkled up her face. "Oh, you don't need to worry—no one will see you here! The shepherds water their flocks at the end of the day. I'm sure there's no one around to see us now." With a carefree smile, Endora pulled her tunic up over her head and flung it onto a nearby rock.

Clearly uncomfortable, Dahlia looked away. She admired how Endora could live so brazenly, unafraid of who might see her or what might happen. A zealous hunger for enjoying life in the moment seemed to free her from the bondage of fear or self-consciousness.

"Suit yourself!" Endora laughed when Dahlia didn't budge from the shore. She waded further in, splashing about in the refreshing, mountain-spring fed waters. Swimming in a lazy circle, she showered Dahlia with questions about life in the big city. Obviously, Dahlia's life was as intriguing to Endora as the Bedouin ways had been to Dahlia. "You don't get overwhelmed by all those people around you all the time?" she asked, eyes wide.

Dahlia squinted as she looked at the distant horizon. The sun was starting to sink low in the sky. "You get used to it, I guess. You hear sounds all the time: cars, sirens, vendors in the street, airplanes overhead. You never feel alone."

Endora frowned. "I guess I like to be alone. It helps me think."

Dahlia knew what she meant. She remembered all the nights she had holed up in the olive oil cellar at home, writing, reading or just dreaming about the future. Dahlia was not surprised that Endora was a shepherdess, preferring to wander in the wilderness away from the camp. It provided the hours she craved to make up stories or practice her hunting skills and flute-playing. "What do you think about when you're alone?" she asked.

A dreamy smile spread across Endora's face. "Artashir, our life together. How our children will grow up like wild little animals, learning to survive on lizards and other creatures they catch when we take them camping in the mountains and teach them to hunt and live off the land." Endora laughed at the look on Dahlia's face. "That doesn't sound fun to you?" she mocked. "You are such a city girl!"

Dahlia stuck out her tongue. "I admit it, gladly!" she laughed. "I don't ever want to have to eat a lizard or enjoy the pleasures of wilderness living!"

Endora reflected to herself for a moment. A distant hawk screeched as it left its high perch and soared down after some small prey. "What is it you want for your future?"

"*Soleado,*" she responded without thinking. It rolled off her tongue as the warmth of the word radiated through her. "It's a place I love, near the sea. I want to grow things, to work the land and produce a harvest to share with the people around me."

"That sounds wonderful," Endora said. A motherly tone in her voice stroked the rawness that last night's events had uncovered. "Your family would be so proud of you. I know you wish you could share these dreams with them."

Dahlia doubted her father would have listened; and if he had, he probably wouldn't have approved. "Endora…" Dahlia hesitated. Did she dare say more? She thought for a moment about the consequences of revealing her identity to her new desert friend. "I need to tell you something about my family, about my father." Her stomach heaved, a light sweat breaking out all over her skin. Maybe she shouldn't force the truth. But Endora deserved to know.

Seeing that Dahlia was physically disturbed by the memory of her parents, Endora waited patiently, knowing that talking about the tragedy would help her heal. "Take your time," she encouraged, splashing about in the shallow stream.

"No, I mean besides their death. It's… it's who my father was."

A cascade of pebbles on the path above them startled the girls, and Endora's eyes grew wide. She gestured wildly for Dahlia to toss her the bright tunic. They heard voices and scrambled to make Endora presentable before the men came around the wall of large boulders. Realizing she didn't have time to put the tunic on, she wrapped it around herself, turning her back to the path, still ankle deep in the stream.

"Endora!" one of the men gasped, and both quickly turned away in exaggerated surprise. Gushing apologies, they covered their faces with their hands, groveling and carrying on as if they feared for their very lives.

Endora stifled a laugh and rolled her eyes at Dahlia as she quickly put the tunic on and pulled her wet hair into a knot at the back of her neck. "You can turn around now, boys. It's ok!"

Still averting their eyes, the two shepherds turned and continued to offer amends for interrupting her swim. "It's just so hot, and we thought we'd water the sheep early today before heading to the lowlands where we might find some shade…"

"And our own throats were so parched; I stupidly forgot to pack a skin of water! I don't know what I was thinking!" the other gushed apologetically.

"Kenan! Jerosh, stop! That's really enough." Endora waved her hand in a dismissive gesture. "I don't think you've done any damage, really. After all, seeing the backs of my legs is hardly reason to beat yourselves up."

"Oh, but we didn't see anything! Really!" the taller one called out, his voice rising sharply.

"No, NO" Jerosh agreed, "Not a thing!"

Endora put her hands over her face and drew in a deep breath. Dahlia held her sides, trying so hard not to laugh that it hurt.

"No, I'm sure you didn't," she conceded in an annoyed tone. "I am mysteriously invisible. In fact, no one has seen me do anything wrong since Artashir and I became betrothed seven years ago!" she added for Dahlia's benefit. "I could run through camp screaming like a mad woman and people would smile and greet me as if I were behaving perfectly normal." She laughed, shaking her head.

"Well, Endora, please don't tell him you saw us here," Kenan said, backing away.

"It would just make things easier for us," Jerosh added, nodding vigorously.

"Don't you want to water your sheep?" Endora called after them.

"No, no; we'll be fine! Thank you! Goodbye!" And with that, the two men were gone.

The girls burst out laughing, unable to contain their amusement any longer. "What kind of bizarre power is that? You could get away with murder!"

"Literally!" Endora snickered. "It's silly, isn't it? Artashir is as gentle as a lamb, but the young men fear him as if he were a brooding, ferocious lion, looking to attack at any moment."

Dahlia reflected on this analogy. On one hand, she could see the gentle side that Endora brought out in him, but Endora's affection blinded her to the dark currents that ran in the blood of the man she loved.

Chapter 11

IBRAHIM STAYED IN Sanzar for a few days while Dahlia settled in. Endora embraced her as a sister and led her around the camp, introducing her to the extended family and close tribes that lived there with them. Daily life revolved around cooking and carpet-weaving for the women. Most sat and gossiped or sang while they wove intricate, nature-influenced designs from lambs' wool. Dahlia found the dyeing process fascinating, watching the pale, natural fiber take on the rich colors extracted from local plants, minerals found in the soil, and even berries that grew wild in the mountains nearby.

The men hunted in shifts, using their off days to work around the camp, mending tent posts or crafting furniture from animal bones and carefully scraped and dried animal skins. Often, hunting trips would last several days as men searched for prey large enough to feed their families through the winter.

Endora begged Ibrahim to stay long enough to join in their wedding celebration, and he agreed. Apparently, Artashir had hoped to marry Endora much earlier, but events had led him away before they had the opportunity. No one talked about what those events were, but Artashir had refused to marry Endora in a quick ceremony before he left, concerned that their separation would be harder on her if they were already married. Continuing with the plans they had made over six months ago, the clan quickly prepared for the wedding ceremony.

When the much anticipated morning finally came, Dahlia watched Endora prepare for the ceremony. "It's important to our people that we wed at a time when we can step immediately into a role of leadership. Since Artashir's parents and several of the other elders are no longer alive, we are prepared to become a couple of great influence among our people." There was no egotistical pride in the way she said it, Dahlia noted. It was simply a matter of accepting the people's needs as their responsibility, and she and Artashir understood that the tribe had chosen them for this task. "Our union makes us fully mature in the eyes of our people; a man cannot lead without a wife, so this is the final step in becoming elders."

Dahlia pondered the people's choice to accept leaders so young. And yet there seemed to be a noticeable lack of middle-aged adults among the tribes. She had accounted it to the harshness of life in the desert, and yet oddly, she had recently noticed a thriving elderly population who accepted their role as caretakers of the children while the young couples went about the daily tasks of the camp. In fact, Berlena was the only middle-aged woman Dahlia had met.

"I must go now." Endora hugged Dahlia to her chest and held her close for a moment. "My hope is that you, also, will accept the opportunity to lead your people when the time comes," she whispered in her ear. "I've seen how Ibrahim looks at you; before long, he will be ready to love again. I hope your happiness together will be as rich and as deep as the joy that Artashir and I find in one another." With a quick kiss on the cheek Endora was gone, leaving Dahlia with an expression of shock on her face.

"Is she mad?" Dahlia muttered to herself, sitting quickly on the edge of the bed to catch her breath. A sudden lightheadedness had overcome her, and her face was hot. Covering her mouth with her hand, her eyes grew wide. *Ibrahim's "feelings" for her?* She couldn't believe it; in fact, it bothered her that Endora should even imagine such things.

Music beckoned to her, and she knew the ceremony was about to begin. Splashing her face with water from the pail, she smoothed back her hair and hurried to the main tent.

⋅⊷⊜ ⊜⊶⋅

Artashir and Endora danced around the floor with their wedding party, dressed in full traditional costume. Lively music and laughter relaxed Dahlia, but she still felt an odd, tight knot in the pit of her stomach. Endora's words had haunted her throughout the ceremony and the drawn-out feast that followed. Several men asked her to dance, but she stayed in the back, sitting behind a group of young girls who giggled and whispered, dreaming of the day when they, too, would wed.

"Look how beautiful she is!" one girl exclaimed. "I hope I look like that when I grow up!"

"I hope my parents find me a husband as handsome as he," another added dreamily.

Dahlia sipped her spiced wine and watched the couple on the dance floor. They were so happy, so natural together. Artashir, for as brazen and bull-headed as he was, treated Endora with all of the respect and gentleness of a knight in shining armor. It was a fairytale evening, one which the people celebrated whole-heartedly, accepting their 'King and Queen' with great rejoicing.

Dahlia wondered if she would ever find anyone who suited her so well; and if she did, who would celebrate her marriage? She had no family, no real friends who knew her for who she actually was. This was just another phase, another short season in her life of exile, but eventually she would have to create a new life for herself. *Would it be here,* she wondered. It didn't seem likely.

Frustrated and feeling desperately alone, she looked around the room. Everyone was fully enjoying themselves—eating, drinking, dancing, laughing. It was a night to celebrate, but she didn't feel like celebrating.

Ibrahim sat across the room, stirring a cup of tea. His eyes were dark, brooding. He seemed uncomfortable and sullen. He looked up and their eyes met. Quickly, she looked away. Then, slowly turning back, her eyes met his again. Feeling completely ridiculous, she quickly got up and moved along the inner wall of the tent searching for a flap through which to escape. She looked back one more time. To her dismay, Ibrahim had gotten up and was making his way toward her. Their eyes met and his arm came up as if beckoning her to stop. Then, he was blocked from her sight as two men stopped in his path to speak, gesturing enthusiastically. They patted his arm and carried on long enough for Dalia to find a hole in the tent and slip out.

The chilly night air slapped her in the face, making her eyes water. She hurried into the darkness, waiting for her eyes to adjust before breaking into a run. At the edge of camp, she found a worn path and followed it out into the desert hoping to get as far away as possible. When she could no longer hear the music, Dahlia looked back. There was nothing there but darkness. Overhead, the stars shone with magnificent brightness.

Dahlia fell to her knees and leaned back, taking in the sheer massiveness of the celestial night sky. "God," she cried out, "where are you?"

A breeze ruffled her hair and the sage brush whispered excitedly. A night owl called out, startled by her voice. "*Who? Who?*"

She heard the heavy beat of its wings as it flew away.

I want to know you," she whispered into the darkness. Another light breeze caressed her face and she looked up in wonder. The moment felt surreal, and yet why should she be surprised that the creator God would use his creation to speak to her? A burst of light lit up the night sky and she watched as a single orb fell across the star-studded expanse.

A lightness overcame her and she laughed to herself. "I want to know you, and I want to understand the purpose you have for me!" she called out. "I want to understand who you are and why I was born into such a time as this! God, I can't believe it's all for no reason! I won't believe it," she whispered, waiting to see if anything would happen. "I want to know why I'm here!" she shouted, "and I want to know why you let this happen to my family!" She muffled a sob, expecting a bolt of lightning to fall from the sky. When nothing happened, she laughed to herself. "What am I doing?" she asked the stars, shaking her head. "Who am I to think that I could talk to God, and who is God that I would expect anything from him?"

She stood. "And how will I know what to do next? I can't stay here forever!" she shouted, shaking her fist at the sky. "I don't want to run anymore!" she cried. "I want to have a life—a fruitful life, a good life! How is that going to happen now?!"

"When it snows, you will know," the small, still voice came. Was it really there, or was it only a memory echoing in the recesses of her mind?

Dahlia sank to her knees again. It was maddening, this voice that she heard, and yet she didn't know if it was real or only a creation of her mind. "What will I know?" she sobbed. "What future can I have? Seljuk's daughter! I'm cursed!"

"I will give you hope and a future," the voice replied.

"Hope and a future," she repeated to herself. "And what kind of future does an outcast have? Will I have to run forever, hoping not to be discovered, living with the shame of my father's sins hanging over me?"

"Hope and a future," came the reply, *"and I have prepared you for such a time as this."*

Dahlia ran her fingers through her hair. Was she going mad?

"What do you want?" she cried.

"When it snows, you will know."

Dahlia sat on the path in the darkness until the cold made her bones ache. Returning to camp, she wondered if it ever snowed in the desert. Would she live the rest of her life here in exile? With a supernatural calmness, she entered the empty tent that she had shared for the past week with Endora. With her mind resolute, she lay on her pallet and silently vowed not to speak to God again until the snow lay in white drifts around her tent.

Chapter 12

"WHERE DID YOU go last night?" came the question in the familiar accusing tone. "Endora was worried about you!"

Dahlia sat beside her fire, hoping he wouldn't gloat at the pyramid of twigs she had carefully constructed and set ablaze. "I took a walk. Just needed to clear my head…" her voice trailed off. He didn't mention why he had tried to follow her. She poked at the chickpeas she was roasting in a shallow pan, then sprinkled some of Endora's seasonings over them. "Would you care for some breakfast?" she asked politely, avoiding his eyes.

"No. I'm going back to Anazir today. There's some business there I need to attend to." Ibrahim cleared his throat. "Do you think you'll be alright here?"

"I'll be fine," she responded with a stony stare. She hoped he hadn't gotten the wrong idea last night. "Do you think there's any snow in the forecast?"

"Not a chance," he laughed. "You should enjoy a rather mild winter here, I imagine. And after that, I don't know. I guess the decision will be yours." Ibrahim got to his feet.

"Do you believe in God?" she asked abruptly.

"God," he said, a look of surprise on his handsome face. "I guess I would say we're not exactly on speaking terms." He turned to go. "And you?"

"I guess it depends on the weather," she said with a wry smile.

Giving her a strange look, he reached into his pocket and pulled out a folded envelope. "I thought you should have this. It's from your father."

Without looking at it, Dahlia took the envelope and tucked it into the fold of her tunic.

"Let me know if you need anything," he added. "Artashir will know how to get in touch with me."

She nodded, and once again, Ibrahim was gone.

⟶▷ ◁⟵

It was the custom among Artashir's people for newlyweds to spend the first few weeks of their marriage out in the wilderness, enjoying the solitude and relying solely on one another for survival. Although Dahlia had only known Endora for little more than a week, her heart ached at the absence of her new friend. She continued to eat her meals with Berlena and Endora's five younger siblings, helping prepare meals and often staying up late playing games with the children or talking to Berlena about Bedouin culture. Everything about this lifestyle was new to her, and she was thankful to have someone who could listen and explain when she had questions. Although the concept of a wilderness survival honeymoon was a very bizarre idea to Dahlia, she found the common practice of arranged marriages even more difficult to accept.

"How long has Nadia been engaged to her future husband?" Dahlia asked one night when the children had gone to bed. She had heard the girls talking about it while they were cleaning up, and it had so astonished her that she'd had to stifle a gasp of surprise. Nadia, who was only fourteen, had mentioned it so calmly, as if it were the most normal thing in the world.

"We chose Samuel for Nadia about five years ago, so it is all she has ever known. It's not uncommon for parents to promise their children to another couple that they respect. It's a way of entrusting a piece of yourself to someone who has played a significant role in your life, and the children accept our choice because they know that our love and concern for their well-being is so strong.

"You see," Berlena's eyes grew moist, "Samuel's father saved my husband's life once on a hunting trip. Years passed, they continued to hunt together and became fast friends; the experience forged a bond between them and as their friendship deepened, the bond grew to include our families as well, and eventually even our futures. By uniting our children, we are including them in the rich relationship we enjoy. Their union will be built on the respect and trust our families share. It's a part of their heritage. What better way to ensure the happiness of our children than to unite them with children who have been raised and shaped by the people we most love and trust? Our bond of friendship is strengthened by the bond of blood."

Dahlia picked at a loose thread on the pillow that comfortably supported her back and arms. The fire had died out, but a couple of small lamps provided a warm glow. "I understand that you love Samuel's family, and that Nadia accepts your choice for her, but … what if she doesn't love him?"

Berlena's eyes grew wide. "Love him? Oh, Dahlia, we have taught our children to love well. Nadia will be a good wife, as she is a good daughter, putting the needs of her husband and family before her own. I have carefully shown her all I know about keeping a tent in order. She performs all of the duties well, and she is not one to complain. She will be a very good wife!" Berlena finished with a rather stern look, as if Dahlia had pushed a little too far.

Laughing, Dahlia apologized. "I don't mean to suggest that she won't be a perfect wife to Samuel. Nadia is a precious, gracious girl with a warm heart. But what I meant was, what if she doesn't *love* him; you know, in a romantic way. What if she doesn't have feelings for him?"

Berlena raised an eyebrow. "Not have feelings for her husband? How could a woman share her bed with a man and not 'love' him as you say? How could she cook his meals and bear his children and work by his side through the seasons of life and not develop 'feelings' for him? You city girls—such strange ideas!"

Dahlia leaned forward, a look of bemused concern on her face. "I only meant that ... well, she might not like him. You know, some people—like Artashir and Endora; they seem to be made for each other. And they chose each other after all, didn't they?"

"Hhhmph! Well, of course they did! Artashir and Endora were matched since childhood. They chose each other because that's the way they are! They know what they want in life and have very strong energy. They were like two magnetic rocks, pulled together by fate. Everyone could see it!"

Dahlia nodded enthusiastically.

"But, silly girl," Berlena shook her head. "Not everyone knows what they want. Not everyone knows who to choose. So, we chose for Nadia. We found someone who we know has been raised well, who will work hard to provide for his family. We chose what's best for Nadia." Berlena's wide smile drew Dahlia in. Putting her head close to Dahlia's, she whispered, "I know who I would choose for you."

Dahlia jerked her head back. "I don't want to get married!"

Berlena turned her head and looked at Dahlia out of the side of her face. "Don't want to marry? What nonsense is that?"

Dahlia crossed her arms. "I just don't. I don't believe God would want me to," she added, as if she had any idea what God wanted for her.

"God?" Berlena retorted. "You have strange ideas, young Dahlia. But I understand you've suffered loss in your life, and I'm sure that in time you will want to have a family... a family of your own."

A strange look froze on Dahlia's pretty face. "Men can't be trusted. They are driven by an insatiable hunger for power. It destroys families, and cities and even countries! I worry that even Artashir will change under the weight of his new responsibilities."

"That's why they have each other," Berlena responded softly. "Of course he will change. A married man enters a whole new world; but they are a team, Dahlia." She shook her head. "Maybe you haven't seen that practiced before, but a people like ours... We rely on one another for strength and support. It's how we survive! No one is strong enough on their own; it takes a combined effort and intentional submission to one another to promote a strong, healthy community. Desert living and isolation have helped us develop this perspective. I can't say that it's for everyone, but it has enabled our people to thrive for centuries. It is our way of life."

Dahlia fidgeted with her hair. It sounded good, but difficult... and so foreign to her upbringing in a city where people were always unhappy with their leaders, and trust was non-existent. Her father had to force his people's submission, and out of a need to have complete authority, he submitted to no one. In Dahlia's mind power equated abuse, and she feared she would never have faith in those who were motivated to choose a life of leadership. She had seen what could happen to a heart eaten up with such ambition.

Since they were talking about serious matters, Dahlia decided to get Berlena's take on another subject that had been much on her mind lately. "Berlena, do you believe God is like a tree?"

"A tree?" Berlena thought for a minute. "Yes, a tree that is strong and graceful. A tree that has many large, shady branches that provide shelter to those who come seeking rest from a harsh world. He provides for us—the way a tree provides fruit for nourishment and kindling for our fires. But I think that I am more inclined to see God as a stream, and we are the trees—drawing our life strength from Him. He connects and refreshes us all." Thinking for a moment, she added, "Like a tree, we suffer and become weaker and more sickly the further we grow from the stream."

Dahlia remembered her dream and the massive old tree she had seen growing up over the river. People had come to it, desperately weary, thirsty for something they couldn't find anywhere else, yet they had hesitated to drink. "Does it ever snow in the desert?" she asked abruptly.

"Oh!" Berlena laughed. "It's been a long time. Let me see, I was just a little girl when we last saw a snowfall in these parts. We didn't know what to make of it—so soft and deep, like the wool on a newborn lamb." The lamp flickered. "Let me get some more oil …"

Dahlia stood to stretch her legs. "No, that's ok. I should head back to my tent. I thought I'd get an early start tomorrow—to beat the other shepherds to the high meadow north of camp. You know the one?"

"Ah, yes …" Berlena's eyes clouded over, and her momentary pause grew into an awkward silence.

"Yes. Well." Dahlia cleared her throat. "Then I'll say goodnight. Can I bring you anything from the hills?" She knew how Berlena loved to collect various sage blooms to season her breads and teas.

Berlena didn't answer. A faraway look she had seen in Berlena's eyes disturbed Dahlia, but she decided that Berlena must be tired. They had stayed up later than usual talking. Drawing a blanket up over Berlena, she bit her lip when a single tear escaped Berlena's tightly closed eyes and slid down her cheek. Without another word, she slipped out of the tent.

Chapter 13

DAHLIA SLEPT FITFULLY that night. She tossed and turned, her dreams filled with dark images covering a valley floor. Like bats they fluttered in the twilight of her mind, too filled with shadows for her to see clearly.

She rose early, wanting to get a start on the day, glad to leave the darkness of her dreams behind. As she went out of the tent, soft wooly bodies crowded around her. Like drifts of winter snow, she thought; but, alas, she was no closer to understanding the direction God had for her. The sheep bleated to her, eager to move up into the hills to find soft green nubs to nibble on. In the winter months, vegetation was scarce and so she would have to take them further than she ever had before. Calling the sheep by the names Endora had given them, Dahlia climbed the rocky path, setting her eyes on the jagged peaks above. She was told that some of the best meadows were just on the other side of the ridge, but when the shepherds told her how to get there, they averted their eyes. She had wondered if it were a holy place, but after talking to Berlena last night, she felt a strange foreboding. Why had Berlena become so withdrawn? Why were there still so many things she didn't know about these people and the secret sorrows they didn't talk about?

As it was, the mountainside was deserted. The other shepherds didn't bring their flocks this way, though they readily admitted it was the best place to feed the sheep this season. Dahlia enjoyed the silence. Living as the Bedouin did, privacy and solitude were rare pleasures.

Just the other night, she had heard two lovers talking as they passed by her tent. It had been a sweet moment, a few brief whispered confessions. Now, Dahlia wondered again if she would ever find someone who would want to walk with her in the evenings, whispering sweet things in her ear.

Winded, she stopped near the top of the path and ate her date cakes and a few pieces of goat cheese Berlena had given her last night. "Fresh!" she had smiled, wrapping it like precious treasure in a thick piece of cloth. Dahlia wrinkled her nose as the tart, salty flavor filled her mouth. It provided a pleasant contrast to the honey-sweetened cake. Refreshed, she climbed a little longer and before she knew it, she had crested the ridge.

Feeling triumphant, she took in the 360-degree views, laughing in wonder at the vistas her efforts awarded her. Below, to the south, lay the camp—dozens of tents all shapes and sizes scattered in several circles. Campfire smoke rose in curling plumes and she could picture the women working over pots of boiling water—cleaning, dyeing wool, cooking. From this high up, they looked like little ants, productively moving about accomplishing the necessary chores of the day. To the north rose another range of mountains; great rocky rows, each ridge higher than the last. They looked like waves on the ocean rolling in great, powerful swells. The highest peaks, rising up in the back, were covered in white caps of snow. It was no wonder that with such mountains to the north and the desert stretching to the south, Artashir's people remained cut off from the rest of the world. They were isolated on all sides by a landscape that was so harsh and desolate that even today it remained undesirable to most.

The sun was already beginning its descent and Dahlia realized it had taken her longer than she had expected to reach the rim. Looking around her, she saw that the sheep had found the high meadow the shepherds had told her of. Spotting a plant that she knew grew only on this side of the mountain, she quickly gathered some of its leaves and put them in the leather pouch she wore around her waist. Berlena loved to use them for teas, and this particular one created a calming affect when brewed, and could even help release the ache of tense, sore muscles. As she plucked a few of the leaves, she remembered her dream and how the leaves on the tree had been called the "healing of the nations." *If only it were that simple*, she sighed to herself.

With the sheep happily feasting on green succulent leaves, Dahlia looked down into the narrow valley that separated her from the foreboding mountains to the north. It was a deep, long plain, its floor hidden in shadows created by the precipitous rock face that rose on either side. Wondering if a river flowed through, she carefully made her way down a path that cut back on itself several times to help reduce the decline.

Before long, the vast plain spread out before her like a waterless sea between the craggy mountains. To her surprise, the entire valley floor was dotted with hand-woven flags tied to tall, gnarled poles—there was hardly an open spot for as far as she could see. She knew the flags were made by the Bedouin; she recognized the woven designs from the carpets and pillows that filled their tents. The edges of the flags were frayed and tattered, weathered by the hot, dry winds that swept through the valley. There were no trees or shrubs to act as windbreaks or to shelter the hand-crafted banners from the incessant blowing. It sounded like thousands of wings beating the air . . . *like souls flying to heaven*. The thought was a whisper in her mind, but it seemed to scream through her head in this eerie, lonely valley. *What is this place*, she wondered.

A vulture circled in the distance, then fell to the earth in a slow spiral. Following a well-worn path, Dahlia made her way down to the field of flags. There was no pattern, no neat rows, just thousands of jagged poles and worn-out flags growing on the valley floor like a field of colorful wildflowers surrounded by rocky, barren mountainsides. When she had finished her descent, deep shadows grew around her. The sun couldn't reach the edge of the valley floor, and she suddenly felt chill in the cool shade. It was then that she saw the memorial marker—one of quiet respect for loved ones lost. *"Rest in the bosom of our land,"* it read. Scrawled beneath it by a hand acting in anger was the one ugly word that painted a picture all too clear: *GENOCIDE!*

Reeling back in shock and understanding, she climbed back up the path and looked out at the sea of flags. *How many of them were there,* her mind screamed.

"Like the sands of the sea," came the unbidden thought, followed by the question: *Are there women and children here, also?* There was no doubt in her mind, though she didn't want to believe it. Who had done this awful thing?

A conversation drifted back, piece by piece. Her father had once called these people "unpredictable." It was a discussion she was asked to leave the room for; sometimes her father got so passionate about what he was saying that it frightened her mother and she would gently usher Dahlia away before she heard too much. Her father had hated these people. He felt that they were unruly and irresponsible—never settling down in one place for too long –so that issues like education and taxes were meaningless to them. For years, the government had ignored the Bedouin, granting them exemption from civil duties as long as they kept to the desert; but, her father had called them "unpredictable," and anything that he couldn't control was considered a threat to be taken seriously.

Now, the question plagued Dahlia's mind. What had happened in this valley of death?

Time stood still as the chill of the valley floor sank into her bones. Frozen to the path, she turned, looking away from the grave marker and viewed the tattered flags once again as they fluttered in the harsh wind. **Like souls flying to heaven.** The tears stung her eyes. They came in a torrent and her constricting throat choked the sobs that heaved from her chest. An anger that she had never experienced before filled Dahlia and she stumbled up the path, her feet carrying her along in a blind fury. Emotions raged through her. Heartbreak for what she had seen. Hatred for the hands that had done it. Shame for the ugly truth that she was the daughter of the one who had sanctioned such atrocities.

What could she do? It was done; this was now just one more piece of the horrible puzzle she was being forced to put together. Through a veil of tears, she felt her way up the steep incline, not stopping when she reached the ridge. With bleating sheep pressing in around her, she hurried along, off the path now, crawling over boulders and ledges, through thick brush and thorny cacti. She wanted to scream, she wanted to tear her eyes out; they burned, as did her chest which was so constricted she could barely breath. Gasping, driven on by the raw pain she felt inside, she felt ready to collapse but unable to stop.

A familiar sound caught her attention and drew her to itself. It was the rushing waters of Endora's stream, the low falls above the pool where she liked to swim. Climbing over boulders, Dahlia made her way toward it. She waded into the shallow current, the icy, mountain spring-fed waters numbing her feet and legs. Wanting to feel that numbness all over, not wanting to feel the pain anymore, she threw off her clothes and waded into the fast flowing stream. She lay down, allowing the water to wash over her, crushing her to the rocky bottom. Her skin went numb as a voice deep inside of her screamed, *I can't bear the weight of what I am, of what I've seen! It's inhumane, it's wrong; I don't want to become what my father did! Help me be different, help me walk in the light! Help me serve others instead of myself and to love and accept when it would be easier to hate and condemn!*

She felt a dam burst somewhere deep inside herself as the tension in her neck and chest released. All of the pain and shame and fear went with it; she felt stripped to the core as the water washed through her hair and over her frozen body. Then she saw her mother's face floating on the sparkling water, gently rocked back and forth by the waves.

Opening her eyes, she smiled sweetly at Dahlia and whispered, "Float, Dahlia. Just let go and float."

Allowing herself to be carried along by the rapid current, Dahlia's body was pushed through the narrow chute that emptied into the pool. Sinking to her knees, she gasped for air, allowing life to flow back into her lungs. She opened her eyes. Just a few feet from her stood two startled gazelles, noses just inches from the water, their eyes glued to her. When she didn't move, they took another long sip and then slowly backed away from the water's edge. As they climbed the rocky hillside above her, they looked back several times, as if to say, "We are watching you." They were witnesses of this moment, the moment of her renewal. It was as if God was once again using his creation to speak to her, saying, "I see you; I am with you. What will you do now?"

Dahlia rose up out of the water and wrapped the thin, blue tunic around herself. Though the shadows grew along the banks of the stream and a cool breeze lifted her wet hair, warmth radiated through her. She felt light, carefree, completely at peace in the rosy afterglow of dusk. Gathering a few dried twigs, she carefully started a fire. Overhead, the faint light of several stars shone as the soft colors of the sky slowly faded into darkness. When the fire was large enough, Dahlia knelt down and watched the flickering tongues of flame. They hungrily licked and devoured the dead branches. It reminded her of something Endora had said about one of God's prophets, of how God had spoken to him out of a burning bush. Although she did not expect God to speak to her now, it would not surprise her in the least to hear his voice. She contemplated what he might say. It was he who had redeemed her, he who had given her hope again. Kneeling beside the stream, she felt renewed, made new. *A new creation.* He could use her as he wanted. She no longer desired control of her life. Everything she had trusted had turned to ash. The truth had tarnished all she had ever loved. She could only be certain of one thing now. God was. She had felt it. She believed it; it was the truth that guided her now. It was the only truth she would accept. She knew it was only a foundation; she believed there was more to learn, and she was going to find it. Dahlia knew that this must be the light that called out to her, and she was now solely focused on seeking it out. It was the truth that had set her free, and she would no longer live in slavery to any other.

Chapter 14

IN HER DREAMS that night, Dahlia found herself bathed in sunlight, a heavy rain shower washing over her in silky steams of water. The raindrops glistened brightly, sparkling like diamonds all around her. She could see each one as they fell in slow motion. Then, they stopped falling altogether and as they hung suspended in the air around her, she watched them slowly crystalize. Dahlia closed her eyes, and when she felt the icy breath of the wind on her face, she felt something awaken inside of her. Opening her eyes, she watched as the suspended snowflakes began to float downward. She reached out a hand and watched them pile up on her palm. *Until the snow lies in drifts around my tent...* Dahlia drew in her breath in surprise when she heard her own voice. *Snow... drifts....*

"You will know," came the reply. The snow fell harder around her until the whiteness was blinding. Dahlia blinked as the heavy flakes fell on her eyelashes. Unable to see, she stumbled forward, her hands reaching out for something, anything. The tips of her fingers brushed a canvas wall and relief flooded her mind. Feeling her way along the side of the tent, she slowly made her way, searching for the opening. There! Pulling back the flap, she slipped inside...

Dahlia sat up with a start. She quickly drew the blankets up around herself. Disoriented, she looked around, but in the grey light of pre-dawn found it difficult to make out her surroundings.

"Dreaming; you're just dreaming!" she muttered to herself, but anxiousness gnawed at her insides, urging her to get up. Quickly, she climbed out of bed and wrapped herself in the blue tunic Endora had made for her. She stepped into her boots and wrapped a thick blanket around herself. It was an unusually cold morning. Stepping to the door flap, she glanced down at the pail of water. It had frozen solid in the night.

She knew before she stepped outside what she would find. The desert floor was covered in a thick blanket of white for as far as she could see. Laughter bubbled up inside of her; she was as giddy as a child! Fresh mounds of snow lay around her like freshly shorn wool on the shearing floor. Suddenly concerned for the animals, she ran around the side of the tent, only to find them bundled together against the back wall, sleeping tightly against one another, snug and warm.

The first rays of sunlight fell across the frozen landscape and it took her breath away. Kneeling down among the sheep, she watched as the crimson sun crept above the low eastern horizon, lending its light to the land. A fiery blush spread over the mountains she had climbed yesterday. Slowly, each ridge beyond the first took on the color of the sun.

Tears streamed down Dahlia's face as she watched in amazement. She couldn't believe no one else was awake yet to share this moment with. Walking quickly, she made her way toward the nearest circle of tents. Her ears perked up when she heard a familiar melody. It sounded like a tune that Artashir liked to whistle to himself, but it seemed to be coming from a pile of blankets on a nearby bench. Looking more closely, she saw the small, wrinkled face peering out. "Hello?" Dahlia offered quietly, not wanting to startle the old lady who continued to hum happily to herself.

"The snow," Dahlia continued. "It's amazing! Is it a miracle?"

The old woman chuckled and rocked back and forth, wrapped in her layers of colorful blankets. In a raspy voice, she replied, "Miracles happen all the time in the desert. We just have to know how to look for them."

"Well, this one certainly took me by surprise! I didn't know it could snow like this in the desert."

"He says to the snow, 'Fall on the earth,'" the old woman whispered.

"I'm sorry?" Dahlia leaned closer. "Has this happened before? Have you seen the desert covered in blankets of snow like this?"

"Never," the wrinkled face chuckled, a look of awe on her face. "But I've heard of more miraculous things than this. There was a time when God covered the desert floor in manna, to feed his people."

"Manna?"

"Dew, from heaven. God provided it for his people and they gathered it up and ate it. It sustained them for years while they wandered in the desert waiting to enter the land he had promised them."

"God did this?" Dahlia paused for a moment. "But if God could do that, why didn't he just show them the way to where they were trying to go?"

"Because they weren't ready to get there," the woman responded matter-of-factly.

Dahlia knit her eyebrows together, perplexed. *What a strange story,* she thought. "This God, what do you know about him?"

"'*This God,*'" the wrinkles crinkled in amusement. "You mean 'the God.' There is no other."

"I don't understand," Dahlia interrupted. "There are many religions, many names for God. How can you claim to know the real one?"

"Oh, they all put their own spin on it, adding sets of silly rules and fables of an immortal being. But they are only shadows and imitations of the true Holy One. *Yahweh.*"

"Yahweh." The name rolled over Dahlia's tongue. It sounded like poetry--concise, complete.

"He is the One." The sage's eyes glistened.

"How did you learn of him?" Dahlia was hungry to hear more. The snow lay all around her, testifying to her that now was the time, this was the moment promised her.

"I suppose I've always known. Didn't you?"

"I don't know. I never really thought about it much before. Until recently. Something happened, and…" She stopped, unable to go on.

"That's usually how it starts," the woman replied. A tiny, wrinkled hand patted its way across the space between them, then covered Dahlia's. It was then that she realized the old woman was blind. "I have seen many things in my life, good and bad; but I have always felt his presence through it all. He is my comforter, my counselor. Even on my bed at night, I talk to him and tell him my heart."

"Does he hear?" Dahlia whispered.

"Why don't you try it tonight? Then let me know what you think."

They sat in silence for a long while. Dahlia contemplated this new name she had discovered. It made God seem more personal—that he had revealed his name to man; that he had provided for his people at a time when they could not provide for themselves; the way he had provided for her when she lost her family. Artashir and Hasan seemed as unlikely a pair of friends as she could have imagined, yet they had shared their families with her.

A figure in the distance caught Dahlia's attention. It quickly grew larger, and as she watched, she began to make out a man, running toward them. *Artashir!* Getting to her feet, she stepped toward him.

"Artashir!" the old woman chuckled, staring affectionately in his direction. "Back so soon?"

"Dahlia, get inside!"

"What?"

"There's no time. Move! Quickly!"

⤖ ⬿

When they were inside the tent, Artashir frantically paced and ranted while Dahlia stood in stunned silence.

"Some men drove into the desert this morning, coming in through the northeastern pass. Endora was out hunting and spotted them from the mountainside where she was perched. She went down to the road to find out what they wanted. When they asked for directions to the camp, she sent them in the opposite direction, but it won't be long before they figure out they've gone the wrong way."

"Who are they?"

"They were in government vehicles. I'm guessing they are some of your father's men."

Dahlia's eyes grew wide. "What do you think they want?"

"The same thing they wanted from your father. Someone the people will follow."

Raising an eyebrow, Dahlia started to say something, but Artashir cut her off. "There's no time now. You've got to hide. Here, in the basket." He gestured to a large basket used for storing un-dyed wool. Seeing the fear in her eyes, he gently helped her climb in. As she curled up in a tight ball, he whispered, "It's ok. I won't let them find you."

Chapter 15

INSIDE THE BASKET, Dahlia held her breath while Artashir spoke to Rashad.

"She is valuable to us; we must find her," her father's top advisor hissed.

"I'm amazed you would even show your face here." Artashir spoke slowly, not hiding the contempt in his voice. "Why do you think we would host the daughter of Seljuk?"

"We have our reasons. We know you were involved with Seljuk's death. Tell us anything you know about her whereabouts!"

"*Leave.* Just leave! Your presence will only surface deep wounds in the hearts of my people."

Dahlia knew Artashir was restraining himself. The anger in his voice was so raw, she worried he might harm the men who had come. What had triggered his reaction? She knew it wasn't concern for herself that choked his voice with rage.

"Artashir, what was done is long passed. We want to see our country healed. It is our deepest desire to move our land toward a new path of leadership and peace."

"*Peace!*" Artashir spat the word. "Your kind will do nothing to bring peace to our land. Your very presence reminds us of the violence we suffered at your hands! What is this 'peace' you speak of?!"

Dahlia waited, trying to breathe quietly while a tense silence filled the tent. Why was Artashir trying to pick a fight with these men?

Rashad cursed. "I don't have to explain to you! To be quite honest, I'm tired of dealing with your kind." Dahlia could picture his dark face, the cool composure that always veiled his true motives. "Why don't you just save yourself more trouble? Tell us where she is!"

"I won't do *anything for you*!" Artashir's restrained voice suddenly rose in pitch. He was breathing hard.

When Rashad spoke again, Dahlia knew he had backed away from Artashir. "I will address this matter once, Artashir. Don't expect an apology; what happened was not our fault. It was simply a misunderstanding." His voice was placating, conniving.

"A misunderstanding! You dare call what happened a mere misunderstanding?"

"Artashir. Artashir, man, listen. We cannot undo what happened. Help us move forward. Our country needs leadership, not a dwelling on the past. Let us talk about that."

"But hundreds died! You know that," Artashir growled. Dahlia strained to hear; his voice was so low. "Explain that to me. Tell me how a misunderstanding resulted in massacre?"

Rashad uttered an exasperated sigh as he settled on a low couch near Dahlia's basket. The stench of his strong cologne overcame her and she tried not to gag. "It was a hard year for the military; the resistance had found a weakness and we lost a lot of men."

"Men. YOU lost men."

"Your people shouldn't have been there!"

"We lived there! Where did you think we would be?!!"

Dahlia cringed as their voices rose to deafening shouts.

"We were told that only your *men* would be there!"

"What does that mean? The *men*! You wanted to obliterate us!"

"NO, no! It was a miscalculation." More quietly, he added, "We were desperate. It was a test, a weapon to bring an end to the fighting."

"A test? Explain that to me! Explain now." Artashir cursed. "I should kill you for coming here!"

Rashad chuckled. "Really, Artashir, don't get carried away." His voice grew cold, calculated. "It was to be for the good of our entire country. But, unity requires a price. We tested our weapon on the least significant population available."

Dahlia's eyes grew wide. Surely Artashir would kill him now. How was he able to restrain himself?

"Lower the gun, Enan. You misjudge our friend's self-control."

Dahlia imagined the burning look in Artashir's eyes as he sat at gunpoint listening to this evil man.

"There were women and children there as well," he whispered.

"Yes, an unfortunate misunderstanding. We didn't know they would be there. I was told that your people stayed in nearby caves during the harsher months of winter, waiting until the men had rebuilt the base camp before returning to the valley floor. It seems we waited too long to test our weapon, mmh?" Rashad exhaled. "How were we to know that your clan would be so eager to rebuild their spring camps in the valley? It's a shame really, especially since we haven't yet been able to use the weapon we tested."

Something fell over with a crash and Dahlia waited, breathless, while a wild scuffle ensued. A hard thud was followed by a sickening silence.

"Are you alright, sir?" one of the men inquired.

"Yes, of course. Damn fool. Tie him up. I want to make a thorough search of the camp before we leave, and I don't want this brazen buffoon muddling up our efforts."

The men left the tent, leaving Dahlia to wonder what had happened to Artashir. She didn't dare come out of her hiding place until the coast was clear. A moment later, her concern for Artashir overcame her fear and she crawled out of the basket. She made her way to his side, then wiped the blood from the back of his head. A large gash was bleeding profusely. She pressed a cloth to the wound and worked to control her breathing. Cradling his head in her lap, Dahlia prayed that God would have mercy on this brave man who had risked his people's lives to take her in.

Time passed slowly and Dahlia was tormented by the thought of the ways in which her presence may jeopardize the safety of these people. They had already suffered so much!

Could her father really have sanctioned such a massacre? To test a weapon? Her heart tore again at the thought. Artashir's tortured voice haunted her. He had lost family, and yet he had brought her here for her own protection. She had never fully understood the kindness of this man.

"Dahlia!" Berlena rushed into the tent and knelt beside her. Working quickly, she pulled an ointment from the cloth satchel she often carried with her and applied it to the gaping wound on Artashir's head, then wrapped a clean cloth around it. After she had propped his head on a pillow and covered him with a blanket, she hugged Dahlia to herself tightly. "You're ok! I was so worried!"

At the sound of concern in Berlena's voice, Dahlia began to cry. "No, it's all my fault! I brought this upon you; your people should never have taken me in! I'm so sorry!" Dahlia sobbed and gasped for air as she tried to speak, but Berlena would hear no more.

"Hush! Hush!" She gently rocked Dahlia back and forth. "They're gone now. Everyone's fine, child. It's going to be alright."

Worn out from the intensity of all that had happened, Dahlia closed her eyes and lay on the floor, her head in Berlena's lap. She opened her eyes and saw Artashir lying like death beside her and focused on praying for his recovery. God had brought the miracle of snow today. Perhaps he would work another miracle on behalf of her friend.

Chapter 16

THEY WALKED SOUTH along the dry bed that was fed by mountain streams in the springtime. It was so deep and wide that Dahlia was surprised it could be bone dry nine months out of the year.

"There's still water there," Artashir explained. "It's just under the surface. If you really dig, you'll find life-saving water in a pinch."

Dahlia pondered what he had said. Right now, she felt like that stream—barren and dry, parched from years of living a lie. But there was living water flowing—just under the surface. She had finally found it and she was ready to start digging.

"You shouldn't be here, Artashir. You need to rest."

He waited a moment before responding. "Maybe, but you never would have found this place without my help. And, anyway, I would have walked fifty miles in the heat of summer just to be rid of you."

Dahlia gasped and shot him a burning look. "I don't feel a bit sorry for you; forget I ever said it!" she snapped.

Chuckling, Artashir replied, "That's the Dahlia I know. Now stop wallowing in all your self-contempt. It's not becoming. Besides, I like a good challenge. A two-day trek in the frozen desert is just what the doctor ordered. A little fresh air to clear my head." He rapped his noggin with his knuckles for emphasis and smiled good-naturedly.

They walked along in comfortable silence for several miles.

"Tell me more about this place, this 'Piedra.'" Berlena had made it sound like a hidden paradise—a meeting place of brilliant minds and creative free-spirits, gathering together in a sanctuary time and the outside world had forgotten.

"Well, Piedra is very, very old. Its early inhabitants carved their dwellings right out of the reddish rock that forms the canyon walls. It's completely locked away and only a privileged few still know the way in. Berlena's people lived there for centuries before she joined our tribe through marriage. I've only been there once myself, with Endora. It is a remarkable place! You have to see it to truly appreciate its beauty."

⊷⊶⊷ ⊷⊶⊷

As night fell in long purple shadows around them, Artashir picked a spot to camp, down inside the dry river channel. Along a washed out bank that provided a cave-like overhang, he built a fire for warmth. They ate the date cakes and jerky Berlena had packed for them and watched the crackling sparks in silence. There were no campfire stories tonight; a heaviness hung between them as Dahlia wrestled with the guilt of what had happened to Artashir's people.

She finally broke the silence. "Do you believe in God?" Her insatiable hunger to know more caused her to question everyone it seemed. She had to know more of this God, *Yahweh*.

"Have you been talking to my grandmother?"

"Yes, I met her today. We watched the sunrise together. It was magnificent, with the snow and all."

"She's blind as a bat and a bit crazy, you know."

"Not as crazy as you," Dahlia snapped defensively. "You shouldn't talk about your grandmother like that."

"You're right. Mmmmh. Where to start. Grandma. God." He snapped a dry twig and tossed it into the fire. "I suppose I don't think of one without thinking of the other. She told me wonderful stories when I was a child—of a boy named David who killed a giant with only a rock and his slingshot. Of a man with long, flowing hair who killed thousands of men with his bare hands. And they all shared a faith in a god named Yahweh."

"Yes, Yahweh! That's the one!"

"That's the only one, as far as Grandma is concerned."

"Is that what you believe?"

"Yes, I suppose so. He's the only god powerful enough to deserve real worship, in my opinion. I know that it was important to him that his people worship him alone. They were to have no other gods."

"I see. So he is a harsh, demanding god."

"No. Not from what I've heard. Jealous for his people, but gentle like a mother with her child. And he had a son, a son he sent to us as a savior. Aaaah! I'm going to get this all wrong!"

"No, it's ok! Go on," Dahlia urged.

"Grandma says God sent his son to redeem his people. Because of their sin. Because he loved them. It's all about love. But the stories I really remember were about the men who led God's people into battle. They were incredible stories—men fighting against all odds, yet God would come through for them and give them victory if they fought his way."

His eyes shown with excitement, remembering the stories from his youth. The stories that had been passed down to his grandmother when she was a child; she knew how he loved to hear about the awesome god Yahweh.

"There was this one time… God's people were told to march around a wall. Not just once, but several times, and then shout and blow their horns."

"A wall?" Dahlia interrupted.

"The walls of a city. A very important city, and God had promised them victory if they did just as he said. Well, they did. And on the seventh day, when they blew their horns and shouted, the walls crumbled before them, allowing them to penetrate and claim the city! Can you imagine?" he shook his head enthusiastically.

Dahlia sat staring at him blankly. How could God love his people and still call them into battle? It seemed so wrong that a god of love could require his people to shed the blood of others.

"The walls, they just came tumbling down. Isn't that crazy?" Artashir laughed. "At least that's how I remember it. You're not listening, are you?"

"Artashir, if he's a god of love, then why is there war?"

Artashir screwed up his lips. "I don't know. I guess because there are so many people who don't want to do what God says. They'd rather do things their way. Then, bam! You've got conflict."

"I don't get it. So many people have lost their lives, have lost love ones. There's so much suffering. For what reason?!!"

"Honestly, I don't know. I'm sure there's a reason." He thought for a moment. "I lost my family this past Spring. I guess you've figured that much out by now. All I know is, someone's going to pay for what has been done. And I intend to kill that man one day."

"Rashad?"

"Yeah, him. He's evil. I know you understand that much."

They sat in silence, Dahlia's heart aching for Artashir and his people. Such senseless violence. Was there no end to it?

A distant jackal howled at the moon.

"Dahlia, are you familiar with the game of chess?"

"Yes, a little." It was a game she used to play with her father. She had loved the pieces of his set carved from olive wood, especially the tiny castle towers.

"Then you know a little about the value of each piece. Take the king, for example. Do you know what he can do?"

"Well, I know that the game ends when he's gone."

"Yes, check-mate. Exactly right. But he's not a very powerful player, if you think about it. Just how much can a king do?"

"He can only move one space at a time."

"One space at a time; meanwhile, the other players move around him, facing battle and maneuvering for his safety. At least, that's what they're supposed to do."

"I don't understand."

"You're father, the king..."

"Yes?"

"They set him up; I think you should know that, at least."

"I don't understand. You killed him; are you telling me now that he wasn't an important part of the strategy?"

"Well, yes, he was important. The country was under his thumb... Sorry, I don't mean to sound insensitive. Your father had been corrupted by his advisors, but he was only an extension of the evil machine that ran this country. It wasn't just him, you see. Rashad, the others, they were the ones doing the real damage. But we had to get to them through your father. We had to cut off the head of the snake."

Dahlia shuddered. "Yes, I've heard it described that way before." She closed her eyes, afraid the tears would escape. "But the game's not over, Artashir. It didn't solve anything. The king is dead, and the fighting hasn't ended."

Artashir sighed. "Yes, I know. That's not exactly where I was going with this. Ok. The bishop—he's pretty fluid. He can move all the way across the board."

"Places where the king can't go," Dahlia interjected.

"Exactly. And the knight—he's my favorite. His pattern of attack is versatile, making it easy to surprise the opponent." A sly smile crossed Artashir's lips while his finger traced in the sand the various L-shaped attacks the piece could make.

"I like the castle."

"You mean the rook?"

"Well, whatever. The rook, the tower. It's my favorite piece. It reminds me of the time my father and I visited an olive mill in southern Spain. It was near a beautiful old village called Zahara. One afternoon, when we had some free time, my father and I hiked up to the old Moorish tower on top of the highest hill."

"They call those strongholds."

"Yes, that's right!" Dahlia's eyes gleamed, her hands gesturing enthusiastically, preparing to explain her reasoning.

"A stronghold provides a deceptive sense of security," Artashir cut in. "A stronghold rarely holds up under battle or siege. It may have seemed impenetrable, but the ones who ran there for security usually ended up regretting their decision."

"Perhaps. But I like the idea of it, don't you? A place people run to, a place that provides protection in the midst of turmoil."

Artashir was quiet. His black eyes, staring into the fire, reflected the red heat of the coals. "It's a noble idea; it just doesn't work in this world. Can't you see that?! There's no sense in trying to find a safe place because there's always someone new trying to hunt you down and destroy you! That's just the way it is!" He spat. "You of all people should understand that. You shouldn't put your hope in such things!"

Dahlia sat with her eyes downcast, trying not to let the tears escape. She knew why Artashir was so bitter and full of anger, but it didn't stop the sting of his harsh words or the way he carelessly trampled her hopes and dreams. "Still, I want to have such a place one day. I don't know how I will make it work, but I believe God can do it. Maybe he's the one who gave me the desire in the first place."

Artashir looked her over. In his anger, he hadn't noticed her retreating inward; he'd been too focused on spewing out the acid that burned in his very bones. Now he saw the stooped shoulders, the water-filled eyes, the way she wouldn't look at him; he'd aimed some of his poisonous arrows at Dahlia and they were never intended for her. "I'm sorry. I shouldn't have said all of that—those thoughts are like angry voices bouncing around my head. Sometimes I can't keep them all inside. I didn't mean to put down your ideas. They're great ideas! More people should dream like you."

Dahlia sighed. "That's it, though. They're just dreams. Here I am again—on the run. A nomad without a home seeking sanctuary with whoever will take me in."

"Just means you're doing field research." Artashir smiled. "You can take all of the good things you've learned while staying with others and create a place that combines the best qualities from each of them. You'll know what it takes to make people feel welcome, even people who are scared or hurting."

Dahlia smiled. "I like that. Thank you."

"So, back to chess."

"Mmh hmm?"

"Who are we forgetting?"

Dahlia thought for a minute. "The pawns?"

"That's right. The little pawns. Most people overlook them, and they're almost always the first players to be sacrificed in a game."

"Makes sense."

"Maybe. There's one thing I've learned in battle, though. It's the seemingly insignificant ones who surprise you the most. There was this scrawny little guy—little hands, big moustache . . . "

"Yes?"

"Well," Artashir stalled. "Never mind."

"What? Did he kick your butt?" Dahlia laughed. "You weren't going to tell me that, were you?"

"Like I said—people will surprise you!" Artashir scowled at her. "Take a pawn, for instance. How quickly can it move?"

"One space at a time. Like a king."

"That's right. But unlike a king, a pawn can pretty much move about unnoticed. They're just not as 'important' as other players, right?"

"I see where you're going, I think."

"Dahlia, you're like a pawn."

"Oh, what? I am?" Her eyebrows shot up.

"Yes, don't you see? You're moving all over the place and no one even knows where you are. You've never held a high-ranking seat, but you're valuable—very valuable. That's what people forget about pawns. They hold unlimited potential."

"I don't think I understand."

"Do you know what happens if a pawn makes it all the way across the board to the other side?"

"No, I guess I don't."

"Well, that pawn can become anything it wants."

"Really?"

"Yes, even a queen." His look was full of implication. Dahlia felt the heaviness of his words. "A queen can do anything. She controls the chessboard... and the battle."

⟶⟩◉ ◉⟨⟵

That night, Dahlia lay on her pallet and stared up at the ceiling above her. The uneven rock reflected the glow of the fire in ripples of shadow and glowing light. She had never felt so free—even though she was on the run from evil men and had no idea where she was going. It was an exciting feeling, and she felt safe with Artashir. She also felt an energy that flowed from the discussion they'd had about the opportunities before her. To join in the battle one day. How, she didn't yet know. But she felt certain that God would make it clear to her.

Remembering the old woman's words, Dahlia reflected on all that she had learned about Yahweh that day. There was still so much to learn;

she'd never dreamed there was a whole history to discover—of kings and battles, a people finding their promised land, and the amazing things God did to help them along the way. She felt like the story was hers, too. There were so many similarities between their story and hers. "Lord," she prayed, "I may wander in the desert for months or even years. But it's ok. I trust your path for my life, and I am so thankful for the friends you have provided along the way to walk this road with me. Go before me now and prepare a place where I can grow in my faith and learn more about you."

She closed her eyes and slept more soundly than she had in months.

Chapter 17

AFTER SEVERAL HOURS of walking, Dahlia and Artashir stopped and stared in wonder. The high desert plateau abruptly ended and before them stretched a foreboding land of shallow canyons and cavernous ravines.

"What is this place?" Dahlia whispered.

"My people call it the Shadowlands. It's easy to get lost in there, so most who have to travel south take the time to go around it. Many of the tribes consider it to be a place of great spiritual significance where outsiders are not welcome. Don't worry; the group you are going to stay with will be more than willing to take you in. It's an unusual place. In times of great religious persecution, a variety of groups have found refuge there."

Like me, Dahlia thought. A weak smile traced her lips, an uneasiness rising in her belly. She looked down at the labyrinth of rock and deep shadows. "Do you know the way from here?"

"I think I'll be able to find it." Artashir's voice lacked its usual confidence.

Dahlia swallowed. What choice did she have? She must trust him as her guide or return with him and face the corrupt men who pursued her. "Lead the way."

A dusty path wound in a series of steep descents and switch-backs. Though the sun was often shut out as the sheer face of rock loomed above them, the air grew warmer as they descended—an inviting breath of welcome. When the path ended, Artashir turned and looked at her. Perhaps she would have to go back with him after all. For the moment, her heart hoped it was so.

"Well, this is it," he announced.

Dahlia looked around her. They were standing in a shallow box canyon; the only way out was to climb the cliff walls or return the way they came.

"You'll go on from here alone."

"But how?" Dahlia eyed the steep walls nervously. Artashir leaned over and began to pull away a pile of dry brush. As she stepped closer, she saw the split in the canyon wall and the narrow opening that had been hidden behind the branches.

"Dahlia, I need to get back to higher ground before nightfall so I can make camp. Are you going to be ok?"

She nodded.

He shook his head. "You'll just have to trust me. It's a straight shot, alright? Whatever you do, don't turn around. If you panic and try to find your way back to camp, you could get lost out here and never find your way back. Just stay on the path and keep moving forward, ok?"

"Ok," she mouthed.

"Dahlia, remember what I said about the pawn? Well, God's got a plan for you, but you've got to keep moving forward. I like to think of God as the the ultimate chess player—"

"Oh! I like that, Artashir!"

He smiled. "Don't forget it, ok? Hold onto your dreams. Trust God's plan, and go where he leads you. It will all work out; you'll see." He brushed a strand of hair out of her eyes.

"Thank you, Artashir. Thank you for all that you've done. You've been such a good friend to me." She grabbed his arm and buried her face in his shoulder. For a moment, she didn't know if she had the courage to go on without him.

Artashir patted her awkwardly on the back and waited for her to let go. When she did, she turned and slipped through the rocks, feeling her way along until her eyes adjusted to the semi-darkness. A tiny slit of sky above her let in just enough light, but a couple of hours more and that, too, would be gone. Dahlia looked back in time to see the branches being placed over the opening between the rocks. Her mouth opened; his name formed on her lips but she knew she couldn't call out for him. This was a path she had to take alone; Artashir had done all he could for her. Facing the dim corridor before her, she moved along, her fingertips tracing the moist cracks in the sandstone walls on either side of her. The strong scent of moss and damp soil were evidence of water, but the sandy path was dry beneath her. Then the canyon grew so narrow that she felt as if the walls were actually closing in upon her. Dahlia's mind was playing tricks on her, and she had to fight the urge to turn and run back to the opening in the box canyon. Artashir was right; she would never find her way out of the badlands on her own and night would soon be upon her. Forcing herself to put one foot in front of the other, she moved along the constricting path. There was no going back.

⋆⊷⊷◉ ◉⊶⊶⋆

The sound of running water was a welcome sound to her ears and as the splashing grew louder, the sandy path widened out into a pleasant cove of ferns and mossy rocks surrounding a crystal clear pool. A steady trickle fell through a split in the rocks, falling several feet into the pool. Stretching out on a rock to rest, Dahlia wondered if she should stop here for the night, not knowing how much further she had to go. Sitting alone in the stillness, she reflected once again on all that had happened over the past few months. She had lost a family but gained the truth. The truth was painful, but a new relationship with a God who performed mighty acts on behalf of those he loved was searing the wounds of her heart. She had found renewal and a sense of freedom that made her feel as if anything was possible. She leaned her head back against the smooth rock wall and closed her eyes. She was exhausted—physically, emotionally. A little sleep might do her good.

⟶▭ ▭⟵

A soft rustling caught her attention and before she could open her eyes, Dahlia knew she was no longer alone.

"Well, hello, beautiful," came a low, rich voice.

Dahlia whipped around to face the man. He stood on a rock above her, strong, tan arms holding a large bow and arrow. Sun-streaked hair framed the deep-green eyes that held hers. He was captivating, and Dahlia felt an unusual calmness as she stared into the stranger's eyes. It was odd, the boldness that came over her, as if admiring a man was perfectly acceptable.

"Imagine my surprise in finding you here," he quipped warmly. He squatted down, his face just a few feet above hers. "Are you lost?"

Realizing that she was still staring at him, Dahlia laughed self-consciously. "No! Well, yes. I suppose I am. I'm going to Piedra. I don't really know where it is, but I think I'm close."

"Well, yes, you are! And I'd be glad to escort you there. If you'd like." He flashed a perfect smile and Dahlia felt herself melting under his casual charm in spite of the nagging feeling that she shouldn't trust anyone just yet.

He reached out his free hand and pulled her up on the rock where he stood. It was an electrically charged moment and Dahlia felt a magnetism to this man that was strange and new.

"My name is Marlin," he said, still holding her hand in his. "And yours is…"

"Dahlia," she smiled shyly and pulled her hand away, running it slowly through her hair. "I'm glad you came along when you did. I was starting to feel a little frightened."

"No worries! We're almost there," he laughed. "I wish I could claim to be the hero to the damsel in distress but I believe you've found us all on your own!"

Relieved, Dahlia exhaled. She couldn't help but beam at him as an overwhelming wave of relief washed over her.

"What are you doing here?" he asked, head cocked to one side.

"There's a civil war going on; I needed to get away." She hoped that would pacify him for now.

He laughed. "And is it any wonder with that madman Seljuk in power. Blood-thirsty bastard!"

Dahlia sucked in a gulp of air. *Is this how it would always be*, she wondered wearily.

"Bloody war. I don't imagine there's any point to it. He won't give an ounce of his power up to the people."

"He's dead," she said flatly.

"Well, God save the queen! It's about bloody time the people did something for themselves! How did it happen?"

Feeling suddenly faint, Dahlia leaned against the rock.

"Are you ok?"

"I'm just very tired."

He wrapped his arm around her waist. A combination of repulsion for what he had just said and the strange magnetic pull she felt toward him caught her off guard, but all she could do was allow this gorgeous, god-like man to help her.

"Hang on," he whispered. "We're not far now."

Chapter 18

"Well, what have you found now, Marlin?" The woman jumped up from where she had been sitting under the shade of a palm-tree reading. The alarm on her face confirmed for Dahlia that she must look as bad as she felt. Her savior had half carried, half dragged her along the sandy path the last mile or so, and as the light began to fade around them, Dahlia felt as if she too were blacking out.

"Hurry, Sarah! I think she may need some medical attention. She's got to be exhausted, but I'm worried there's something worse."

With arms supporting both sides of her now, Dahlia allowed herself to be carried along. A warm, balmy air soothed her chilled, clammy skin. The presence of caring people melted away her fears.

"Lie her down here," the woman whispered. Dahlia felt Marlin's warm hands arrange her limbs on the soft bed. Another set of hands smoothed back her hair. The last thing she remembered was her shoes being removed and strong hands gently massaging her feet and swollen ankles.

⤜⧫⤛ ⤜⧫⤛

When her eyes opened again, a kind-looking older woman sat beside her bed reading a book.

"Well, hello there," she chortled when she noticed that Dahlia was awake. "I've been wondering when you might come back to us. It's quite a rest you've taken!"

"Really?" Dahlia raised herself up on one elbow. "Did I sleep long?"

"Over fifteen hours." The woman smiled warmly. "I think you must have needed the rest. Where did you come from?"

Dahlia thought for a moment before answering. How much to tell? "The northern Bedouin camp at the foot of the mountains. My friend Berlena sent me."

When the woman heard Berlena's name, a shadow passed over her face. "Berlena. How is she, dear?"

"You mean because she lost her husband?" Dahlia tried. In the short time that she had known about the tragedy surrounding the valley of death, she had not considered that Berlena was so recent a widow.

"Oh, it's too terrible. We don't like to talk of what happened. But she and her children; they're ok?"

"Yes, yes, they're fine. In fact, Endora just married."

The woman beamed, the fine lines around her eyes crinkling slightly.

"We left a couple of days ago," Dahlia said quickly, trying to change the subject. "The day after it snowed."

"Well, then, no wonder your ankles swelled up so! You must have walked almost fifty miles, and in two days! That trip normally takes four. What possessed you to come so quickly? And in the dead of winter?"

"It's a long story." Dahlia sat back in exhaustion. "It didn't feel like that much. Is it really fifty miles?"

"Perhaps a couple less. You must have been in an awful big hurry; but don't you worry. We all have our reasons for coming to Piedra and no one will ask you yours. You're here now; that's all that matters."

Dahlia was relieved but curious. "You mean you don't talk about it—your reasons for coming here?" She cocked her head to one side.

"Oh no." The woman chuckled. "It's best we all just look forward together. Some have left behind dreadful pasts, painful memories; no reason for dwelling on all that."

Well, that's a relief, Dahlia thought to herself.

"How are you feeling now?"

"Much better, thank you."

"Between exhaustion and dehydration, your body's had quite a go, but you should be feeling up to your normal self before you know it."

Dahlia smiled appreciatively and folded her hands on her lap. A soft, lavender blanket was wrapped around her legs; the linens felt like the finest silk. The sweet scent of rosemary permeated the room. Earthen, white-washed walls reflected the light that shown in through a single, high window. Though simple and rather sparse, the room had a luxuriously comfortable feel. Two straight-backed chairs composed of weathered gray wood stood in one corner. The wood, bleached by the desert sun, was rounded and smooth from years of surviving blistering desert winds and sandstorms. A large painting of a desert sunrise hung on the wall opposite the bed.

"That's beautiful," Dahlia remarked.

"Our Sister Marcela painted that. She is quite talented."

"Does she live here?" Dahlia sounded surprised.

"Oh, yes! Everything we have here was made by one of us. That's what we do—we make things. I made the blanket on your bed."

It's so soft!"

"Yes, we take pride in the simplest of comforts. We don't have a lot, but what we do have is made well. Quality of life, not quantity of possessions. Don't you agree? After all, most of us came here without anything. Like you. I'd say you traveled lighter than most."

"Oh!" Dahlia looked down. "Yes, I lost all I had in the war."

"Poor dear, that's terrible! I'm sure the others will be curious to hear more about that later. We do lack news of the outside world here. Not that it really matters much. You kind of get used to not knowing." She glanced up at the window. "Well, you must be hungry! I'll get you something from the Cook House. Try to rest a bit more if you want. I'm sure Marlin will want to make you something special himself, so it may take a little while."

Dahlia stared blankly at the woman but the heaviness of sleep pulled at her eyelids and before long, she succumbed to the weight of them.

⇥⊜ ⊜⇤

"My, you look even better today—if that's possible," Marlin said dreamily when she opened her eyes again. A delicious aroma wafted around her and she felt her stomach growl ferociously. "How are you, dear?" he asked as if they had known each other for years.

"I'm fine," Dahlia replied blankly, bewildered by the peculiar behavior of this stunningly handsome man.

"I think you'll like what I brought you. It's a velvety rabbit stew simmered in some of the best wine I could swindle from Sister Naomi. She will love you, I'm sure, but she is a slight bit stingy with her exceptional brew, I'm afraid. Generosity is not a fruit she's familiar with."

Dahlia laughed. Marlin talked so funny—not only in the way he used words but with his strong Aussie accent.

"You've got such a beautiful smile," Marlin said, leaning forward on one elbow.

"Marlin!" cried the older woman as she ladled up a bowl of soup on the small bedside table. "Stop smothering the girl and let her eat! I declare, you act like a love-sick child!"

Dahlia laughed and nodded in agreement. She'd never seen a man act so silly.

"Don't mock me, Dahlia." He gave her a playful glare. "It's not every day that a breathtakingly beautiful woman like yourself lands in our midst. Besides, I don't believe in hiding my feelings."

"Obviously," the woman quipped, rolling her eyes at Dahlia. She handed a steaming bowl of stew to Dahlia and broke off a piece of bread. "At least he can cook. That's one thing I can say for this sad, ridiculous boy."

"My, I am the lucky one," Dahlia teased, feeling emboldened by Marlin's excessive compliments.

"Well, what do you think?" He watched as she savored the first mouthful. "I hope you like it."

Overcome by her appetite, Dahlia ate the stew quickly, ignoring the question.

"Poor dear; she must have been starved half to death." The woman put her hand on Marlin's shoulder and watched as Dahlia finished the last drop.

"Get her some more, Sister Sarah." He took the bowl from Dahlia's hands and passed it along. "And some more bread if we can spare it."

"Of course."

"Oh, thank you!" Dahlia said eagerly, attempting manners as she took the second steaming portion. She ate more slowly this time.

"Well, what should we do today?" Marlin inquired when she was almost through.

"I don't know; what is there to do here?"

"Don't you wear the girl out after she's just recovered, Marlin." Sarah gave him a stern look.

Marlin ignored her. "We can hunt, or you can show me what you do."

Dahlia knit her eyebrows together. "I don't know what I do."

"And of course not," Sarah quickly interjected, taking the empty bowl from her hands. "It's only her first day."

"Well, I've always hunted!" Marlin objected. "And Sister Sarah knits and Sister Marcela paints. Brother Albert tends the garden and Samuel builds furniture. Dahlia, what is it you like to do?"

Speechless, Dahlia tried to come up with a response. "I... I just don't know. I guess I always thought I might like to teach, or maybe even run an olive mill. But I'm not sure."

"I don't think we can grow olives here." Sarah looked very concerned. "And we haven't had children here in over a decade!"

"Oh." Dahlia raised her eyebrows. This might be serious. Did she need to do something in order to stay? She racked her brain for something, anything useful. "I can tend sheep!" she said emphatically.

"Wonderful!" Sarah exclaimed. "That will come in quite handy. Our dear Brother Edgar of Ireland is growing a 'wee bit frail' as he likes to remind us, so I'm sure he wouldn't mind the help."

Marlin beamed. "You're amazing! I bet you could do anything."

Dahlia gave him a strange look. Pulling the blanket up, she peeked under it to see what she was wearing. *Not enough*, she thought. "Could you both give me a moment to get dressed?"

"Of course." Sarah fluttered about, readying the tray to carry out and reaching for the blue tunic Dahlia had worn in to Piedra. "I had this laundered for you."

Dahlia held it to her face, breathing in the heavenly scent of fresh lavender. "Divine!" she breathed.

"That's the work of Sister Chan. Her tiny hands can force freshness into the most worn out of threads," Sarah admonished. "I'll take you to meet her later. You'll be wanting to have her make you some new clothes."

While Dahlia dressed, she mulled over the bizarre circumstances she now found herself in. No one seemed to be from Piedra, but they all lived and worked together as if they were family. She wondered how she would fit into the mix.

Chapter 19

EXPLORING THE COMMUNITY was the most fascinating experience she'd ever had. As they walked from building to building, Dahlia was as stunned by the architecture as she was by the rhythm of motion and activity that she found in the hidden city. Each person was busy at work in some useful way—weeding a large garden, scrubbing white-washed walls, building tables, mending fences. Several ladies were busy tending the animals at the Barn House, as Marlin called it. There were chickens, goats, cows, horses and even peacocks. When Dahlia commented on the exotic, showy birds, Marlin replied, "Beauty to accentuate the utile. Work is hard, this life is hard. Without beauty, it would not be worth it."

Dahlia watched the shimmering blue-green birds as they strutted about with the chickens. She'd never thought much about the conscious effort to add beauty to her life, but it seemed to be a very intentional practice here.

"I'm curious about the buildings," she said later as they walked along the corridor which formed the community's center. Tall, orna-mented façades were carved directly out of the canyon walls. The color of the stone was a soft, pinkish coral, just as Artashir had described.

"The buildings were carved from the sandstone walls over three thousand years ago. Can you imagine the gifted hands that did this?" Marlin gestured enthusiastically.

Dahlia admired the Romanesque pillars and arches. Statues carved inside of arches hewn from the rose-colored rock looked like the Greek gods of ancient mythology. They passed an amphitheater carved from the very side of the mountain.

"Amazing," she said breathlessly.

"Even more impressive are the mosaics inside many of the buildings. I'll take you to see them later. Would you like to see the view from the top?"

Dahlia nodded enthusiastically.

"Come on then!" Marlin grabbed her hand and pulled her up the steep steps leading to the top of the amphitheater. As the sun set behind the towering rock walls of the city, the buildings shown a brilliant red.

As they sat overlooking all of Piedra, Marlin explained how the hidden architectural jewel had been passed from culture to culture, often a hub of trade and at times a refuge to the persecuted. It had even been the burial place of several prominent Greco-Roman rulers. He pointed to a tomb that more resembled a Roman temple, carved from the side of the canyon wall opposite of where they sat. Dahlia admired the elaborate façade as it reflected the burning colors of the setting sun. Far below, the workers were making their way back from the various Barn Houses and Wood-working Shops, some from the fields and others from the ancient aqueduct and Cistern House where the city's water was stored.

"Ah, the workers coming in from a full day's work. Isn't that a beautiful sight?" Marlin pointed to various workers and identified for Dahlia who they were and what work they performed for the community.

When Dahlia remarked that it seemed quite providential for each person to possess such a beneficial and specific skill, Marlin nodded in agreement. "Need necessitates function. That's how things work so perfectly around here. It is quite providential indeed that you have arrived to help Brother Edgar in his time of frailty."

"I'm glad I can be of assistance," Dahlia agreed. "I would hate to be a burden to the people."

"Oh, you could never be a burden!" Marlin looked at her with those flashing emerald eyes. "If you should choose to stay, I would make it my life's work to do all I can to make you happy!" He stood in dramatic emphasis and Dahlia sat back in stunned silence. "All of this should be yours," he added earnestly, pointing to the city below them, "And we could enjoy all of it together."

"Marlin," Dahlia laughed, "how can you say such things? You hardly even know me!"

"Oh, but I don't have to know you. I can see that you are good! And what is all of this toil without someone beautiful to share it with? I could make you so happy! Don't you believe I would?" He sat on the stone bench and grasped her hands in his. "Tell me that you'll at least think about it. I won't take 'no' for an answer."

Dahlia sighed. Perhaps it would be best if she agreed. Then, at least, when she declined, he would have to accept that she had taken the time to give his proposal some serious thought. "Marlin, I don't know why you have chosen me as the recipient of this appealing proposal, but I am deeply touched by your earnestness." She paused. It felt like she was rehearsing a part for a Shakespearian play. Stifling the sudden urge to laugh, she continued. "Would you allow me the time to consider all that you're asking? I've hardly had time to learn what my life in Piedra is to be."

As he listened to what she had to say, Marlin's face took on a very serious look. "I will have to work extra hard to convince you of my merits. I will not be able to rest until I am sure that I have won your heart."

"Oh, Marlin, please rest! I do not want to be the cause of your exhaustion and inability to work. It seems a crime in this place."

"Yes, you're right," he agreed earnestly. "But every waking moment shall be dedicated to winning you!"

"Ok, agreed. Now, where do we eat?"

·─⟫═◉ ◉═⟪─·

Sitting in a grassy meadow under the graceful arch of the aqueduct, Dahlia watched her sheep with great pleasure. Brother Edgar had agreed to give Dahlia the flock as her occupation while he stayed back and carded wool in the Sheering House. After a list of lengthy instructions and several days of thorough training, Dahlia felt quite confident that she would be successful in her new profession. With over fifty sheep and all of their needs, she knew there would be moments of mayhem, but for the time being, they were content to stay in the meadow and eat while she rested nearby.

At any moment, she expected to see Marlin come over the hill toting a satchel of delectables for their lunch. Lately, he had been on a ham-kick, since the butcher had slaughtered a large hog for the community. Ham and savory potatoes, or a slice of ham slathered with Marlin's special stone-ground mustard sauce wrapped between two thick slices of bread. Her stomach growled.

Dahlia's heart skipped a beat when she saw him. The sight of this tall, muscular man striding toward her still took her breath way. It was only when he started talking that she found herself absolutely unable to take him seriously.

"What is it today, Marlin?" She rose to greet him and was surprised when he gave her a quick peck on the cheek.

"A selection of sausage and cheeses for your dining pleasure, my dear. An array of seasonal fruits. And a draught of wine," he waved the small satchel mischievously.

"What's the occasion?" Dahlia laughed. "You know Sister Naomi will want your head when she finds that missing."

"It's worth it! You see, we're celebrating the completion of your first month here at Piedra—refuge to the lost souls of the world." He poured the deep red wine into a small earthen jar and handed it to her. "And here's to your decision to stay and embrace the rewarding life of work and personal satisfaction. Look and see what your hands have done."

Dahlia's eyes followed as his hand motioned toward the flock of pink, healthy bodies. It was true; in the past month, she had cared for all of their needs, even birthing three lambs and helping Edgar sheer the thick wool to be used by the community. She stooped to pick up one of the soft little bodies barely a week old. It squirmed in her arms, working its mouth in an effort to find the milk it craved, and Dahlia set it down beside its mother. "I *love* doing this," she sighed. "I had no idea it could be so fulfilling—to manage and care for the needs of these precious creatures."

"Well, it takes a special person." Marlin raised an eyebrow and rubbed his palms together. "I look at this healthy flock of yours and all I see is lamb chops and mutton stew. A little dab of mint jelly, a few sprigs of rosemary. Aaah, and a loaf of soda bread, wouldn't you say, Brother Edgar?"

"Hello, laddy," Edgar greeted cheerfully as he slowly made his way toward them with the help of a crooked walking stick. "What brings you ou' this way?" he asked in a stilted brogue. "Ah, I shoulda noon; 'tis the lass you come fer."

"That it is, that it is," Marlin laughed. "But I'd be delighted for you to join us. Would you sit for a bite?"

"Don't mind if I do, now. Let's have the blessin' quick though; what you brung smells a mite divine!"

Chapter 20

With the springtime coming early to the lowlands, Dahlia filled her time with picking wildflowers in the meadows while the sheep grazed. Marlin's twin sister Melissa had shown her how they could be pressed, then added to a starchy mixture which, when dry, was the most lovely paper Dahlia had ever seen. It seemed wasteful to use such beautiful things for common use, but then everything made in Piedra seemed like a piece of art—not to be held onto, but to be used and enjoyed on a daily basis. It was an extravagant and delightful practice.

The only mystery was Marlin's strange obsession with her, and Dahlia meant to hold him off for as long as she could. Surprisingly, no one else knew of his proposal and Dahlia certainly had no intention of telling anyone. Marlin was, after all, a bit of a charmer and he certainly had his way with the women of the city. Wherever he went, he flirted and charmed, and the women loved to flirt back, relishing the momentary attention of his extravagant style. It kept Dahlia in stitches. When she asked his sister Melissa about it, she simply rolled her eyes and gave the excuse: "He was raised in this community, spoiled by the attention of all the women who felt sorry for him because our mother died when we were young. Since we have no father, the community raised us themselves, lavishing every good gift on us they could, as we were the only children. You can imagine how such a thing would go to his head; Marlin thinks the sun sets and rises around him, and as long as he lives here, I imagine it will."

Dahlia nodded understandingly. "But why do you both stay, then? Don't you wonder about the outside, and what life might hold for you out there?"

Melissa shook her head. "I need nothing of that life. I have my mother's diaries and they are filled with the miseries and evil choices that dwell out there. My life is here, even if it means I'll never marry."

Dahlia's heart went out to her. In many ways, their lives were the same. "Perhaps a handsome stranger will arrive one day and your hopes for a family will come true."

"Oh, no! That's not for me. I have no need of a family."

Dahlia was surprised at her bitterness; there was a dark secret locked in Melissa's heart, one it was obvious she still grieved.

"Besides, no one here can marry. It's not of our ways, you see."

"Oh!" Dahlia was taken aback. "No one? Even if they wanted to?"

"I can't imagine why anyone would want to, but no. Not if they want to stay in Piedra. You understand, don't you? We're all here by our own choice, forsaking the tragedies of our past and living from this day forward—embracing the beauty and healing balm of production and communal living. To pair off and invite all of the troubles that come with marriage would only invite heartache into our midst. Heartache is exactly what the people of Piedra have left behind; we don't desire that kind of drama. It's an unnecessary evil."

Dahlia stood in a sort of stunned silence. She had never considered marriage in that way before, but even more importantly, she saw Marlin's proposal in a new light. He could not have her and have his life in Piedra, too. It simply would not happen. All the more reason, she thought, to reject him gently.

Not long after, Melissa offered to show Dahlia the famous mosaics left on the walls of the rock-dwellings by early inhabitants. Dahlia was most interested, though, in the wall-paintings left by the group of Christians who had lived in Piedra several centuries after Christ's death.

They spent hours examining the drawings, and Dahlia absorbed every detail Melissa could offer about the life of Christ and the practices of the early church. When darkness had fallen, they found themselves at the entrance to a cave far from the city's center.

"This one is the most interesting to me. I rather think you'll like it; should we come back tomorrow when it's a bit lighter?"

Unable to resist, Dahlia stepped into the dark cave. "Let's look at it now!"

Melissa lit one of the torches that lay on the floor by the entrance. "As you wish," she smiled. "Follow me!"

As Dahlia's eyes adjusted to the dim light, she noticed a corridor that emptied into the stone room where they stood. It was like a gaping black mouth fringed with sharp stalactite teeth. Dahlia shivered. She hoped they wouldn't have to go deeper inside to find the cave paintings. A damp, musty smell pervaded the room, and a steady drip-drip echoed up the dark passage from chambers deep inside the mountain. A sudden draft nearly blew out the torch and Dahlia's heart skipped a beat.

In the flickering light, Dahlia saw the image of a man on the wall before them. His hair was long and flowing, a robe of white draped his slender frame. He stood with arms outstretched, palms facing up in a welcoming gesture toward a demonized man. Behind him stood a circle of men with shocked expressions on their faces. An aura of light shown around the gentle man's face, causing it to be illuminated unlike the faces of the men who stood with him. Around them were tombs and broken chains—shackles that the people had tried to use to contain the mad man.

"Who is he?" Dahlia whispered. She reached out to touch the kind man's face.

"He is the one I told you of—Jesus. They called him the Christ. Messiah."

His face shown with compassion and a sense of deep understanding was easily read upon it. He was like a skilled and gentle trainer, reaching out to a wounded lion. He was a man with the understanding that the wild animal had the force and ability to tear him to shreds, but with the calming confidence of one who knew he could end the pain and suffering *if* the wild animal would allow it.

Melissa touched the outstretched hand. "He was said to be the son of God, sent to save the world from itself."

Dahlia remembered Artashir telling her that. That God had loved the world and sent his son to save them from their sins. "What happened here?" Dahlia touched the face of the tortured man, a wild mix of fear and pleading in his wide eyes. The broken chains were still shackled around his ankles. It was obvious that he was ready to submit to the gentle savior, but a feral animal could not be trusted and this man bore every mark of one completely twisted by his own inner pain. The expression on his face showed fear and wonder and surprise at the man in flowing robes who reached out kind hands in welcome.

Melissa took Dahlia's hand and led her down the dark passage-way. They were deep inside the mountain now. The flickering light of the torch fell on the next set of paintings, lending them an eerie life-like movement. The tortured man had fallen at Jesus' feet, and with his hands gripping the sandals of the robed man, he looked back at a herd of pigs with a look of wonder in his eyes. The man named Jesus seemed to be speaking and the herd of pigs, with the same haunted, tortured look in their eyes, were running toward a sandy seashore. Several of the swine had already entered the waves and the herd seemed doomed to a watery death.

"It was an evil spirit?" Dahlia asked, examining the bewildered look on the man's face. His eyes were wide with wonder, yet a serenity had replaced the wild edge in his eyes.

"A legion of them."

Dahlia stared at the once demon-possessed man. She had wondered what it was that Jesus offered the man with his outstretched hands. Perhaps Jesus offered him freedom, though not freedom from the chains that had bound him; the wild man had already set himself free from the physical binding. It seemed that Jesus offered him hope, freedom from the war that raged inside of himself—the battle in which evil spirits had the stronghold and tormented the man day and night.

"I guess we all have our own set of demons that war inside of us." Melissa's voice was hollow.

For a long moment, Dahlia reflected on her own inner conflict—the overwhelming desire to defend her father's name weighed by the growing desire to protect and help the people that he had oppressed. Even now, a new longing to take control and impose her own ideas on the helpless and harassed populations seemed to grasp at her heart, though she knew the only way she could gain real control would be to force the people back into a tyrannical form of government. It was the only way to unite the country and stop the fighting. With the taste of freedom fresh on their balled up, bloody fists, the people could hardly see the need to compromise and work together; they would seek freedom to the point of anarchy now that they had removed the dictator and his imposing government. It seemed hopeless.

"Do you see the cuts on his arms?" Melissa asked, pointing to the jagged lines that marked the wild man's arms from the wrist to the elbow. "This was a man filled with despair and self-loathing; he was unable to find peace, though he roamed freely wherever he went and no man could stop him."

Dahlia ached for the poor man. She understood his pain; she had felt that way herself before. As she pondered it, she was reminded of the war that still raged across Al Cazar. Her country desperately fought to free itself, to the point that it had cut deep wounds in its own land. A self-mutilation designed to free it from the pain caused by its own inner struggle, yet there seemed to be no end to the horrific battles. Would her people ever agree to a solution? Would they continue to live as a fragmented nation, seeking self-rule as the city of Lamirya had? Could a country survive such division? How would a people so diverse and so self-absorbed ever find peace again?

She thought of the massacre of the Bedouin. Under her father's leadership, the military had chosen to dispose of them in an effort to obtain a solution to the endless warring, producing a weapon that would put a violent stop to the uprisings. At so great a cost, could such a weapon really be worth the unity it might bring? And how long would the people live in fear of the hated leadership before the grumbling started again, leading to more uprisings and violence? The people were determined to have a say in the way they were ruled; the resistance had at least proven that. They thought that by freeing themselves from the current leadership, they would be free to make their own decisions, form governments they were happy with, and choose leaders they could love. *Was it even possible,* Dahlia wondered. How many limbs would be severed, eyes gouged out, to obtain a so-called freedom? Was self-rule really freedom after all?

"What did Jesus do with the man he set free?" Dahlia asked.

"Nothing."

"Nothing?"

"He wouldn't even allow him to join his disciples in their travels."

"I don't understand. Why did Jesus bother freeing the man if he didn't plan to help him start over? Where would he go after living among the hills and tombs for so long?

"He sent the man back to his own people. Jesus told him to share the good news of all the Lord had done for him."

"And what if the people still feared him and tried to tie him up and mistreat him? He had been such a crazy, evil man before!"

"Look at his eyes, Dahlia. A man who has found inner freedom knows no chains, however tightly they may bind him. He had found freedom within, an inner peace that could not be rocked by physical bondage."

Understanding flooded Dahlia's mind. The face of the one called Jesus seemed to glow in the soft light of the torch, and her own heart soared with the enlightenment Melissa had shared with her. "It's so beautiful! I understand now; I really do! Isn't it amazing? I have felt that freedom before; when I was at my darkest moment, I experienced the freedom to let go of my anger and fear." She looked at Melissa, her eyes filled with tears of joy. She wanted to share her moment of renewal with Melissa, to tell her of the night she had been washed clean in the waters of the stream under the starry desert sky. One look at Melissa, however, sucked the joy right out of her. "What's wrong?" she cried, reaching a hand out to comfort her friend.

Melissa wiped at the tears flowing down her cheeks. She quickly turned away, a hardened expression covering her beautiful face. "You wouldn't understand. You can't know the things that haunt me or the pain that is mine to carry in this life."

Dahlia dropped her hand to her side. A chill swept through her, and for a moment, she felt as if she were looking at the wild, tortured man who had lived among the tombs. What pain had chained itself to Melissa's heart, strangling it to the point of so much self-hatred?

Melissa walked back up the steep, rocky passageway. Dahlia hurried to keep up. "I might," she called. "Melissa, please wait! I want to help you!"

"You can't! No one can. And no one will ever know the secrets I have to carry. Not you; not anyone!" She smeared the torch across the earthen floor, leaving a dark, sooty scar. Before Dahlia could reach her, she had fled the cave and disappeared into the darkness of night.

Kneeling down in the dark cave, Dahlia felt frantically about for the torch. Realizing she didn't have anything to light it with, she stopped her futile efforts. Sitting alone in the pitch black room, she pictured the painting again—the gentle attitude of Jesus as he reached out his hands toward the crazed, demon-possessed man. A gesture of welcome... Welcoming to talk, to walk with he and his friends, Dahlia wasn't sure, but she felt she knew this man—that she might want to be known by him. This was a man who cared for the individual; this Jesus had a heart for each person he came in contact with—healing, walking with, eating with, celebrating life with, teaching. He didn't condemn, he didn't judge based on race or social class; he found each person right where they were and he offered—in a very personal way—the very thing they sought after: HOPE. Compassion, understanding, acceptance. Was there any other man like him? Was there any other god who could claim such a perfect desire to know and love his people?

As she knelt on the sandy floor of the cave, Dahlia prayed to the God she was finally coming to know. "Jesus, thank you for loving me! Thank you for giving me hope! I don't know you very well, yet, but I know that you know me. I *feel* that you love me. It's enough—for now."

Chapter 21

"Brother Edgar, do you know about Jesus? He's the one…"

"Yes, yes, I know, lass! Doesn't everyone? Now wrap the wee thing up an' take it aw'eh while I tend to the mother!"

Lambing season was in full swing and Dahlia now saw a new side of Edgar. He seemed to thrive on the energy of bringing the 'wee little ones' as he called them into the world. Stressful as it was, Dahlia was delighted by the joy of seeing the soft little lambs laid beside their gentle mothers. They worked around the clock, taking turns sleeping when needed, but for several weeks they had lived and breathed the excitement of tending to the flock while multiple births occurred seemingly back to back. The incessant 'baaaahhh-ing' of the babes attracted the attention of jackals and other desert animals of prey, so several men had been assigned to guard the flock by night.

On the night that Marlin took his turn, Dahlia joined him beside the fire holding one of the little lambs who yet seemed to have a rather weak hold on life. They talked and talked of so many things while the northern star and moon slowly danced their way across the night sky. Marlin told her stories of the aboriginal people near his family's home in Australia and Dahlia followed with stories she had learned from Artashir around the campfire.

"Do you ever think about going there?" she asked as they watched Orion slowly turn on his side.

"I'd like to. I suppose it would be hard to leave Piedra, but it's where my people are from and I long to learn more about them. Their ways, the animals… Australia is filled with a wondrous variety of animals! They say that when God got bored creating animals for the world, he went to work on Australia."

Dahlia laughed. "I've learned some about the animals there. The kangaroo, the plata… platapospherous?"

"You mean the platypus," Marlin corrected. "I've often wondered how they'd taste. Peculiar, I imagine, don't you?"

"Marlin," Dahlia giggled uncontrollably. "You think of the silliest things! And always about food!"

"Food is my favorite thing; you should know that by now!"

"Quite right," Dahlia agreed. "I'm thankful to have benefited from so many of your kitchen experiments." Just that night, they had enjoyed skewered kebabs over the fire—seasoned snake meat and a variety of succulent roots roasted slowly over the glowing coals.

"Perhaps you'd like to go with me; start a new life somewhere else— far from the pain you've experienced here?" For once, Marlin had a calm, serious expression. Their relationship had grown so that she had to pause to consider before she knew what to say. She had to admit that her heart had felt a slight twinge when he spoke of going so far away, 'returning to his roots' so to speak.

"I don't know what to say." Dahlia looked at him in the soft light of the fire. His chiseled face and deep green eyes stared back. Eternity seemed to yawn between them as she allowed herself to take in all of the sweet adoration that shone on his face for her. She may never find someone who would love her as deeply as she felt loved and cared for by Marlin. *So what is wrong*, she asked herself. Why couldn't she jump up and down and reply with joyous kisses for the wonderful man who continued to offer her his heart? "I think… I would like that very much…" Her voice trailed off to a whisper. Her hand grabbed his and

Marlin allowed her to hold it while the tears began to slide down her cheeks.

"But…" he prodded gently.

"I don't know," she whispered. "I know that I want to be loved—the way that you want to love me…" She choked down a quiet sob. "But I just don't seem ready to accept it. Does that make any sense?"

Marlin swallowed hard. "I've never felt like this before, Dahlia. I just want you. I think that's all I really want. It's hard for me to understand why that's not enough."

"Do you ever wonder about the God who created all those amazing animals in Australia?"

He bit his lip. "That's a strange question."

"It's just, I have this strong desire to know and live for God, and the more I learn about him, the stronger it grows. I feel like I'm on a journey. It's the only thing that seems to matter somehow. Like I'm meant to live for him alone."

"Like a nun?"

"A what?"

"A nun. Sister Naomi was a nun before she came here. She lived in a tiny room and would go for days without talking to anyone. 'Vows of silence,' she called it. So that she might grow closer to God."

"Oh. I don't know. I don't think I want to do that. It seems kind of lonely."

I agree. Can't you come with me and live for God? I'll let you go for days without talking, and I'll feed you if you forget to eat."

Dahlia laughed. "Marlin, why are you so bent on having me? There are plenty of beautiful women out there who would love to have a shot at you. I'm quite certain of it."

His face fell. "But not you." Like a child, he sulked in silence and Dahlia felt certain that she could never return his love in the way he wanted her to. "Marlin, I've never had a friend as good as you. You are precious to me. I wish you could know how much I mean that!"

His sad eyes looked at her. If she had seen in their depths flashing sparks and an intensity that refused to take no for an answer, she might have changed her mind; but, as it was, she knew that Marlin loved the idea of a romance more than he might possibly love her. Their futures did seem very different, after all. She pursued knowledge of God, and he possessed a spirit of wanderlust which would take him back to the 'land down under' for a bit of a 'walk-about' as he called it. They would have to let each other go. Perhaps the time was already closer now than she'd realized.

⊷⊷⊙ ⊙⊷⊷

Springtime burst over the land in waves of pastel blooms that sprouted from prickly cactus branches and dry sagebrush. Dahlia took long walks with the flocks and contemplated the future. How long did she dare stay among the people of Piedra? Where would she go? Marlin loved her still; his actions showed the greatest care. She knew that if she removed herself, he would heal. He would move on and find someone else, Dahlia felt certain of it.

Yet she had nowhere to go. Still, staying in Piedra could not possibly be an option. Life there was strangely void of purpose for Dahlia. It seemed as if it was the place where the hurt and heart-sick came to heal, yet never left. And she had come and found healing. Unlike the inhabitants of Piedra, however, she no longer felt the need to hide away—she didn't want to! The light that she had dreamed about now lived inside of her. It burned and seared her very soul; it was something meant to be shared! She thought of the image of Christ reaching his hand out to the demon-possessed man: the invitation to embrace love and peace, followed by the command to stay and tell others how much God had done for him.

Dahlia thought of the people of Piedra—how they had come to find healing, yet in hiding from the world, they had become trapped in the process. The people of Piedra knew what it was to want to be loved and accepted for who they were; they had spent years running and hiding from a world that treated them with contempt and hostility. Each had a personal story of heartache, though no one talked about them. Perhaps true healing would never come until they told their stories, until they made themselves vulnerable again and faced the very world that had scarred them.

With this thought, Dahlia saw Ibrahim's face flash before her. It took her breath away; she felt her stomach twist and heave as she remembered the raw pain that had marked his face the night they had sat together on the beach at *Soleado*. He had been a broken man, overcome by grief in the loss of his young wife and child. She saw him so vividly in the dream she had had several times before where she helplessly watched him dive into the stormy sea and swim away until he was lost in the darkness. In Dahlia's dreams, he had shown no fear, had simply slipped into the dark sea without even a cry for help. In her dreams, she had turned and moved toward the light—determined to save herself.

Understanding dawned upon her. It was exactly what they had done in real time. She, drawn irresistibly to the light, had turned to it in hope of finding healing while Ibrahim had embraced the pain that overcame him and had gone back into the turmoil that swept their country like angry waves on a storm-vexed sea. Unable to find peace in his own life, Ibrahim had chosen to offer himself as a sacrifice to the people who hurt as he did, pouring himself out in an effort to bear their burdens and rebuild what had been broken in the war.

Honey bees buzzed from flower to flower as Dahlia sat on a lichen-covered rock. The scent of spring lingered in the air and the flock quietly nibbled at fresh sprouts along the edge of a mountain-fed spring. Purple shadows warned that evening was not far off, yet Dahlia sat and wondered at what Ibrahim had done. Their reactions, as opposite as could be, were like two pieces of the same puzzle; without each, the picture was incomplete. Dahlia had chosen healing—from the one source that could grant healing, and Ibrahim had chosen service to others while his own heart lay in a bloody heap. He would never find healing without the truth, and she would never find fulfillment without carrying the truth to those who were broken and lost.

The answer lay before her. It was time to move on. Hiding in Piedra was attractive; it was a comfortable ideal, but she knew that the truth she had found was meant to be shared. It was for the 'healing of the nations.' All the dreams that had haunted her for so many months now finally made sense! The weary who came to the stream desperate for a drink; the tree that grew over the stream—the tree that represented life, a life of abundance that could only be found in God; and the stream that represented his truth flowing from it. *And the leaves...* She dared not hold the knowledge to herself any longer, but must make preparation to move out right away! What to tell Marlin; would he understand? Sister Sarah and the others, and Melissa; would they believe her? They had sat on top of the truth for so long; had they become calloused to it? Why didn't they see it? The cycle of healing could not be completed without carrying healing to others, and Piedra had become a place of ingrown service and self-centered existence.

She hardly noticed her feet moving as she followed the sheep along the well-worn path.

"Edgar! O, brother Edgar," she called as the sheep wandered slowly into their pens. "Tell me, please, about Jesus! What is it you know—how is it that you know about this man who healed the broken?"

"Ah, lass! It's an old story—old as time itself. Ev'ry town bek' home has a church built in his name to be sure. People don' believe it much anymore."

"Believe what?"

"That he was the Savior. That they be needin' savin', child."

"But what do you think?"

Edgar rubbed his whiskers with his old wrinkled hand and thought for a minute. "Do I believe that the son of God came an' was born as a wee baby—to grow up and save the world? I dunno. It seems a bit of a stretch. Don' see why not tho'. Everyone needs a shepherd after all." He winked at her. "That's what they call 'im, you see. The Good Shepherd. Come to lead his flock to the livin' waters."

"The living waters! Why do you say that?" Dahlia pictured the weary people in her dreams, crawling toward the bank of the sparkling river, desperate for a drink.

"That's wha' the Scriptures call it. The water of life."

"Scriptures? You mean it's written down somewhere?"

"Whar' ye been, gal? Under a rock?! There's a Bible on ev'ry mantle bek' home! Cushioned with a doily. Don' ye have one then?"

Dahlia stood in stunned silence. A whole book to read about God and the Christ! Speechless, she imagined how she might find such a book. Did Edgar have one with him? She had to know. "Brother Edgar, do you have such a book?" she whispered.

He scoffed at her. A stern look replaced the excitement that had shown on his face just a moment earlier. "No, chil', I left that nonsense back at 'ome. I've moved on."

"Well, could you tell me just a bit more?" she begged.

"A bit more? Lass, there's thousands of stories! Where to begin? Hogwash—that's what it is. Stories made up to soothe our restless souls."

Dahlia took a step back. *How could he say that,* she wondered. *Why did he not believe?* "You mean, you don't believe in God?"

He didn't look at her. Busying himself with settling the sheep in for the night, he dismissed her questions. Realizing that she wasn't going to get anything else from him on the subject, Dahlia prepared the feed for the chickens. It was hard for her to imagine that someone had actually seen the scriptures that told of the one true God and yet did not have the faith to believe them. Working quietly in the stalls, she played the conversation over and over in her mind. *Scriptures, thousands of stories, living waters.*

As the sun set behind the rose-colored cliffs, she slowly wandered from pen to pen, checking on the animals one final time before heading back to the Cook House. She didn't feel much like eating at the moment. As she neared the sheep pens, she heard the thick brogue and lilting voice singing softly to the sheep:

"Know ye not that lowly baby was the bright and morning Star?
He who came to light the Gentiles and the darkened isles afar?
And we, too, may seek his cradle; there our hearts' best treasures bring:
To love and faith and true devotion for our Savior, God, and King." *

*Cecile Frances Alexander, 1853

145

Chapter 22

DAHLIA HAD TO duck her head to enter the low earthen doorway that led into the Laundry. The fragrance of lavender was so intense that Dahlia stopped for a moment just to enjoy the pungent scent. "Good morning, Sister Chan!" she called.

"I'm back here!" came the reply.

Dahlia made her way past tables laden with freshly pressed and folded garments. Stacks of plush blankets and bedcovers were carefully bundled and tied with strands of undyed wool. Following the sound of the loom whirring softly, she entered another room where vats of water for washing lined the walls. In the back corner, the tiny oriental woman sat facing the large loom, weaving colorful strands together. Though she couldn't be certain, Dahlia believed it must be a tapestry featuring several large white water lilies. "Oh, that's beautiful! Sister Chan, your work continues to amaze me!"

Chan bowed her head humbly in response, not taking her eyes from her work. Her fingers moved quickly, pulling threads together and working them into the pattern.

"I'll be needing some city clothes. Do you think you could make them for me?" Dahlia felt as if she were intruding. In a community where money was not used, the weight of such a request may not be appropriate. "I know you probably won't approve, but I need to return to my home."

The fingers came to an abrupt stop. "Not approve? Why would you think that?" For the first time that Dahlia could remember, Sister Chan made eye contact with her.

"I … just… I thought maybe people in our community wouldn't agree with my returning to my previous situation." When Chan didn't say anything, Dahlia rushed on. "I have some things I need to take care of. There are people who are hurting, and my country is in trouble! It's all a big mess, and I just feel so strongly that God is telling me to return to the city and face the troubles I left behind. Does that make any sense?"

A warm smile spread across Chan's face. "You are going back then. And for the right reasons!" She clapped her hands. Dahlia found the enthusiastic response rather bewildering. "I knew it was just a matter of time! You're not like us; you're so full of life and spirit! We will make you a fine wardrobe. I have a feeling you're going to accomplish a lot when you return home!"

"Sister Chan," Dahlia shook her head. "I don't understand. You're happy I'm going back? I'm glad that you are willing to help me, but I thought it was contrary to the philosophy of Piedra. I mean, why don't you want to go back to your home?"

Chan shook her head, sad eyes foretelling a sad story. "You don't need to know the details of my past, but there is no returning home for me. My country has chosen its leaders, and there is no place for me there now. To return could mean death; but I believe you can still help your country."

Dahlia's eyes grew wide. "You know who I am?"

Chan nodded gleefully as if they shared a wonderful secret. "I didn't want to frighten you, and it is our unspoken policy to leave our pasts behind and never speak of them. So when I found a letter in your tunic upon your arrival, I hid it away. I prayed that one day you would be ready to have it back. It seems that day has finally come."

"A letter? Oh, Sister Chan, from my father! You've read it?"

"Yes. But no one else has! Your secret is safe with me. But you're ready to face your destiny; I can see it in your eyes!"

Dahlia nodded, then shook her head. "No, I'm not sure what the letter says; it's from my father. Sister Chan, he was such an evil man." She bit her lip. "I'm a little afraid of what may happen when people find out that I'm still alive."

Chan crossed the room and pushed several bins of soap aside. Behind them was a small wooden box that she took down and blew off. "A laundress knows many secrets. You never know what you'll find in pockets." She gave Dahlia a sly wink. After rummaging through the box a moment, she retrieved the yellowed envelope. "Here. It's time you read this. I have complete confidence you are the daughter your father believed you to be. You have no reason to be afraid. It seems there are good people on your side, ready to help. It's time you sought them out and joined the fight to help your country overcome its bitter struggle."

"Oh, I don't know if God is calling me to that. I'm just one person, Sister Chan, and not one that anyone in my country would trust now. But I do have a dream—a vision that is becoming clearer. I do want to help people! I'm just not quite sure how..."

Sister Chan pressed the letter against Dahlia's heart and gave her a stern motherly look. "If you fail, then at least fail trying to help those you love. Men may judge you and others may try to harm you, but you are made of the stuff that moves you to try! So go, pour yourself out for a worthy cause; take your dreams and make them happen! Don't stay here with the cold and timid souls who have locked themselves away from the world. We have given up on our dreams."

A tear made its way down Dahlia's cheek. "I wish you could help your people, Sister Chan," she whispered. "I can tell that you loved them very much."

"My people are here now. This is my family." Chan smiled. "I tend to those who are broken and mourning, and once they make their home among us, I do my best to make their lives as comfortable as possible. Every once in a while, one like you comes along and I get to watch the wounds heal. You are strong; go and live for all of us!"

⊰⊷⊷⊷⊷

In the stable, Dahlia found a rusty bucket to sit upon. With trembling fingers, she took the yellowed envelope from her pocket and held it on her lap. She had forgotten that Ibrahim had given it to her. It was a painful reminder of her past, and for a moment, she wondered if she were really ready to face the people of her country. Whatever she found here, it could not change the disappointment she felt for her father. Perhaps it was best if she didn't find out more. Would the contents of the letter tear open old wounds? Sister Chan didn't seem to think so.

"Thank you, God, for her encouragement," Dahlia whispered. "You are my Father now, and I will do whatever I can to serve those who were most hurt by my father's actions. Help me know what it is you have for me. I'm ready to go. Please lead the way."

Unfolding the letter, she stared for a moment at the first line. *"My dearest friend:"* She saw the familiar slant to the letters, the way her father crossed his t's with a swirl. Tears filled her eyes and blinded her for a moment.

"My dearest friend: It pains me to write to you after so many years of not having spoken. It seems our lives have taken different courses since our time together at Cambridge. Do you remember how we hotly debated all things political? It seems we never could see eye to eye on such things.

I know it grieves you to see what has happened in our country. It seems we are poised at the edge of a dark precipice—and I fear the worst now. I have done all I could to exert an influence of control on our divided nation, but I have failed. The fighting grows worse every day now and my military advisors seem bent to do us all in with their madness.

Your book was a helpful reminder; Edmund Burke was always a favorite. You have proven to be 'the good man' while I have done nothing to help our people work through this strife—I'm afraid all of my attempts to stifle the fighting have only made it worse for all of us.

There is something I need you to do for me. It concerns my daughter Dahlia. You would like her very much—she has her mother's heart and my political ambition. She, all the time, challenges me with her Western ideas, studying democratic process and telling me what countries around the world are doing to provide freedoms for their people. She lives in a world of textbooks, ignorant of how things really are; she just doesn't understand our ways. But perhaps she's right. Change is bound to happen, and with the world growing smaller all the time, it may even happen in her lifetime. I have great hopes for her. And a tremendous fear for her safety.

So I ask a great favor of you. There will come a time when I am no longer able to watch over her. It may be sooner than I thought. She has plans to go to school in London, and I am thankful that she will soon be far away from all of this.

I am leaving her my estate 'Soleado'. It is all that will be left for her when the government fails. The deed is enclosed. I'm sure you realize the fullness of what I am asking, and while you have every right to decline, I know you would not.

It grieved me to hear of your son's loss. I wish it was in my power to restore the country to what it once was, but it seems I have failed, tremendously. Grievously.

Please forgive me.

Your friend,
Seljuk

Chapter 23

The more she talked, the faster Marlin chopped. Soon the potatoes were paper thin, folding over on themselves like a long line of white-topped waves crashing onto the seashore. With an overdramatic flourish, he tossed them into the popping oil and snatched up a large, wooden spoon.

"I won't let you go!" he snapped, waving the slotted spoon at her, slinging drops of hot oil around the room. "You are a bigger fool than I thought! All this talk of helping your people—you're so naïve! How do you think they'll respond, really?"

"Marlin," Dahlia raised a hand hoping to silence him. "You're overreacting. You've hardly listened to what I have to say. Does it not mean anything to you that I feel God is calling me to do this? I've never felt more certain of anything in all my life!"

"God! All this talk of God! And returning to the people that killed your father! This is why we don't talk about the past—stirring up feelings that are better left buried. Don't you see—you're dreaming up this huge heroic ideal where you get to save your people—people who don't want to be saved, let me remind you! They just got rid of one tyrannical leader, and now you want to go and sell them something new. What? What do you have to offer them? And what makes you think they'll even listen to you? You're the last person on earth they would want to get advice from on how to solve the country's problems!"

Dahlia got up, ready to leave. She didn't need this. What she needed right now was encouragement and support. Marlin was too blinded by his love for her to offer either of those right now.

"You're trying to play the martyr! Just like the Christ you keep talking about! Your Jesus. Do you know what happened to him? I bet you don't!" Marlin's green eyes flashed, his mouth twisted in an angry scowl. "Yes, he came to save the people—but guess what? They didn't want saving, and certainly not by him!"

Dahlia turned around. Marlin knew about Jesus? "You know about the Christ?" she whispered excitedly.

"More than you know, obviously." Marlin snapped up a mess of fried, crispy potatoes and gave them a heavy dusting of grainy salt. He angrily sampled one, the loud crunching sound grating on Dahlia's nerves.

How could he eat at a time like this? "Tell me what you know," she hissed.

"They crucified him. Do you know what that means? It was meant to shame him, an excruciating death—public and painful. That's what his people did to him!"

The hair on Dahlia's arms stood on end. *Could it be true? How could such a thing have happened?* "Why would they do that?" she whispered breathlessly.

"Why? Why do people hurt other people? That is exactly the kind of question we try to avoid here at Piedra. Because it really doesn't matter, does it?!! People hurt people—it's just what they do! Fear, selfishness, misunderstanding; and there are plenty of other reasons why, but it doesn't make any difference. Pain should be avoided, but you want to walk right back into it!" Marlin smashed the crunchy potato flakes with his fist. "Can't you see that? You're walking right into their mess. They'll take their anger and frustrations out on you! I don't need to tell you how it will end."

Dahlia ignored his last comments. Her problems really didn't matter right now. "But Jesus helped people! I've heard the stories. He was kind and he only wanted to help!"

"It doesn't matter! Dahlia, I can't let you go! I won't let you go!" Marlin had transformed before her very eyes—like a little boy throwing a tantrum when he couldn't have his way—he ranted and pounded the wooden spoon on the table.

Dahlia sat down with a heavy sigh. It was more than she could take at the moment; a sudden weariness filled her heart.

When Marlin saw the look on her face, he stopped abruptly. "You're going anyway, aren't you? You don't care what happens!" he cried in disbelief.

"It's not that I don't care; I'm very much afraid! It's just that… I know it's the right thing to do. I know it with all my heart! It burns inside of me—this calling to return to those who were hurt by my father! To help however I can. It's just something I *have* to do."

Marlin knelt down beside her, placing his heavy head in her lap. "Please don't go," he sobbed. Like a mother calming a little boy, Dahlia stroked his head and shushed him gently.

⇥☙ ❧⇤

Dahlia stomped into the Barn House. A fire burned inside of her and she would not let Edgar ignore her questions this time. "They killed him? You knew they killed him and you didn't tell me?!"

Edgar sat with his back to her, his hands working the wool patiently. "Aye, gal. I thought ya knew. It's a crucial part of the story!"

"What? That a good, loving man should die? On a cross? What kind of twisted fate is that? How could such a thing happen? How could his own people turn on him like that?!!"

Edgar stopped and turned around, a keen look on his face. "It had to happen, it did. The sacrificial lamb? Don'cha know, lass? It's the most important thing he did!"

"What? You mean he *let* them do it? Are you telling me he knew they wanted to kill him?"

"Yes, child. It's how it had to be. The people needed savin' from themselves. He was the sacrificial lamb. I thought ya knew it."

A sacrificial lamb. Dahlia thought back to the season of Ramadan. At the end of the holy month of fasting, the people would purchase sheep and cart them home—all across the city. Then, they would string them up in alleyways and side streets, slaughtering them for a special feast. Because her father was a secularist and not interested in religious practices, the celebration was not one she had personally experienced. Instead, it had been a frightening time, one she dreaded every year.

"Why did he have to be the sacrificial lamb? Couldn't the people slaughter sheep instead?" she asked. "How could they kill a man? A good, kind man?"

Edgar's face softened. A misty, far-away look filled his eyes. "Because he was the perfect man—without blemish. He was the ultimate sacrifice—the payment for our sins. His blood for our freedom. It was the only way, and he gladly paid the price. Out of love. He was by very nature God, perfectly righteous, but humbled himself and came to dwell among men. He took on their sorrows, and the nature of a servant, lovin' the unlovable and giving himself up—even to death on a cross!

"Aye," Edgar wiped a tear away, "It's a glorious story! The perfect picture of humility and self-sacrifice."

Dahlia sat down for a minute. This was not what she had expected at all. It didn't make any sense; her heart grieved for the man she had only heard about, yet she was in awe of what he had done. She knew it was for his people, and that it was for her if she could accept it. Drawing in a deep breath, she knew she already had. "Do you think it's wrong for me to want to go back to my people, Edgar, and help them? Marlin says I'm playing the martyr, but if I don't go, I don't think I will ever find peace again!"

"Ah, lassy! 'Tis a spirit of humility you have, then. Looking to the interests of others—'tis the attitude of Christ ye have. 'Tis what would be expected of one who chooses to follow Him."

"Then you think I should go?" Dahlia's eyes filled with tears. It was the confirmation she needed. Once again, the truth had set her free!

Time flashed by in a feverish flurry of activity and goodbyes. Dahlia made her rounds and told the few friends she had made in her short time at Piedra what she could about her reasons for leaving. Most looked at her wistfully as she told of the passion she had for helping her people in their great time of need; it was as if they longed to find the courage to face their own sorrows. Sister Chan slipped a bundle of special-made clothes into her room when she wasn't there; Dahlia was undone by the simple, versatile wardrobe bestowed upon her. Exquisite tailoring made the few casual pieces fine enough to be dressed up or down depending on the situation. All fit perfectly in a sturdy backpack she was meant to wear on her trek back to the city. It was an amazing gift.

⊶⊶⊙ ⊙⊷⊷

On a moonless night, only two days before she planned to depart, Dahlia sat under the bright stars, soaking in the calmness of the desert night one last time. Before long, she would be among sights and sounds that would be all too familiar—the rush of the city and noise in every direction.

She sat and prayed—for wisdom, clearness of mind and unwavering courage. "If you could face the people that hated you, then you will help me face the people who hated my father," she whispered.

The call of a jackal startled her. For a moment, she thought of Artashir and wondered if she should seek his help. Somehow, she felt certain that she must not. After all, he and Endora had the burdens of their own people to worry about now.

As she walked past the Cook House, sounds of laughter floated out the open doorway. A crowd had gathered to play cards and a frenzied game of Dutch Blitz had the group throwing cards around the table in animated chaos.

"Dahlia!"

From the corner of her eye, she saw someone get up from the entry step and move toward her.

"Melissa!" Dahlia squinted, trying to see her face in the darkness. It had been over two weeks since they had last spoken—the night that Melissa had shown her the cave paintings. Dahlia knew she was being avoided, but she didn't feel that pressing Melissa to open up would help her wounded friend.

"I have something to tell you!" Melissa greeted her with an enthusiastic hug and kiss on the cheek. "You won't believe it when I tell you— but you've set the community abuzz with the news of your returning to Anazir! Most people think you're crazy but Marlin and I, we've decided you're right!"

Dahlia was shocked. How could Melissa have had such a change of heart? And Melissa had been so upset before—unwilling even to talk of the outside world.

"We're going to Australia! We've decided to go and meet our family and see the land we come from. Marlin's so excited—he's filled my ears with stories of the Outback and strange animals; he can hardly wait!"

"Oh, Melissa, that's wonderful! You'll finally have a fresh start. I'm so happy for you!"

"Well, it won't be that easy. In fact, it's unlikely that my mother's family will want to see us at all. You see, she led a ... colorful life, so to speak." Melissa looked down; she seemed reluctant to speak of her mother, but a determined spirit had replaced the bitterness that once enslaved her. "For so long, I have been ashamed of her, and how Marlin and I were conceived ... My mother's journals leave no clue as to who our father might have been. She had so many ... clients."

"Oh," Dahlia tried not to sound shocked. "I'm so sorry."

"It's ok," Melissa laughed. "I'm over it now! You have helped me realize that our lives are not defined by the actions of our parents." She nodded decisively. "If you can go back and face your people, then so can we! If our family won't accept us, then we'll move on. But we can't stay here! It's time to live our own lives. I won't be condemned for my mother's mistakes any longer. Her lifestyle cost her her life; she came here to die a slow and painful death, but we were given the best upbringing possible among a group of people who loved and accepted us without judging us for our mother's choices." Melissa began to tear up. "I've been filled with bitterness for so long, angry at my mother and at the world that allowed such things to go on; I didn't want to accept that she was responsible for what happened. It was her own choices that destroyed her, and I am the one who chose to bear the guilt for her actions—living under the weight of her sins. Well, not anymore! I feel so free!" Melissa twirled around like a little girl, arms outstretched.

Dahlia laughed and grabbed Melissa's hands. "I'm so happy for you! But I know you'll be missed here. This is your family!" She nodded toward the merry group inside. "I know they'll miss you and Marlin very much."

"Yes, I suppose you're right. But we all have to grow up sometime. I'm done hiding out. There's a whole big world out there!"

Chapter 24

DAHLIA AWOKE AT dawn, too restless to sleep any longer. It was time to go. Everything was ready; she had nothing else to keep her in Piedra. She packed the last few items in the satchel Sister Chan had made for her and placed a jar of water in the side pocket. In the other side pocket were the carefully wrapped travel snacks Marlin had prepared. It was a three day trip to the main road and she didn't want to put it off any longer.

Marlin and Melissa would go with her as far as the road, then they would go their separate ways. Dahlia had made it clear that she didn't want them to come to Anazir with her. Whatever troubles faced her in the city, she would face them alone.

Dahlia headed down to the sheep pens to say one last goodbye. Dawn was breaking with a rosy glow that lit up the eastern sky. A few puffy white clouds low in the horizon completed the picture. She would miss the beauty of the desert.

"Brother Edgar," she called. He came out of his hut, rubbing sleepy eyes and tucking in a wrinkled shirt.

"So, there's no stoppin' ye now, eh?" He gave her a sly wink. "That's a brave gurl! I've got somethin' for ye." He stepped back inside for a minute. "Sister Chan asked me to give this to ye. Don't read it'all in one settin'." He gave a hearty laugh as he slapped the heavy, leather bound book into her hands.

"What is …" Dahlia traced the gold, imprinted letters with her finger. "A Bible? Is this the scriptures you've told me about?"

"It's all there; every word of it."

"Oh, I don't know how to thank you! I can hardly, oh, but, wait! I can't take it. You need it here, Brother Edgar. You said you didn't have one, and if Sister Chan gives me hers…"

"Dahlia. Gal, listen, you've helped me face me past—somethin' I never thought wou'd happen. It seemed *impossible!*" He spit the word out with a laugh. "You see, I once tended to me own flock, in Ireland. They call them 'churches,' and I was the 'shepherd.'" He looked out at his sheep fondly. "Me wife 'n I. Ahh! When God took her, I grew bitter. Then they took me church, too!" Tears filled his eyes and Dahlia couldn't help herself. She hugged him around his neck and held on tight for a minute. *All this pain around me,* she thought, *and I never even knew the root of it. Why do they keep it all bottled up inside?*

"I wandered fer a'while, a restless soul with a hard and stubborn heart. 'Twas no good! I've lived so long like that—hard and blinded by me anger. Well! No more, I say!" He wiped the tear from his cheek. "I've got a new callin' from God—to a new flock. One right here!" He pounded the Bible. "Ya see, I don' need it—not this; got it all right here!" He tapped his head, then his heart. "I've been knowin' these words for a whole lot longer than you could imagine; it's time I share them with the hurtin' people right here."

"That's wonderful, Brother Edgar!" Dahlia hugged him again. "Tell Sister Chan 'thank you!' This means so much!"

"A word of warnin', lass." He thumped the leather cover soundly. "The words within that book will change ye, wait 'n see! Be prepared, eh? Theh' don' let go of ye, no matter how far ye run."

Dahlia nodded. She believed she understood what he was telling her.

⊷⊨◉ ◉⊨⊶

They had walked for two and a half days, and with the sun sinking in the western sky, Dahlia hoped they were getting close. It had been a special time with Melissa and Marlin—reading the Bible aloud together at night by the light of the fire and discussing it through the day while they walked along the dusty path that led them north toward the mountains.

"Look!" Melissa cried. "The road—there it is!" The three of them stood and stared, suddenly feeling the weight of the futures that faced them.

"We can go back now, and I'll never mention any of this again," Marlin said. "I'll make a big pot of stew, bake some herbed bread—"

A truck appeared in the distance, and Marlin fell silent. It was heading west.

"This is me," Dahlia whispered. She hugged her friends; without looking back, she approached the road. Two men dressed in work clothes eyed her suspiciously as they pulled over. Showing no sign of recognition, they agreed to give her a ride to the next city and waved her toward the back. Dahlia climbed into the truck bed and huddled between a few scruffy goats and baskets of undyed wool.

As the truck pulled off the side of the road, she saw Melissa and Marlin standing in the brush, waving goodbye.

Chapter 25

THE CITY WAS abuzz with chaotic energy; it was nothing like Dahlia remembered. Buildings and streets looked much as she had last seen them, but without the overbearing presence of armed military guards, the citizens moved about without restriction, enjoying the freedoms of carrying on commerce and trade at will. Open-air markets spilled onto crowded sidewalks, demonstrators held signs supporting this or that local agenda, and displaced refugees lined the sides of buildings holding signs pleading for food and assistance. It seemed everyone wanted something and all were freely voicing their opinions and needs to their hearts' content. The noise and bustle overwhelmed Dahlia after her time in the peaceful desert region, but the one positive thing she noticed as she cautiously made her way along the busy streets was the overall preservation of Anazir following her father's death; except for the hillside neighborhood of Guardi, the majority of the capital city was unscathed.

With the hood of her jacket pulled over her hair and sunglasses to cover her eyes, Dahlia felt safe walking among the residents of her city. There were no longer I.D. checkpoints as there had been during her father's reign, and the majority of the people seemed caught up in their new lives, enjoying doing whatever they pleased, unconcerned with the people around them. Unlike the city of Lamirya, whose residents had bonded together in the arduous process of rebuilding, the citizens of Anazir had simply taken their new-found freedom and run—right back to the things they had been doing before the year of curfews and insanity. They had forgotten the short bondage they had endured in the war that had mostly been fought outside of their city. All that remained now was the hard-nosed energy of commerce carrying on; except for the throng of dirty beggars and refugees—and a few belligerent demonstrators littering the streets, a visitor would never have known that a civil war had swept through the city.

Looking at the yellowed envelope, Dahlia ran her finger over the address. She knew the street name; it wasn't far from Guardi or the presidential mansion where she had lived. A short walk from the city's center the roads narrowed and led up into quiet residential neighborhoods that grew along the rocky ridge. Except for the occasional car or motorcycle, Dahlia was mostly alone as she walked up the steep sidewalks lined with young poplars whose willowy branches were just beginning to sprout new, spring leaves. Dahlia was startled by a woman—tossing a large carpet over her balcony railing and beating it with a stick. The muted sounds of old men talking on a sidewalk bench or shouting at a televised soccer game in a corner bar echoed off the building walls. She turned left when the narrow alley she had been following emptied onto a wide boulevard that ran along the hillside. Between apartment buildings, she caught glimpses of the city below. When she reached building #23, she stopped and stared at the long list of names and apartment numbers on the doorbell pad. #4B, *Saran*, was near the bottom. She drew in a long breath and let it out slowly. Raising her hand, she quickly pressed the button. "Hello?" came the call.

"Dahlia Seljuk." She replied. As soon as the words escaped, she realized what a foolish thing she had done. She hadn't told anyone her full name in months; what had possessed her to blurt it out now? And to a complete stranger!

The buzzer rang, and the door to the building clicked open. She leaned against it and paused. Did she dare go up? How could she be sure it was safe? The foyer was lined with a simple white marble, the floor an artistic blend of white and black mosaic tile. Tasteful and modern, nothing fancy. She placed her hand on the metal banister and took the first step. Three flights later, she turned and faced the closed door to #4B. Her heart pounded in her chest and she contemplated turning and running back down the steps. Before she had the chance, the door opened and Dahlia knew instantly who was standing before her. The crisp, white button-up shirt, sleeves rolled up to the elbows; the perfectly straight nose and ruggedly handsome face; the piercing, dark eyes. The only difference was the light peppering over the temples and the kind expression that looked back at her in surprise.

"'I'm sorry for your son's loss!'" she blurted, then covered her mouth with her hand, realizing she had echoed the words from her father's letter aloud.

"It's alright, Dahlia," the man said with a sad smile. He stepped back, gesturing her graciously into the apartment. "It was over two years ago. And besides, our family has suffered less than many. We have that to be thankful for."

Dahlia, downcast, entered the room and followed him to a large white sofa.

"Please, sit down," the man said. "My wife will bring you some tea. Excuse me for just a moment. I need to let her know that you're here."

The sound of children playing in the alleyway below echoed up through the open windows. Dahlia looked around the room and found the airy, open space to be bright and clean. The modern, white décor seemed strangely foreign after her stay in the desert.

A young boy in a soccer jersey smiled down at her from a framed photo on the mantle. Ibrahim hadn't always been so sullen and serious, she mused. Remembering the reason why quickly sobered her.

"Ah, Dahlia!" a cheerful little woman exclaimed as she came into the room carrying a tea tray. "You look so much like your mother."

Pleased, Dahlia smiled shyly. "Except for the curls; I didn't get them."

"Oh, but you've fine, thick hair. So beautiful, isn't she, Saran?"

Nodding, the man settled in an armchair across from her and took the tray from his wife's hands. "Let me serve you, please. Sugar cubes?"

The attention made her feel suddenly very self-conscious, and more homesick than she ever remembered feeling. Dahlia nodded, tears welling up in her eyes.

"Oh, excuse me! I've got a roast of lamb in the oven." Ibrahim's mother smoothed her apron and disappeared into the kitchen.

When Dahlia realized she was trying to hide behind her steaming cup of tea, she set it down and looked up at Saran.

"Well, I'm sure you have many questions," he offered.

"A few," she nodded emphatically. "I'm not really sure where to start."

"Of course." He set down his cup of tea. "Why don't we start with your father."

"You were his friend?"

"Yes, a close friend. We roomed together at Cambridge. We knew each other a very long time."

"It's just… Well, I never heard about you." Dahlia bit her lip; she felt she could trust this man. She desperately wanted to know more, and perhaps he could provide the answers she had been looking for.

"We had a falling out, many years ago. Before your father took office even. You see, your father and I had very different ideas about how our country should be directed. We had studied political science together and developed strong theories on how the leadership of Al Cazar needed to be shaped. Your father's political career took off; mine did not. And then he was elected into office. The country chose him; I felt it was my duty to respect their wishes and not try to influence your father any longer."

"But, my father always listened to advisors!" Dahlia interjected. "They were very important to him."

"I know; I thought I was counted among that special group, especially since we had been so close in our youth. But your father outgrew our relationship; when I didn't affirm his decisions the way his military advisors did, I was kindly asked to butt out. And so I did. After all, Dahlia, it was what the people wanted. There was no mistaking the enthusiasm with which the country rallied around your father in his early years as president. They loved him, and he brought some good changes to our nation."

"So what happened? When did things begin to fall apart?"

"I don't know. Perhaps it was right before the last election—your father's second time around. A variety of strong candidates were popping up and some questionable things that had happened in your father's first term were brought to light. You see, in order to accomplish so much, your father made deals with many powerful men; that sort of thing has a way of working out poorly in the end. Especially since much of the existing leadership was severely corrupt. Perhaps your father compromised more and more in hopes of pulling the country together and in the end lost his ability to please anyone. Authority has a way of undoing men; I suppose it clouded your father's judgment, causing him to lose sight of what the people really needed. Unfortunately, when a man becomes that controlling, a fall from power can take the whole country with him."

"And that's why you had him killed? Were you trying to prevent more damage to the stability of the nation?" Dahlia knew she sounded angry. She didn't care.

"I was disappointed in your father, Dahlia. I wish now I hadn't been so willing to step out of his life, but pride has a way of stopping us from saying the things we need to say. When I walked away from our relationship, I lost any ability I had to influence him. Even if I had found a way to remain in his life, I don't know that he would have listened. Towards the end, your father became irrational, vengeful and destructive."

Dahlia knew it was true. She knew she could trust this man. His testimony was the bridge to the memories of the man she remembered her father to be in her youth. If Saran had stayed in her father's life, perhaps he wouldn't have morphed into the monster he had become. Would he have handled the country's problems differently? Would it have saved her family in the end? Dahlia mentally kicked herself back to the present. It didn't matter anymore—but this window into her father's past added an element of humanity to him that the recent truths she had learned had tainted. That he had made such deep mistakes, had chosen such evil advisors, and had used such horrific methods of control—she would never understand the dark powers that had taken hold of him. She only understood that it all came down to choices: he had chosen darkness, and she had chosen light.

"Let's talk of why you're here now. I have something for you— something I hope you still want."

Dahlia nodded.

Saran cleared his throat then leaned forward to stir his tea. "What I have," he sat back and took a sip, "is the paperwork that will make *Soleado* yours. It would be my honor to help you become the rightful owner of your father's estate. Is that what you want?"

"Oh, yes. Very much so." Dahlia's eyes gleamed.

He smiled. "Then that's what we shall do. We will draw up the papers tomorrow—make it official. And you shall have your father's beloved *Soleado*. What will you do with it?"

Dahlia's eyes searched the room for an answer. How could she explain the dream she had; it was still a fuzzy idea that she liked to play with—at night when she should be sleeping, or out under the desert sky while the sheep grazed. "I'm not sure exactly . . . yet. I have a plan . . ."

Saran waited. "A plan?"

"I want it to be a place . . . for others to come . . . and find healing—and hope . . . after suffering through the war." Dahlia set down her teacup. "And I want to grow things—oh, olives, lavender, sunflowers, and—I don't know what else!" She laughed. "But I can hardly wait to return there. It is my home now, at last. I'm ready to go home." She nodded, averting her eyes. Perhaps she had shared too much.

"That's quite a vision." Saran smiled. "But I think I can see it. Your father would like that, too. He loved to grow things." He looked down. "He loved to work that land. It was when he was at his best."

Dahlia nodded in agreement.

⤛⟿ ⟿⤜

As they drove north, Dahlia admired the familiar landscape. Olive groves stood in perfect lines, stretching out for miles all around them. The trees' silvery leaves glimmered in the pale spring sunlight. She enjoyed the company of Saran very much, and as they drove along the highway, they discussed democratic theory. Dahlia enjoyed the opportunity to speak openly about her political views. Her father had always discouraged any discussion of elections or civil rights—but Dahlia's imagination ran wild with ways to incorporate such practices into the new government that would eventually be formed. It seemed, from what Saran shared, that many cities had already elected representatives as they prepared to meet and discuss new leadership at a national level.

"It will be the first election in over ten years," Saran added. "The people are very eager to make the most of this opportunity. We have great hopes that they will handle their new freedoms well ..."

"But?" Dahlia waited. "It seems you have some doubts."

"Our people are so diverse. Our countrymen have struggled and fought over religious and racial differences for centuries. I don't know that such a varied population can ever agree on one set of governing rules."

Saran raised his hands above the wheel. "Will they ever allow an elected of-ficial to rule them as one people—or will they continue to bite and devour one another as they have for generations?" He shook his head. "It seems we always end up with some form of dictatorial rule; the military has per-formed almost a dozen coups in the last century alone. What will it take for our people to find a common ground—to live in unity?"

"Perhaps this war has helped unite them," Dahlia interjected. "They have learned to fight together for a common cause—one that is precious to them all."

"Perhaps . . ." Saran shook his head. "But it doesn't change the root of the problem. Our populace is too diverse. They want different things; they have conflicting values."

Dahlia rubbed her forehead. "Maybe the only way they will ever be one nation again is under a strong leader who can persuade them to remain as one."

Saran looked over at her. "You're starting to sound like your father," he warned.

Dahlia sighed. "You're right! I don't know anymore. I used to think I had all the answers to our country's problems. I studied and schemed; I examined history and how democracy had evolved in Western civiliza-tion. I had it all figured out, and then my world turned upside down. Nothing is what it really seemed, after all; not even my family."

Saran nodded. "You've been through a lot this year. I can't imagine how it's been for you."

"What I've come to realize," she turned to look at him, "is that there is no real solution—not in us. We spin our wheels trying to figure out how to make a broken system work—but no matter how hard we try, it's still broken."

"I'm a pragmatist, Dahlia. I don't believe in giving up. Is that really what you're suggesting? That we sit back and watch our country fall apart?"

"No, I believe we were created to try—to work together and find ways to use our gifts to help others. But the solution is not ours."

"Whose is it? How do we achieve anything then?"

"In Christ alone," she replied earnestly.

Saran raised his eyebrows. "You didn't learn that from your father," he retorted.

"No, but it's what I believe now . . . With all my heart."

Chapter 26

When they got out of the car, Dahlia wondered how she had allowed Saran to talk her into coming. Her stomach was tied in knots and her mouth was suddenly very dry.

"They're rebuilding a school," Saran explained, pointing out the various piles that would be recycled into the new structure. Mounds of mortar, piles of steel, a long line of window frames to be re-paned. Doors, desks, books; everything had been salvaged and set aside, ready to be used.

"Ah, there he is!" Saran strode toward his son. Dahlia trailed behind him, concerned how Ibrahim would take her impromptu visit.

He looked relaxed, she noticed, as he talked to the men who were working with him. A set of blueprints was rolled out over a long board set up on saw-horses. One by one, the men took their orders and wandered off to start the afternoon tasks. Each loudly delivered the instructions they had been given to a group of men who worked with them, and before long, the lot was a beehive of activity.

When Ibrahim was alone, Saran approached and patted his son on the back.

"Dad!" he exclaimed and the two men embraced. When he saw Dahlia, she thought he looked genuinely glad to see her, though obviously surprised. After a brief round of pleasantries, Saran excused himself to find coffee for the group.

Dahlia looked at Ibrahim sheepishly and waited to see what he'd say when his father was gone.

"Would you like to see the plans?" he asked with a casual smile that Dahlia found more than a little unnerving.

"I'd love to!" she replied, disarmed by his unusual openness. Walking around the saw-horses, she joined him in front of the elaborate drawings. A front perspective showed the long, clean lines of the future school. Large window groupings would allow plenty of sunshine into the classrooms and an inviting entryway was supported by sturdy, wooden beams covered in some sort of flowering vine. "It looks lovely," she breathed. It was the most inviting school Dahlia had ever seen—with window boxes for flowers and even a gated garden plot off to one side.

Ibrahim gestured to the marble pillars that lined the front of the building. "We salvaged them from the local courthouse. Only eight were left after the bombings," he explained. "The people were very proud of them, were adamant that they be incorporated into the design as a symbol of hope for the future of their children. I just can't seem to make them work in the design—with so few. Do you see what I mean?"

Dahlia examined the drawing for a moment. The pillars—spaced symmetrically along the front of the building—did seem rather sparse standing so far apart. "They just seem sort of lonely," she agreed. "Perhaps you could group them in pairs here, and here," she pointed to the simple beams that supported the gabled entryway. "That may make them feel a little more dramatic—and substantial."

Ibrahim erased the singular pillars and grouped them in pairs on either side of the entryway, then sketched decorative caps and bases to tie them into the structure. Dahlia liked standing next to him while he worked. She could feel the creative energy oozing out of him as he pondered and sketched. It was clear why he had become so successful;

he was confident and skilled, willing to try new things. And he had an artistic flair that complimented his vast architectural knowledge.

"Your father showed me some of your completed works on the way here—the new hospital at the south end of town, and a fresh produce complex near the city's center. They're wonderful!"

"Thank you," he beamed.

Dahlia looked up at him, melting before the warm, unguarded man who smiled back at her. Reconstruction had been good for him, she realized. He was using the gifts God had given him, and it seemed to be the process of healing he had needed. "I'm so glad to have had the opportunity to see the work you're doing here. I had no idea how talented you were!"

Ibrahim laughed. "Don't sound so surprised." Dahlia noticed a dimple on the left side of his face that appeared when he smiled.

"It's . . . just . . ." Dahlia stammered. She felt herself growing flustered as Ibrahim grinned at her in amusement. Why did she allow herself to become so unraveled around him? "Well . . ." she waved her hand as if grasping for words. "I've only seen what you did to my house," she blurted.

Ibrahim stepped back.

Dahlia gasped. "I mean . . . Oh, I didn't mean to . . ." She stopped.

Ibrahim's astonished face flushed before her. His mouth opened as if he were about to say something.

Dahlia bit her lip and waited, wondering why she had said what she did. *What were you thinking,* her mind screamed.

"Dahlia, I'm sorry," he said in a low voice.

"No, Ibrahim. Please don't apologize—I didn't mean . . ." she faltered. What could she say?

"You must hate being around me. It must be torture—a constant reminder of what I did to your family, of the pain I brought into your life."

Dahlia's mouth fell open. She had to stop this; he shouldn't bear the guilt for what had happened. "Ibrahim, please!" Dahlia shook her head, desperately wanting to stop him from continuing. And then the thought hit her. *Is that what he thinks of when he looks at me?* Her mind began to race as she realized why he might feel the way he did. *When he looks at me, does he only see the flesh and blood of Seljuk—the one who killed his wife and child?* She shuddered.

"These hands," he continued, "you should know . . . that I have vowed never to use these hands in judgment again. It is not my place to pass judgment, to destroy . . ." He quickly rolled up the drawings they had worked on together only a moment before. "I will spend my life building what I can, helping restore the broken walls and dwellings of our land." He gave her a weak smile and the light seemed to fade around them. "I won't impose on you again, Dahlia. I'll leave you to your healing." He took a step backwards, shame and grief written on the lines of his face. "I hope you have a full and happy life. Please try to forgive me for what I've done."

I already have, her mind screamed, but her throat was choked by a swelling knot as she felt her eyes filling with tears. "Ibrahim—I have," she croaked.

He nodded, pressing his lips together as he waited for her to continue.

Unable to speak, Dahlia wiped the tears away, desperately wishing she could find the words he needed to hear.

"I hate that I have brought so much pain to your life, Dahlia. I give you my word that I will respect your right to heal and move on without my presence to remind you of that awful day."

As Ibrahim walked away, all of the joy she had felt a moment ago—while working by his side—went with him.

Chapter 27

"Dahlia, there's something I need to speak to you about."

She looked blankly out the window, her mood reflected in the grey afternoon showers. Dahlia watched as a single raindrop slid down the passenger window creating a wet streak across the glass.

"I've debated involving you at all, but I feel you should know." Saran gripped the steering wheel with both hands. "I would feel like I was repeating past mistakes if I wasn't completely honest with you. It's just that you've been through so much already. Sometimes, when I look at you, I see the same grief that I've seen in Ibrahim's eyes. It's almost too much to bear, to know that he's had to deal with so much loss in his young life . . . as have you."

At the mention of his name, Dahlia flinched. She turned to look at Saran. His face was anguished as he continued to speak, looking straight ahead.

"It's so much to ask of you—it was too much to ask of him. To take advantage of his grief and anger, to ask him to orchestrate . . ." Saran stopped. He turned to look at her, saw the wide eyes staring back at him. For a moment, he seemed to panic, realizing where the words were taking him. A look of resolve appeared and he started again. "They have a chemical weapon." He stopped, letting it sink in.

"Who does?"

"The military, what's left of it. Your father's men."

"But—I thought the war was over! Hasn't the military been disbanded?"

"There's still a remnant . . . There's always a remnant—lurking, waiting, scheming for an opportunity to regain control."

"Rashad?"

"Of course. And others; we don't know how many. They've worked their way back into the city, spreading propaganda, looking for sympathetic ears."

"How serious is it?"

"They're planning a coup. Perhaps. Or, just one last act of terror—retaliation for the people's betrayal. What we do know is that they have a powerful weapon. They tested it last spring. It was horrible—it spreads out in a cloud of death, slowly strangling its victims . . ."

Dahlia shuddered; a wave of nausea ran through her as she pictured the sea of flags on the barren valley floor, the merciless desert wind whipping their frayed ends. *Like souls flying to heaven.*

"We just don't know when they will use it, or where. But, if they have it here in Anazir, it could kill thousands of people."

She nodded, understanding. It was clear that the situation was very serious; it was not clear why Saran thought she could help.

"Dahlia, you could find out what Rashad's plan is."

"Me?" she gasped.

"Of course. He has no reason to mistrust you. Perhaps you could go to him and learn his plan."

Dahlia's heart began to pound. As much as she didn't want to acknowledge it, she felt a certainty deep inside that this was part of God's plan. She had been shown the next step; now it was up to her to take it.

⇥⊚ ⊚⇤

Under the cover of a moonless night, Dahlia approached the imploded palace. Its dark form stood outlined against the blinking city lights below. A wave of sadness followed by a hollow numbness set in like a damp chill on a rainy, winter's night.

Spotting the armed guards before they saw her, she chose to find a more indirect route inside. Skirting the rocky hillside, she made her way down into the grove of cedars that grew below the house. She climbed the low wall that encircled the back gardens, then followed the path Hasan and Artashir had cleared for her. Memories of their time here together seemed like distant dreams.

A classical piano piece crescendoed from the speakers of an old record player, and as she approached the terrace, Dahlia saw Rashad sitting alone at the kitchen table. Through the gaping hole in the kitchen wall, she watched him, head back, eyes closed as he smiled and waved a hand along with the music. A single candle lit the room and she strained her eyes to see if any guards were standing in the shadows. When she felt certain that he was alone, she crept up the steps and stood before him.

As the piano piece slowly ended, fingers touching the keys so gently and softly that the music seemed to simply fade away, Rashad let out a long, deep sigh. Dahlia cleared her throat.

His eyes blinked open and for a moment, as his eyes adjusted, she could see the fear written clearly on his face. "Dahlia!" he exclaimed, recovering from the shock. A hungry look replaced his momentary panic and he leaned forward eagerly. "We've looked everywhere for you!" he cried, moving forward to embrace her as though she were his long, lost daughter.

Dahlia took a few steps back, putting up arms to ward him off.

Seeing the alarm on her face, he backed off, physically demonstrating his respect for her personal need for space. "You've been through so much, my dear. Forgive me. I have waited so long for this moment . . .

It has weighed so heavily on my heart that my closest friend's daughter was out there alone, suffering!"

Dahlia looked around the kitchen; like a caged animal, she noted various routes of escape as she listened, regretting deeply her decision to come here. How could she trust him after all she'd learned?

"It's ok, now, dear one. You are safe here with us." Rashad sat in his chair, placing his hands squarely on the table and leaning back in a relaxed pose. "Tell me now, how is it that you've finally found us after all these months? We've been so worried."

Forcing herself to breathe normally, Dahlia moved toward the sink and placed her back against it. From there, she could see the doorway leading into the room and the gaping hole that led onto the terrace. So far, they seemed to be alone. "I was afraid to come home." She was afraid to say too much. How could she win his trust, she wondered, when every move he made seemed to be so falsely sincere?

A forced sadness filled his eyes, and he shook his head in sorrow. "Oh, Dahlia. What have they done to you? It's been months, and yet you've had no time to mourn the loss of your parents. Have you been running all this time?"

She had prepared for this moment; she knew they would want to know where she'd been. Without betraying the trust of her friends, she needed to be as honest as possible. Rashad obviously knew more than he let on. "I stayed in the desert for a time; one of my captors took me there. And I went to *Soleado*. It felt like a safe place in the midst of all that's happened."

Rashad nodded sympathetically. "Did they hurt you?" His eyes burned with anger; she couldn't give him reason to seek revenge on the men who had protected her.

"No! Not ever; they . . . took care of me and made sure I was safe. They didn't really want to be responsible for me. They said they didn't know I was at home when . . ." Her eyes filled with tears. It seemed surreal now to stand in the kitchen this many months later, still feeling the loss of her parents while knowing all that she did. "I'm ok," she whispered.

"I'm glad." He sounded sincere. They sat together for a moment in silence. "Do you want to talk more tonight? Perhaps we should wait until morning . . . give you a chance to rest. Would you like that?"

"Yes." She felt safe; perhaps this would be easier than she had imagined. She would stay here with Rashad; he seemed to feel responsible for her.

"Come, there's a bed set up downstairs. You'll be safe there." He led her to the cellar door and opened it wide. "Take this candle; I think you'll find everything else you need down there." With a warm smile, he gestured for her to go first. When he didn't follow, she turned and looked up at him. "Goodnight, Dahlia. I'm so glad you've returned."

She nodded, then watched as he closed the door. She waited until she heard the click of the lock.

Chapter 28

SHE HAD FINALLY fallen asleep, lying on the bed she had made for herself the day after the explosion tore her life apart. Lying alone in the darkness, she had prayed for hours, asking for wisdom, protection and faith that God would give her courage in her time of need. She had felt such peace since coming to know the truth about Yahweh, and the sudden intrusion back into her old surroundings had brought with it the familiar fears and confusion. Who could she trust; how long would she be forced to stay with Rashad and his cronies; would people like Ibrahim always hate her for what her father had done? The thoughts whirled at tornadic speed through her mind until she finally fell asleep repeating the comforting phrase to herself, "The Lord is my shepherd, the Lord is my shepherd."

Upon waking, she got dressed and quietly made her way up the stairs. Slowly, she turned the knob. Surprised to find it unlocked, she prepared herself for the discussions ahead.

"Dahlia!" the rotund, spectacled gentleman sat at the kitchen table drinking black tea. When she entered the room, he quickly rose and moved toward her. Obviously warned by Rashad to keep a safe distance, he suddenly stopped and stood before her smiling awkwardly.

"Benahim, I'm so glad you're here." She gave him a quick hug and breathed a sigh of relief. Of all her father's men, he was the one she most trusted. It seemed hard to believe that he could ever have approved the dark deeds the military had carried out under her father's regime.

"Please, sit. Rashad will be joining us soon, but I wanted to have a moment alone with you to catch up." Graciously serving her bread and jam, he moved nervously, as if uncertain of how to treat her. These men had known Dahlia all of her life, and yet an unspoken curtain had been drawn—a curtain of mistrust. Both parties wanted to know just how much the other knew. "Would you like some tea?"

"Of course, thank you." She smiled, trying to set him at ease. "How have you been this last year? So much has happened!"

"Ah, yes! But, I'm much more worried about you," he forced a nervous laugh. "Are you sure you're ok?"

"I'm fine. Really. It's good to be here with you." She sipped the tea, then blew on it for a moment. Memories of Hasan and Artashir around the large, oak table at breakfast came flooding back; Hasan humming the call to prayer, Artashir—with his unkempt mane of coal black hair—sitting grumpily in his chair trying to wake up, spewing hot tea across the table when it burned his tongue. She smiled to herself.

"I'm glad." Benahim leaned forward and took her hand. "You look more and more like your mother every day."

Dahlia's smile widened. "Thank you." Looking away, she added, "I can barely picture her sometimes. Maybe . . . I'm just afraid that it will hurt too much." She shook her head. "I don't know. I miss her so much." A tear dropped from her chin to the table.

"I know. I'm sorry," he whispered.

"Oh, how selfish of me! Benahim, how is your family? Nadim, the others?" She'd hardly had a thought for them all these months, but suddenly she was very curious as to where they were and what had happened to them after her father's assassination.

"They're ok. Out east, in Molocca. We have family there; it seemed safer."

"Good. That's good. And everyone else? Did they all go east when Anazir fell under attack?"

"Yes. It's safer there, for now."

Dahlia stared blankly at him. Reports from Saran indicated that the fighting had stopped, which made her wonder why the families hadn't returned with the men. Months had passed, and their homes were here. Perhaps Saran was right; could it be that Rashad intended to use the weapon in the capital city after all?

"Dahlia, good morning!" Rashed breezed into the room. "Benahim, it is good to have her with us, is it not?" Benahim smiled at Dahlia in response. "It seemed we would never find you; like looking for a needle in the haystack! We searched near and far, following every lead. And," he clapped his hands for effect, "here you are! Incredible, is it not?" He sat and the two men looked at her, as if waiting for a response.

Dahlia looked from one to the other, then stirred her tea and took a sip. "Benahim was just telling me that your families are still in the east. I'm glad to know that they're alright."

Rashad looked at Benahim, then back at Dahlia. "They've been so worried about you. Sanshan wanted to come and look for you early on; we had to convince her that it wasn't safe." He rubbed his mustache thoughtfully. "Perhaps you'd like to talk to her. Should we arrange a phone call?"

"Maybe later. I'm not sure I'm ready to talk with anyone just yet. Tell her I said 'hello,'" Dahlia forced a smile.

"Of course. You've been through enough, Dahlia." Rashad moved closer to her, taking her hand in his and patting it mechanically. It was as if he had planned out this move in his head, as if it were a tactical part of his strategy to win her trust. Dahlia pulled her hand away and pressed herself as tightly as she could against the back of the chair. Clearing his throat, Rashad continued. "She'll be glad to know you're alright. I'll send word today. As for you, well, we have a lot to discuss when you're ready. But right now, we feel that it is our duty to care for you, to let you rest, to provide the protection and guidance that your father would have wanted you to have. It's the least we could do!" He turned his eyes to Benahim. "The daughter of our dearest friend. If only we could have found her sooner! How she must have suffered, alone, in the wilderness with those nomads." He shook his head. "I've lain awake at night assuring myself: if we find her, *when* we find her, she will have everything she deserves! A comfortable home, the education she planned for, the opportunity she has always wanted—to lead her people."

Dahlia's eyes grew wide. Was she hearing him correctly? What schemes did her father's advisors have up their sleeve?

"Yes, Dahlia," Benahim exclaimed, "we know that you have long been zealous in finding a solution to our country's problems. It is something we have often discussed with your father, and we believe it's what he would have wanted."

"I'm sorry, I don't understand," Dahlia interrupted. "What are we talking about? What exactly is it that you're doing here? Is this why you've been looking for me?"

"No, of course not! We simply wanted to make sure you were alright." Rashad shot Benahim a warning glance. "Let's not overthink this. Benahim just meant to say that we know our country's situation has weighed heavily on us all, and you have a unique opportunity to help us find a solution."

"Yes, a solution. You are such a bright young lady!"

Dahlia raised an eyebrow. "So, you're here to see what happens in the elections?"

Rashad feigned surprise. "Elections? Surely you don't believe the people have been able to organize an election already?"

Dahlia blinked. "I don't know. It just seemed likely that communities are ready to enact some sort of formal leadership. I just assumed . . ." Had she given too much away?

"What do you think, Benahim? Could the people who could barely get along under military edict possibly find a way to effectively communicate and organize a national election?" Both men laughed.

"Why did you say that I could lead the people?"

The men stopped and looked at her.

"Why do you think the people would want that, that my father would have wanted that? He always discouraged any interest I had in political issues. You know that."

"Now, really, he was very proud of your political understanding. You are so much like him, Dahlia!" Rashad reached toward her.

"No, Rashad." She jerked her hand away. "I'm not. And he never wanted to discuss our country's problems with me. He saved those discussions for you. That's how it always was. He listened to you!" She knew her anger was getting the best of her; she needed to slow down and think about what she was saying, but the way they had thrown the subject at her out of left field had her reeling. "Do you really think my father had any idea what his people wanted?" Dahlia shook her head. "You never understood the people of Al Cazar. None of you did. So many years have been wasted controlling instead of serving. No wonder the people hated him."

Benahim sat back, a shocked look on his round face.

"Serving! Yes, that's it, Dahlia." Rashad guided the dialogue so masterfully, not for a minute losing sight of the direction he wanted to go. "This is exactly what we believe you can do for Al Cazar. You can be a public servant, like in America!"

"Yes, a servant!" Benahim nodded his head vigorously, enthusiastically, his eyebrows knit together in a quizzical expression. "You will be a great servant!"

Rashad shot Benahim an annoyed look. "It is how every great democracy begins, Dahlia. We know how you have studied this philosophy. It is very noble, this dream of yours. We believe you are just the person to pull it off. It can be a great transition, a wonderful change for our country. You! You can make it happen!"

Dahlia wanted to stand up and scream. Instead, she covered her eyes with her hands and sighed. Rubbing her temples with the palms of her hands, she began to shake her head. "This is why you've been look-ing for me? This is the plan you hatched in the months since my father was killed?" She looked at the men incredulously.

"Yes, Dahlia, now is the time for change," Rashad whispered. "A fresh start, a new beginning. A new way."

Perhaps the men were right. Dahlia took several long, deep breaths. Her palms were starting to sweat. "I don't understand. Why me? Why now? Don't you think my father could have been the one to lead our country into democracy? Did you ever encourage *him* to bring change to Al Cazar?"

"You know how your father was, Dahlia." Rashad shook his head sadly. "He was a good man, but... Well, some people just aren't ready for change."

"And your father was one of those people." Benahim stood and crossed the room to the window. Looking out through broken panes of glass, he added, "He just wouldn't listen to reason."

Wouldn't listen? Dahlia's heart ached. Could her father really have been that stubborn? Could he truly have been so hardened in his quest for authority that he would force an entire nation into submission, even against the counsel of his trusted advisors? She thought of the book she had found in the rubble outside his office. *Evil prevails where good men do nothing.* Was he blinded by his own ambition or was there a great strug-gle inside the man she never really knew? Did he ever really love this country, or did he just love the idea of ruling?

A tear slid down her cheek. "How could he have done the things that he did? Why didn't you stop him?"

"Oh, Dahlia. Sweetheart, there's so much you just don't under-stand." Benahim patted her knee. "Terrible things have happened, and none of us can change that now. Don't you see? This is the opportu-nity we've all been waiting for! Together, we can help our country find healing."

Dahlia blinked. Isn't this what she'd always wanted? A chance to help? And these men were going to support her. They would open the door for her to bring healing to this war-torn country. It all sounded so good! "You have no idea how long I've wanted this…" She paused. Her mouth felt dry, like sand was filling it up, making it difficult to speak. *Is this the course you have for me?* She closed her eyes and prayed. *Maybe these men have been sent by you to encourage me.* An uneasiness in her spirit made her doubt it.

⊷⊨◉ ◉⊨⊷

After the odd discussion she'd had with Benahim and Rashad over breakfast, Dahlia spent the day working in the garden below the terrace. It felt good to work with her hands, to feel the warmth of the sun on her back. Her mind swirled with bits of their conversation twisting and worming their way to her heart. *You could lead the people, it's time for change, this is the opportunity we've all been waiting for.* The seductive promise of power was tantalizing, and Dahlia struggled to know if her heart could handle the power that would come with leading a nation. In her heart, she knew she was too young to have the experience and wisdom needed to take on such a task, but everyone else had failed; God had prepared her for such a time as this, hadn't he?

As the sun set below the mountains, she joined Rashad beside the fire and looked out over the city. He smiled sweetly at her and, with a fatherly gesture, invited her to join him. It reminded her of Hasan, the kind friend who had been with her through the darkest hours of her life. Holding a steaming cup of tea in her hands, she admired the familiar setting—the scent of burning cedar, the crackle and glow of the fire, the warmth radiating towards her. There would be no stories tonight, no talk of loved ones left behind for a season, only Dahlia and Rashad and the secrets that were buried behind her under the crumbled mess she once called home.

"Dear one," he started, then waited for her to look at him. "We overwhelmed you with a lot of talk this morning. Please don't feel that there is any pressure for you to take on more than you are ready for. We are just so excited to see you, to continue with our life's calling to help our country, to lead the people well." He slowly poked the fire with a long, dry twig. When it suddenly ignited, he dropped it and drew back his hand as if it were a snake that had attempted to strike at him. He cleared his throat, quickly regaining his composure. "Having you with us here is like having a piece of your father—to help us in our calling. You are so much like him."

She knew the words were meant to cajole her, but a violent shiver ran down her spine. "I'm not that much like my father; perhaps you have misread my intentions." Dahlia looked warily at Rashad and prayed for wisdom in her response. "I care about the future of our country, but I don't have the fervor that my father had for leadership. Power can be such a seductive thing . . ." She didn't dare say more; her father's men did not need to know that she had learned of the evil methods they had used under his authority.

"So true! What a wise one you have become, Dahlia. And with your gentle manner and humility, well, we shall see what time will do for you. I believe you may become a great leader yet. Just wait and see!" He smiled, emboldened by her willingness to talk. "Your father also had doubts about his ability to lead; he often wondered if he was doing the right thing for the people. As his advisor, I felt it my duty to bolster his administration at every turn. I offer you that same service; when you are ready, I will ensure your transition into power. You will have my full support, and the people will not resist! How could they?" He smiled excitedly and Dahlia wondered what tactics he might use to ensure the people's acceptance of her authority should she choose to move forward with their plan. Remembering the reason that she was there, she searched for words to pry out information about a possible weapon.

"How can you be so sure that the people will follow someone like me?" She fished for a helpful response. "Strong-fisted control and a reign of terror; this is the legacy I have to live up to! What makes you so sure they are ready to hear from the daughter of Seljuk?" The name twisted her lips, the way it felt to eat something that was sweet and sour at the same time.

"We have ways, Dahlia. You don't need to worry about such things; it is beneath you. I assure you," the hungry gleam sparkled in his eye, "should you decide to move forward with this plan, you will be well taken care of. The people will love you! You see, we will have complete control over the circumstances surrounding your path to leadership," he continued. "They loved him, you know? Even after all that happened between your father and his country, they loved and revered him. Don't you see? He was their king; they wanted to be ruled!" Rashad gave her a sad smile. "They just didn't know how. In the last election, your father won by a landslide. It was just those rebels—trying to stir up dissension—that questioned the outcome."

"Yes," Dahlia nodded. "That's what the media said."

"It's true, darling." Rashad smiled earnestly. "It's all true. Your father worked so hard to hold this country together. And if not for an unhappy, divisive bunch of terrorists stirring up trouble, your father might have brought great progress to this nation."

Progress. It was a word Dahlia loved. How she had hoped for her people to find a way past the fighting, to be prosperous and civilized. "Rashad, that so-called little band of terrorists overthrew the government! Don't you feel you've underestimated the people's determination to enact political reformation? They staged a revolution, and they won! Rashad, they assassinated my father!"

"Oh, Dahlia, Dahlia," Rashad's eyes blurred, his voice filled with anguish. "How you have suffered so! I promise you, this is the time for you to speak! The people are ready for leadership and you are just the voice to bring it. You have the heart of your father and the progressive ideas to win the people's favor. They will love you!"

Misguided as he was, Dahlia couldn't help but be caught up in the dialogue; he was so earnest in his argument.

"Look to the city below you. This is your city! It is young and vibrant, eager for progress. No! We cannot hold it back! You can lead them on from here, you are the cord that binds the past to the future—the transitional piece. No one else could do what you *will* do! Your father's men, his entire military will stand behind you! The people, they will embrace you! All of this," he gestured to the shimmering city below, "is yours! I can guarantee it."

Dahlia's ears perked up at the telling words. Perhaps Rashad would reveal a glimpse of his plan.

"We have discovered a way to communicate with the nation—to send a message to them in their time of need. All we need now is a unifying voice, a gentle call to follow as we lead them along the path of healing."

Tears swelled in her eyes; his words were that convincing. But they were poisoned by the truths she could not deny; all of her father's hopes and dreams for leading his people lay crumbled around her. The people had violently rejected such a regime; he had battled for control until his own motives were twisted and ingrown while the people's fight for freedom echoed from province to province in one bloody battle after another.

"Will you be that voice, Dahlia? Can you lead your people like your father never could?"

It was intoxicating, heady even. Dahlia remembered the conversation she'd had with Artashir the night they camped in the desert on the way to Piedra. She envisioned the pawn approaching the far side of the chess board, unseen, unscathed. Perhaps she would become a queen after all . . .

As if on cue, a distant jackal howled. The sound drew her attention and the hairs on her arms stood on end. Dahlia instinctively looked to the moon which hung full and low in the sky. She thought of the desert and the peace and quiet she had so enjoyed there. She longed for it now. The wind changed suddenly causing the fire to flicker. Goosebumps rose on Dahlia's arms and she felt an uneasiness in the pit of her stomach.

Rashad continued to talk, listing all of the ways they would improve the situation of their country, offering hope and peace to a war-weary people. Dahlia knew it was too good to be true; the false-front of serving the people and doing what was best for them was just a pleasantly wrapped re-gift of the service the military had provided her father during his unending term as president. Rashad droned on and on and Dahlia tried to capture the message wrapped in all of the things God had shown her over the past few months. What exactly was he preparing her for? If not to lead, then what? If she rejected Rashad's plan now, would there be ominous consequences? She shuddered to think what might happen if she agreed to their plan and the people rejected her; the weapon Saran warned her of might very well be the means of assurance Rashad had in mind. It disgusted her to think that someone could be so eaten up with power—that he would be willing to sacrifice thousands in order to gain the position he once maintained under her father's rule.

"Rashad, what if the people aren't ready like you say? What if they look at me and see my father instead?" She thought of Ibrahim and winced. "So many have suffered under his heavy hand. They won't so quickly forget."

"Of course." Rashad nodded understandingly, calmly consoling her every doubt. "You'll have to trust me on this. Your father always did."

The jackal howled again, closer this time. Dahlia could almost feel the desert breeze on her face, smell the pungent sage, hear the sound of the wind rippling through the quiet desert valley, snapping the colorful fabric of hundreds of shredded banners. She tried to stop the progression of her thoughts but instantly she was there on the shadowed valley floor, standing among the poles that marked the graves of Artashir's people. *Like wings beating* . . . Dahlia snapped back to the present. She had to find out what Rashad's plan was. That's why she was here, after all!

The call of the jackal was almost upon them. Surprised, Dahlia realized she had never heard a jackal's call before her time of living in the desert among the Bedouin. The animals didn't live near the city, and with the heavy rains of springtime, it was unlikely that jackals would brave civilization in search of food or water. A sickening realization began to sink in and Dahlia stared up at the hillside from where the sound had come. Unable to see anything in the darkness, she strained to hear any sound of movement among the trees. The howl came once more and she made a slight gasping sound.

"Are you ok, dear?" Rashad stopped his ranting and reached out to touch her arm. "You seem suddenly distracted; is everything alright?"

Suddenly, she *knew,* as she looked into his cool, black eyes. Dahlia stared at Rashad, the color draining from her face. Trying not to alarm him, she swallowed hard. "I'm fine. Just a sudden chill, I think." She smiled weakly as she realized the inevitable truth: *she was looking into the eyes of a dead man.* It was only a matter of time.

⊷⊨⊚ ⊚⊨⊷

Lying on her bed that night, Dahlia realized her time was running out. With Artashir waiting in the hills nearby, it would not be long before he took matters into his own hands. Whether or not he knew of Saran's recent concern she could not be certain, but regardless, she needed to find out about Rashad's plans for the secret weapon of mass destruction. Lives were at stake. The weight of it all seemed to crush her chest.

In the quiet of her cellar suite, she rolled the conversation back through her mind. These men, who had been the force behind the decisions made under her father's regime, were offering her the chance to step into his shoes. Whether her father had been puppet or henchman was still uncertain, but she was being given an opportunity—one she had dreamed of for years. What she did with this opportunity was yet to be decided, but above all, she knew she must seek help from the only Advisor she could trust. Thumbing blindly through the pages of the worn Bible, she looked for something, anything to give her clarity at this moment. She knew the words of Rashad and Benahim were too good to be true; as much as she wanted to believe them, their intentions could not be trusted. More importantly, she felt certain that she could not trust herself under the influence of unlimited power. As much as she felt the need to see her country in capable hands, she could not provide the kind of leadership Al Cazar needed.

Yet one question remained: *What kind of leader did the people of Al Cazar need?* Who could withstand the temptations and pressures of such a position? And who would best understand the people's needs at this moment in time? Kneeling in the center of her bed, she closed her eyes and breathed in deeply. As Artashir's grandmother had instructed her, Dahlia chose to call upon the Lord—seeking answers from the only One who holds perfect wisdom.

Opening her eyes slowly, she saw the bottles of olive oil lining the walls of the cellar come into focus in the dim candlelight. They stood like little green soldiers lined up for battle. Seeing them reminded her of *Soleado* and she longed for the warmth of her home, the calming rhythm of the waves, the restoring rays of the sun. More than ever, she felt the darkness closing in around her here. All this talk of what would be—woven with lies from the one who had fed off of her father and now longed to do the same with her; it was maddening! Exhausted, Dahlia lay on her bed and flipped through the pages of the Bible that Edgar had given her. She had found a collection of Psalms in the center of the book that had become especially comforting to her. They were written by a man named David—the one Artashir had told her had slain a giant with a simple slingshot as a boy. She loved the way David spoke to God and had grown to love the warrior who often seemed to be fighting the same daily battles she fought—against loneliness, betrayal, rejection and guilt.

Tonight, Dahlia opened to Psalm 63 and noted that David had written it while he was in the desert. "We have so much in common," she whispered, her breath causing the light of the candle to flicker softly.

"O God, you are my God," the psalmist began. "Earnestly I seek you; I thirst for you, my whole being longs for you, in a dry and parched land where there is no water."

Dahlia could feel the dry, scratchy throat calling out to God. Her own soul yearned as David's did for that which only God above could give.

"I have seen you in the sanctuary and beheld your power and your glory."

She remembered the radiance of Christ depicted on the cave wall by the early Christians of Piedra, his figure animated by the flickering torch light as he reached out his hands in welcome.

"Because your love is better than life, my lips will glorify you. I will praise you as long as I live, and in your name I will lift up my hands. I will be fully satisfied as with the richest of foods; with singing lips my mouth will praise you."

She paused and drank in the beauty of the words. They echoed all that she had come to feel for the Lord. Stretching out on the bed, she held the bound pages close to her chest.

"On my bed I remember you; I think of you through the watches of the night. Because you are my help, I sing in the shadow of your wings. I cling to you; your right hand upholds me.

"Those who want to kill me will be destroyed; they will go down to the depths of the earth."

The line startled her, but the next line was like a blow to her gut.

"They will be given over to the sword and become food for jackals."

She sat in stunned silence for a moment before reading the final line. With the knowledge of what Artashir had come to do weighing heavily upon her heart, she read it again.

"They will be given over to the sword and become food for jackals. But the king will rejoice in God; all who swear by God will glory in him, while the mouths of liars will be silenced."

Again, she was reminded of the choice she had to make. It was a burden, this daily struggle to know what to do, who to trust. Some things were crystal clear while others were fuzzy concoctions mixed with subtle half-truths and flattery meant to sway her from her course. She hated that she often felt her own niggling desires twisting themselves up into all of it until she hardly knew what was right. But usually, when she lay down at night, alone with the Word open before her, the truth could be found—in black and white—and the deception fell away.

The pawn had reached the other side of the board, metaphorically speaking, and the time to act was now. The opportunity lay ripe before her. All she had to do was act and the Lord would give her the words in her time of need.

Dahlia rose and, taking up one of the bottles of oil, broke the neck off against the wall. Instinctively, she poured it over her hair, running her fingers through it, savoring the rich, heavy scent of freshly pressed olives. She remembered the night, almost a year ago, when the explosion had rocked her world and how the oil had felt in her thick, matted hair. *For such a time as this,* called the words to her spirit and she acknowledged the anointing a second time. The first one had been to a time of personal awakening for Dahlia, marking the path to truth on so many levels. This time, it was a personal declaration, a vow to follow the path set out before her, whatever the cost.

Chapter 29

DISCUSSIONS BEGAN TO formalize as Dahlia vocalized a willingness to play along with the crazy political ploy Rashad had hatched. Within two days, he had divulged his plan to present her to the nation as the answer to their political problems: she would be their savior—understanding, gentle, and wise beyond her years. It would be done on national television, and would be—by Rashad's telling—an outstanding success.

To keep herself busy and to find time to think without being disturbed, Dahlia worked in the garden for hours on end, imagining ways in which she might pry out further information concerning Rashad's plan in the event that the people did not immediately accept her offer to lead. He managed to divert all attempts, assuring her that he had everything under control. His cool, calm exterior was impossible to break through and as Dahlia's frustrations grew, she wondered if she would ever find the answers she was seeking.

At the close of the second week, she noticed increased activity among the guards; something was happening, and Rashad's attention was highly distracted. He spent less time with Dahlia and left Benahim to keep an eye on her while he attended to other business.

Then she saw it. In the garden where she had cleared a large area for planting a bed of squash, the ground had been disturbed. Significantly. At first, she wondered if one of the men had been killed; she would not have been surprised at all to hear that Rashad had shot one of his own men for insubordination and buried him in the garden. However, when a new guard was assigned a nearby post, she realized that the garden plot was being guarded. No one said anything to her as she went about her work planting and tending the spring seedlings, but the guard kept a careful eye on what she did in and around the squash bed. The answer to her question was almost certain; the feared weapon of mass destruction had indeed been brought to Anazir as Rashad's plans advanced. It was buried in the vegetable garden, and in the event that it was needed, would be brought out and used to force the people into submission.

In response to her growing certainty of Rashad's plan, Dahlia made her intentions clearly known: she would accept the role as leader of the country with Rashad as her top advisor. Together, they would help the country move forward. Almost simultaneously, her father's advisors began to make appearances, offering her their complete support and humble service as she might need it in her future role as leader of Al Cazar. It was surreal, the way in which they accepted her and promoted her among themselves—never letting on that they had ever been a part of any other regime. Talk was of the future and what they could do together to make things better. She was never privy to any discussion of what would happen to the people should they refuse the military's decision to appoint her; she had only to think about what she would say when she was finally given the opportunity to address the people, and the time was drawing near.

Rashad's plan included hijacking the local office of the national broadcasting station. A small company had recently begun broadcasting soccer games on Sundays, and as the people returned to somewhat normal lives, the ratings were beginning to rise. In fact, Rashad revealed to her that within a week's time the championship game would be shown nationally. It was the first time in over ten years that anything had been shown nationally without the approval of the government. Reports predicted that thousands of viewers around the country would gather in tearooms, bars and living rooms to watch the game, and it was Rashad's perfect chance to present his plan to the people.

Rashad began to prepare Dahlia for the upcoming broadcast and was so attentive to her needs and concerns that she could almost feel herself becoming sucked under his influence. He had proven himself to be so crafty in his manipulation that Dahlia sometimes wondered who was playing whom. His manner of handling her was so smooth, so effortless, that it felt as if she could do anything she wanted. She knew that if she went forward with his plan, she could count on his full support; his heart's desire was to regain the power he once knew and she was the tool with which he would do it. If he ever doubted her sincerity, it never showed, but she maintained a strong understanding that should she ever cross him, the consequences would be lethal.

On the day of the broadcast, Rashad gave her a special outfit to wear—a smart, navy blue suit with a stylish silk blouse that had a soft, pearlesque sheen. When she appeared at the top of the cellar stairs, dressed for the much planned production, he was waiting to escort her to the car.

"Ah, Dahlia. You look magnificent," he whispered, shaking his head. With an air of complete confidence, he held out his arm. Bolstered by his calm assurance, she bravely linked her arm in his and walked with him to the waiting car. Guards, standing with shoulders back and rifles at their sides, lined the walk. They did not look at her, but clicked their heels together loudly in respectful acknowledgment as she passed. She had walked such a line before, but only as the daughter of Seljuk, trailing behind him in awe of the respect his position commanded. Now, the attention was for her alone; she was to be the first in command.

For the first time in almost a month, Dahlia left the palace grounds. An armed escort sat beside the chauffer; Rashad sat next to her in the back. No one spoke and she was left to her own thoughts—thoughts of what she would say and how the people would respond. The time had come—she had been prepared for such a time as this.

⋯⊨● ●⊨⋯

The drive through the city was uneventful, surreal. Familiar sights were seen through new eyes, eyes that had been opened in so many ways. The entourage arrived in front of the national broadcast station which was an empty shell of what it once had been. It had sat vacant for years; all major media and television programs had been broadcasted through government agencies after her father's second election. Tight control had limited what the country was allowed to see and know.

Several armed guards jumped out of the van in front of them and ran into the building. A few shots were fired and the building was secured. Dahlia prayed no one was killed. When one of the men returned to the entrance, he waved them on. The armed escort jumped out of the car and opened Dahlia's door for her. She waited until Rashad got out, then took his arm when he offered it. With a heavy heart, she allowed herself to be moved inside. This moment was covered in hours of prayer and thought, but the task she was about to undertake would be anything but easy. In teashops and living rooms across the country, the national airwaves, hijacked by Rashad's men, would present her to the people as the hope they had been waiting for.

Chapter 30

DAHLIA STARED INTO the black eye of the camera, counting the seconds between each breath she took. Three, four, five, exhale. Looking into the small black, luminous hole, she was reminded of the eye of a whale she had seen once off the coast of Lamirya. It had been a desperately hot day, she remembered, and so they had gone out on the water with a fisherman in his small, colorfully painted boat. Sitting next to her mother, Dahlia had watched in stunned silence as the whale suddenly appeared, moving in a smooth, graceful arc up and out of the water less than twenty feet from their boat. The single eye had watched them as they stared back at it until the whale slid back into the water, its humongous tail gliding soundlessly into the sea. Her father had ordered the fisherman to take them back to shore immediately, certain that the whale would return and capsize their boat at any moment; but Dahlia had not been afraid. She hoped she might see it again, feeling as though the animal had chosen that moment to look at them, to examine them closely—and Dahlia had felt that it had communicated so much in that one, brief instant—from the single, black eye that watched them. Curiosity, understanding, trust.

Staring into the black lens of the camera, Dahlia thought of all who would be watching her today. She needed to start slowly, to give the people time to gather. Across the country in cafes and homes, people would call to their friends and neighbors, "Look! It's Dahlia, daughter of Seljuk!" They would feel so many things; this she knew. Anger, bitterness, shock, disgust, confusion. She had to give them time to let it sink in, for they would not be able to really hear what she had to say until those emotions had run their course.

Rashad signaled that they would be live in five . . . four . . . He counted down with his fingers and then a red light turned on accompanied by a low-grade buzzing. Dahlia stared at the black eye, could see a tiny reflection of herself in the glass lens.

"Hello," she whispered, then licked her lips and took a deep breath. "My name is Dahlia. Dahlia Seljuk." She glanced up at Rashad who sat nervously perched at a desk behind the camera. Several of the men she knew as her father's advisors stood behind him and they all waited tensely.

"Go on!" one of them mouthed.

"Some of you are wondering how I can still be alive; many of you know that my family was killed in a bombing almost a year ago now." She swallowed hard. "God had mercy; he allowed me to live, and I have spent these many months learning what plans he has for me—his purpose for granting me life."

She could see the hungry gleam in Rashad's eyes, almost sense him rubbing his hands together greedily.

"It's not a course I would ever have envisioned for myself, but I am so thankful for the opportunity I have had to learn more about the people of my country. At this time, especially, I know that many have suffered and grieve the loss of family and home—all that was familiar to them. I, too, have had to accept a life changed forever by this war.

"Before I go further, I feel compelled to . . ." she saw Rashad's hand rise sharply. The words caught in her throat. Even if she'd wanted to say it, her voice had disappeared. Tears flooded her eyes, the weight of grief for her people shuddered through her and she wiped at her eyes.

"I'm sorry," she whispered. The camera's eye stared back, unblinking. Dahlia tried to picture them behind the lens: young and old, shocked and surprised to see her on the screen before them. Ibrahim's flushed face floated before her—the way he had looked in the last moment they spent together—pained, by the very sight of her. The tears stung, her nose burned and she had to fight the urge to get up and run. *For such a time as this*, the familiar words steadied her.

With a deep breath, she opened her eyes and held her hands out to the camera, palms up—the ways she had seen Christ reaching out to the tormented man. "You don't know me; I hardly know myself. I was daughter of Seljuk, and I am a daughter of this nation. This war has torn my life apart; like so many of you, I have almost been crushed by the darkness that has swept our land." She steeled herself and focused on finding the right words. "But it's time to put down our weapons, to move forward together! Only we, as a people who have lived through the darkness of these past years, can wipe the tears away—looking to our neighbors, our countrymen for support. Putting aside our differences, we pick up tools—to rebuild, to replant, to restore the land of Al Cazar. Her cities, her fields, her people. Together, we can accomplish great things; together, *we will rebuild*. We will not wallow in our sorrows; we will not bite and devour one another any longer. We will not sit back and shrug at the overwhelming task ahead of us.

"Seljuk is gone. For better or for worse. The mess is left in our hands now. We cannot say that we are too young, too broken by grief, too weak to fight anymore. The battle ahead of us is for the building of a nation—the reconstruction of our homes and lives! We can gather the strength we need from each other, from the trials which have tested us, and from God—who will not desert us in our time of need."

Rashad leaned forward. She wondered how much longer she had. The sound of a scuffle outside the door momentarily distracted her, but Dahlia resolved to see her speech through to the end. This was her only chance!

"The elections loom before us; let us not lose sight of the significance they hold. Many of you have fought for the opportunity to choose a leader who will guide you in this time of reconstruction, this era of change. And I," her voice faltered, "I want to offer my nomination for this important position." She saw Rashad stand, knocking over his chair in the process. He held up a hand, ordering her to stop with his eyes. A gun shot was fired and Dahlia's heart stopped; were they going to kill her now? She rushed to find the concise words she needed. "Ibrahim Saran—he will lead our nation through the reconstruction and restructuring of our communities and country!"

"Stop!" Rashad shouted. "Turn it off! Somebody pull the plug!" he cried as he rushed toward her. Knocking the camera over, he reached out and slapped her across the face. Momentarily too stunned to move, Dahlia sat in shock, ears ringing, as she heard the door being kicked in behind her. More shots were fired, and although she mentally understood the need to take cover, she found herself unable to do anything. A loud skirmish was taking place just behind her, and all Dahlia could do was stare at the black eye that stared up at her from the floor. Rashad backed away, looking now at the men who were fighting behind her. He yelled orders that nobody followed in the uproar.

"Dahlia!" a familiar voice bellowed. "Get out of the way!"

Reaching up to touch the hot mark on her face, she turned and tried to see through the tears that stung her eyes.

"You!" Rashad growled. "I should have known! What a fool I've been!"

Dahlia watched as Artashir fought off the men around him, then gasped as rough hands grabbed her wrists and pulled her backwards. She knew it was Rashad, could smell his ghastly cologne, and struggled to breathe as he forced an arm around her neck.

"How did you find us?" Rashad asked, biding for time.

Artashir's men tied up the guards and waited for an order. With machine gun at the ready, the desert jackal stood coolly before them and assessed the situation. A tense jaw muscle twitched, the unending stream of anger that lay just beneath the surface threatening to boil over. "I've never stopped hunting you; I've waited many months for this moment . . ."

"So now what?" Rashad laughed. "You'll kill Seljuk's daughter? The nation's new hero? I don't think so! You—who kept her alive all this time. I should have known! You've brainwashed her—I don't know how you did it! What could your kind offer the daughter of a king?" He spat the words, tightening his grip around her neck. "Really, Dahlia," he whispered in her ear, "how could you be on this animal's side? It's beneath you; you've thrown away the chance to rule!"

"Let her go!" Artashir commanded. He took a step forward, eyes narrowing.

With her eyes, she pleaded for Artashir to stop; she knew the cold, murderous look in his eyes. He had vowed to kill this man and today was the day. "No," she mouthed, "not like this."

"Let her go!" Artashir repeated. "I won't say it again."

Rashad laughed. "Of course! Just a babe, she is. And since you won't kill an innocent one, I believe I'll take my leave now." Dragging her in front of him, Rashad moved forward. "Move out of the way or I'll break her neck." Rashad placed his other hand on her throat, moving it tightly up against her jaw. Dahlia tried to swallow, to cry out, but he had choked off her airway. "Put down your weapon and step aside."

Artashir hesitated for a moment, then did as he was told. "You're hurting her," he growled. Dahlia watched as he bent down, never taking his eyes from Rashad. As the room began to grow black around her, Dahlia heard a sickening thud and felt the hands loosen around her neck. Unable to support herself, she fell to the floor. From a horizontal viewpoint, she watched as Artashir grabbed up his gun and ran to her before her eyelids gave out.

"Dahlia!" he yelled. She felt him shake her shoulders. "Someone get her out of here! Now!"

Her eyelids fluttered open and she watched as Benahim reached down to help her stand, gently guiding her by the elbow. "Are you ok?" The concern written on his face was sincere and Dahlia realized he must have knocked Rashad out from behind.

"Thank you," she smiled weakly.

Benahim sighed. "I should have done it a long time ago. Nothing but a bully!"

Out of the corner of her eye, she saw Artashir standing over Rashad, the long barrel of a gun pointed directly at his head. "No!" she shouted, running back to his side. "No, Artashir. Not like this! Please."

"This is none of your concern, Dahlia."

"But, Artashir, please! Don't do this; he hasn't hurt only you. So many others . . ."

Artashir placed his foot heavily on Rashad's chest. They watched as his eyes fluttered open, then grow wide with realization.

"Let the people judge him for the crimes he has committed. They have every bit as much a right as you."

Artashir turned and glared at her. "You don't know!"

"I know, I don't. I wasn't there; I didn't witness what your people went through. I'm sorry." She pleaded with her eyes. "But your people weren't the only ones hurt; there have been so many others. They deserve to know the whole truth and have a voice in his judgment. It's not your place to decide his fate alone." She waited; he didn't seem convinced.

"Get her out of here," he said in a low voice. Two men stepped forward and took her arms. Gently, they led her toward the door.

"Please, Artashir. Don't do this. It's time we started acting like one country, one people. We can't act separately and pretend that our actions don't affect the rest of the nation. You have a responsibility to all the others . . ."

"Get her out of here!" he shouted.

She allowed the men to pull her along. They stepped over the fallen guards whose wrists had been tied behind them. Through tears, she saw more men entering the station. "Dahlia!" one called as he ran to her.

"Saran!" She felt his arms wrap tightly around her and, exhausted by the emotional rollercoaster of the past hour, she leaned into the security of his embrace.

"I've been worried sick. How many days has it been? No word, no message that you were ok. I came as soon as I heard what was happening." He held her at arm's length. "Are you alright?"

With tears streaming down her face, she nodded.

Looking past her, Saran zeroed in on Artashir. No one moved as they waited to see what would happen next. Dahlia didn't turn around; she didn't want to see. Saran released her and went to Artashir. Standing next to him, he placed his hand on Artashir's shoulder. No words were exchanged, but after a moment, Artashir backed away and allowed the men to bind Rashad's hands. Saran began to give orders, and Seljuk's men were pulled to their feet. Suddenly remembering that she was still there, Saran came back to her side. He placed his hands on her shoulders and looked into her eyes. "We have a great deal to talk about, but now is not the time. You need to rest; will you be ok?"

Dahlia nodded. Saran gestured to a young man, and he came forward quickly. "This is Aalim, my driver. He will take you wherever you want to go. Are you sure you'll be alright?"

Finding her voice, Dahlia assured him. "I'll be fine; please, go with your men." She looked at Artashir. "Take care of him. Endora must be worried sick; please get word to her."

"Of course."

"Saran, I almost forgot to tell you!" Dahlia looked around her. Was it safe to say it here? "You know, the secret . . ." She stopped. Leaning forward, she whispered in his ear.

"The garden? Under the squash."

She nodded.

Shaking his head, Saran laughed. "Well done, young Dahlia! Well done." Turning his attention to his men, he continued issuing instructions. The political prisoners were lined up. Making eye-contact with Benahim, Dahlia stopped in her tracks. She wondered if she should say something on his behalf, then realized to do so would be as equally wrong as Artashir condemning Rashad to death. These men were equally guilty of the crimes they had committed together and it was for the people to decide their fate. She nodded her head in farewell, and with a brave smile, he did the same.

⋆⇥⬤ ⬤⇤⋆

Outside in the sunlight, Dahlia looked around, surprised again at how quiet the streets were. No one ever would have guessed at the events that had just taken place inside the modern-looking building. As she peered back at the reflective walls of windows, Dahlia wondered what was happening inside of the cafes and living rooms of the nation.

"You were so great in there!" young Aalim exclaimed. "Were you ever afraid for your life?" His eyes shown with excitement; she wondered how much he had heard.

"So you all listened to the broadcast?"

"Most of it; they had you on all the airwaves!" He held the car door open and Dahlia climbed inside the white sedan. Aalim jumped in the front. "As soon as he saw your face, Saran had us running for the car. We found you on the radio and listened on our way over. The streets were empty! I guess everyone was holed up watching their TV's.

Everyone thought you were dead!" Aalim pulled away from the curb and watched her in the rearview mirror.

Dahlia sat in silence and watched as the buildings began to pass by faster and faster. She turned around just in time to see Artashir and Saran leading the prisoners out of the building.

"Where to?"

"What?" Dahlia faced forward.

"Where would you like to go?"

Dahlia thought for a minute. They were passing through the modern downtown, and would quickly be heading up the hill in the direction of her house. The imploded mansion, the mound of mortar and stone. "Take me to *Soleado*," she said.

Aalim looked at her in the mirror. "Where is that?"

Dahlia smiled. "I'll show you the way."

Chapter 31

As they drove along the westward-leading road, Aalim talked and Dahlia listened, asking questions occasionally, or stopping him to point out some familiar roadside spot she recognized from childhood trips to her father's estate in Lamirya.

Aalim's story was a familiar one, immediately resonating with Dahlia's own childhood memories. He was the only son of a planter who had owned a small farm in a northern province of Al Cazar. When the fighting reached their town, his father had immediately joined the resistance, tired of the taxes and restrictions imposed on them by a government who was out of tune with the pressing needs of the area. When Aalim's father was killed in a battle on the eastern front, the family followed dozens of other misplaced families who sought refuge from the fighting in the capital city of Anazir. His mother found lodging for them with a distant relative, but it was an awkward situation and, weakened by grief and stress, his mother succumbed to a terminal illness not long after. While his sister was placed with a family in a nearby village, Aalim fell under Saran's radar. When he became aware of the boy's situation, Saran decided to provide a position for the boy in hopes of keeping him from joining the resistance. Under the protective wing of Saran, Aalim ran messages for resistance leaders, and proving himself responsible in that area, eventually became Saran's personal driver when he was old enough to handle the responsibility.

Saran had become a father-figure to him, but Aalim still missed his younger sister Ghizlan and the emotional stress of their separation weighed heavily upon him.

When he had finished telling her his story, Dahlia sat silent for a long while. They were getting close now, and the evening sky was a brilliant blush of color. "Roll down the windows," she whispered. Aalim did as she asked and they rode the rest of the way breathing in the salty sea air. As darkness fell, she worried, wondering if she would be able to find her way, but an innate homing device seemed to lead her to Soleado and as the first stars became visible, she directed Aalim into the long drive that led to the seaside estate.

"Are you sure this is the way?" he asked nervously as the road continued to wind through brush and washed out gullies.

"Absolutely!" she gasped as the excitement began to build inside her. "We're almost there! Can't you hear the waves crashing?"

Aalim watched her in the rearview mirror. He hadn't asked why she had wanted to be brought here, but now he needed to know. "What is *Soleado*? Are we allowed to be here?"

Dahlia laughed. "Soleado is home! This is my home; it is a refuge to my weary soul."

⇥⊶◉ ◉⊷⇤

In the flickering candlelight, long shadows gave the dusty furniture and cobwebbed corners a ghostly appearance, but nothing could dampen Dahlia's mood. With Aalim's help, she swept the terrace and made beds out of couch cushions. They slept out under the stars, listening to the waves and enjoying the fresh night air. In the morning, Aalim drove into to town to buy some food and call Saran to tell him where they were. He couldn't wait to tell Dahlia the good news.

He found her in the olive grove, trimming dead branches from the overgrown trees which were beginning to flower. "They found the weapon!" he called. "Right where you said it would be."

Dahlia climbed down the ladder and dusted herself off. She took the fleshy peach Aalim offered and bit into it. "And Artashir? Have they managed to calm him down after yesterday?" She worried for Endora; they had so many issues of their own to take care of in the camps, and yet Artashir had left it all to avenge the death of his family and people.

"They have convinced him to stand as a witness in court when Rashad and the other generals are brought to trial. Saran's got his hands full with the aftermath of it all." He examined the work she had done on the tree. "Not bad; it should produce a healthy crop this year."

"Do you think so?" Dahlia smiled. "I can't wait to see how many of the trees have survived. It's been a long time since they were tended."

"You'll have your hands full. This grove goes on for miles. Driving out this morning, I tried to count the rows. I'll wager you've got over five thousand trees here, plus fields that are fallow with wild poppy and sunflowers growing in them. This is quite a farm!"

"Yes, quite." Dahlia didn't want to correct the boy. It was one of the largest olive plantations in the country, and the trees stretched for miles in both directions along the coast. "I hope to see it up and running again one day. For now, though, I will do what I can to turn it back into a working farm. Perhaps you'll come and help me, now that the fighting is finished?"

Aalim's eyes grew wide. "Do you mean it?" He put his hand to the back of his head and smiled, looking out over the rows of silver-foliaged trees.

"I do. I think I really mean it." She laughed. "In fact, that is exactly what I mean! And I want you to bring Ghizlan here, and together we can turn this into a home." She laughed again, longer and harder. "Then, others will come. There will be many who need a home, like you, and this will be a haven to them all. Don't you see," she held her hands to her mouth. "It's what God's been preparing me for! This is what I'm called to do!"

Aalim whooped. His boyish enthusiasm got the better of him, and he picked Dahlia up and swung her around. "Ghizlan and I will have a home! A real home, with trees and land to work!" He stopped and set her down, a forlorn look in his eyes. "What will I tell Saran?"

"I think he'll understand. No, I'm sure of it." Giddily, Dahlia linked her arm in his and together they walked back to the house.

Chapter 32

THEIR DAYS WERE filled with cleaning the house and repairing rotten boards, weeding and planting seeds that Aalim had brought back from town. At night, they made lists of things to do the following day, lists that ranged from items they would need to purchase to designs for garden plots and flower beds. They had found most of the tools they needed in a large shed behind the garage, and Aalim had already set about turning the garage into his own personal workshop. He mended chairs, tools, got the tractor running, built a new table for the terrace to replace the old, rotten one, and built a bed for his sister. Together, they cleaned out one of the bedrooms on the sea-facing side of the house. They scrubbed the windows, painted the walls with a gallon of faded yellow they found in the garage, and cleaned up a couple of comfortable chairs to create a sitting area on one side of the room. Aalim couldn't wait to show it to his sister; Ghizlan hadn't had her own room since they had left home nearly three years ago.

Their excitement intensified as they began to make plans for their first return trip to Anazir. Dahlia would retrieve her few remaining items from the presidential palace on the hill, and Aalim would gather up his belongings before they headed to the village where his sister was staying. "She's going to love it here!" he repeated again and again.

In preparation of their return, Saran sent word to Hasan that Dahlia had returned home to Soleado. It was of utmost importance that they meet with Hasan and return to Anazir with written confirmation that the province of Lamirya was ready to take part in a national election. Most provinces had successfully elected leadership at the local level and each had to send written and signed documents confirming their approval of the proposed process for electing a national leader. It would be a long and complicated procedure, and in response to Dahlia's national broadcast, people were calling out for her to step into the position of moderator. Others felt they could not trust Dahlia in light of her connection to Seljuk's regime, but an overwhelming majority felt she was the right person for the task. Resistance leaders agreed, and on their behalf, Saran had convinced Dahlia to make another appearance on national television. The people had been won over by her personal plea to elect Ibrahim as leader and found her sincerity and youthful zeal too pure to be corrupted. Simply put, they felt they could trust her. Still, Dahlia's whereabouts were kept secret, with only Saran and Hasan aware of her actual location.

⊷⊶◉ ◉⊷⊶

It was a perfect summer evening, the afternoon sun sparkling on the water below, the waves lapping rhythmically onto the beach. Dahlia carefully arranged the flowers in a vase on the table, then set it for two using the fancy plates and linens she remembered from her youth.

"So, you've finally come home!" Hasan exclaimed as he walked out onto the terrace. Dahlia ran to greet him, exuberantly kissing both cheeks as he carried on about what a lovely young woman she had grown into.

"I can't have changed that much!" she laughed. "It hasn't been even a year."

"Ah, but you were only a girl when I found you; and now look at you!" Tears sparkled in his eyes as if he were looking at his own granddaughter. "You've grown up so much in these last months. When I saw you on TV that day . . ." his eyes welled with tears.

"I've learned so much, Hasan." She gestured for him to sit at the head of the table, then lit the candles while he settled in.

"You are all grown up," he repeated reflectively as he watched her bring out the food. "And how I've worried that the things you would learn would poison you, that the truths you faced would fill you up with bitterness."

Dahlia stopped, one hand on a glass, the other holding a pitcher of water mid-air. "Let's not talk of those things, Hasan," she answered solemnly. "I've chosen to let it go because it's not my place to judge; what's done is done and I meant what I said that day about moving forward. As a nation and as individuals. I cannot bear to think on it anymore."

Hasan nodded in understanding. "The trials are almost over. They will not call you as a witness. Artashir has testified that you were ignorant of the on-goings of your father's regime. Do you wish to know the outcome of the trials?"

Dahlia shook her head. "I am finished with that. I hope that the people's judgment will bring closure for those that were hurt most by my father's regime, but I have found a different kind of healing." She smiled at Hasan. "Perhaps we can speak of that one day. I have learned so much in the past few months—good things, things that have restored me!"

Hasan nodded. "I can tell. You're not the same Dahlia I knew last fall. It would appear that you blossomed in the desert this winter. Dahlia, our Desert Rose." He smiled mischievously. "I'm not the only one who's noticed, either."

"What do you mean?"

"I had a visitor last week, a concerned individual who was checking up on you."

"Saran? But, why didn't he stop . . ."

"Not Saran." Hasan laughed. "Ibrahim. He came under the guise of wanting to check up on a local school he helped start, but I think there was a more personal interest involved."

Dahlia flushed. "Oh, I feel so terrible about that. He never wants to see me again!"

"Really?" Hasan sounded surprised. "Is that what he told you?"

"Well, not exactly; he said he wanted to give me space to heal."

"Poor lad, he must feel terrible for his involvement in your father's . . ." Hasan couldn't bring himself to speak the word.

"No, Hasan," Dahlia cried, "for what my father did to his family!" Her chest heaved as she remembered again the look of pain on his face that day. "Every time he looks at me, he's reminded of it!" She couldn't hold the sobs back any longer.

"No, no, child," Hasan comforted her. "It's not like that. I'm sure of it!"

She shook her head wildly. "It is! You had to have seen his face . . ." She wiped her eyes with a linen napkin, then set it down in frustration.

Hasan patted her hand. "He asked about you. Did I tell you that? He wanted to know how you were, if I had checked up on you yet, if you might need anything that he could provide. He seemed very concerned for your well-being."

Dahlia sniffed. "Really?"

Hasan smiled thoughtfully. "Perhaps the two of you will become friends yet. I suppose only time will tell. After all, it would seem your futures are somewhat bound by the circumstances our nation faces. Have you considered that?"

Dahlia's red-rimmed eyes stared back at him.

"Dahlia, you nominated him to be the next leader of our country, and now the people want you there throughout the electoral process. Haven't you thought of that?"

She shook her head, her eyes growing wide.

Hasan laughed. "It may be a moot point. Ibrahim has his fingers in a lot of stews right now, and the best that I can tell, his heart is torn between honoring your wishes that he lead and continuing in the work that he has been doing these past ten years."

"I hadn't thought about that. His work is very important! I suppose I thought he could lead by example, showing our country how to restore itself throughout the rebuilding process."

"Yes, but there is a lot more to be done by our first elected leader; there will be a government to establish, a constitution to write, offices to be filled, accountability to be set in place. We've fought so hard to have this chance to start over. The first leader cannot fail; we have to get it right the first time. That's a lot of weight to put on one man."

Dahlia nodded. Her eyes gleamed in the candlelight. "It's exciting, though, isn't it? We are witnessing the birth of a new nation!"

Hasan raised his glass. "To a new nation."

"A new nation," Dahlia echoed as they clinked their glasses.

Chapter 33

THE TRIP TO Anazir went smoothly—a well-planned, concise visit that allowed Dahlia and Aalim to slip in and out again unnoticed. They met briefly with Saran, passing off the necessary documents he had requested. Then, he prepped Dahlia for the short broadcast she would make.

"Just speak to the people as you did before, Dahlia. They love you, and you are the only voice they trust right now. Remind them that what we are undertaking as a nation is bigger than one man can bear; it is critical that they inform their elected representatives of their provincial needs and plans so that our elected leaders can best provide for them in the future. We don't want any one area to feel as if their voice hasn't been heard in the upcoming election process."

Dahlia nodded, taking rapid mental notes. She could already feel the perspiration breaking out in beads on her lip. "What if I don't know what to say?"

Saran took her hand in his. "Just speak the truth. Don't make promises we can't keep. The people need to know that this is going to be a very arduous task for our new leaders and that they will do their best to take all of the people's concerns into consideration. We'll all do the best we can, won't we?"

She nodded, heart fluttering. She thought of Sister Chan and how she would never have the opportunity to help the people of her home country. This was Dahlia's chance to make a difference, to help her own people. "Why do they trust me?" she whispered.

"Dahlia, the people are thirsty for peace. They need someone who can lead them to it. It doesn't matter why; it only matters that you help them find it by working together. That's the key. We must put aside our differences and work together."

"What if they won't, Saran? What if the people won't work together?" She remembered the people in her dream, crawling toward the stream of living waters and yet unable to drink from it.

"We have to try. And I believe they will listen to you. You have become a symbol of hope for them, like a shard of light in the darkness. You can be the catalyst, the agent of change we've all been waiting for. It's a gift you've been given—embrace it, use it. Your people await your voice."

Following the broadcast, Aalim and Dahlia drove to the home where Ghizlan was staying. They quickly collected her things and left, not wanting to draw attention to themselves. Once on the road again, brother and sister began to gush enthusiastically, full of questions about each other's lives since they'd last been together.

"I have waited so long for this day!" Ghizlan cried, unable to contain her excitement any longer. "When I heard that you had found us a home, I could hardly believe it!" She shook her head, tearing up. "Mama would be so happy. How I wish she were here!"

Dahlia sat quietly in the backseat, allowing them to catch up with one another. They had a lot of ground to cover after three years of separation. Her own mind wandered to the broadcast and she rolled the words over and over again in her mind, searching for anything she could have said better. *Did I cover it all*, she wondered. *Did the people understand the role they must play in the coming reconstruction?* She prayed that they would listen and heed her warnings of the danger of divisions and divisive arguments. Such a fragile situation—so long had the people lived in government-imposed isolation from each other, and so strong was the desire for freedom boiling under the surface. Would they now be able to compose a picture of freedom that would be acceptable to all, without damaging the differences and needs of the others? Would they strike a balance of government rule and citizen liberty?

The closer they got to Lamirya, the more her mind wandered to the work ahead of them at Soleado and she quickly forgot the monumental national issues. Pleasant thoughts of cultivating fields and mending rock fences replaced all other worries and soon all she thought of was the meal she planned to cook in celebration of Soleado's new arrival. Dahlia watched the young girl as she talked with her brother about the things she had been learning in school. Ghizlan had a soft voice and gentle nature, interrupted only momentarily by occasional enthusiastic outbursts that revealed a fun-loving spirit. When she laughed, it seemed as if shackles were falling off of her, as if with each burst of laughter Ghizlan was shaking off the sadness that had bound her since her parents' death.

Dahlia couldn't wait to take her to the beach, to chase sandpipers along the water's edge, to show her where to find the best seashells, to sing around a campfire as the waves lapped the shore under a bright, starry sky.

She thought of Ibrahim and how he had looked in the moonlight, sitting on the sand beside her. Perhaps he had been transformed most by the months following her father's assassination. His zeal for reconstruction was legendary and Dahlia couldn't wait to visit the school he had started in Lamirya. Hasan had told her that it was a cutting-edge educational center, focused on architectural design using all of the ingenious techniques Ibrahim had implemented in his efforts to find innovative ways to re-use the broken buildings available. Hasan's grandson Timon was in his second year at the school. The proud grandfather had bragged that Timon had already won an award for reintroducing a traditional thatched roof design, a technique long forgotten in more modern cities. The boy would spend his third and fourth year apprenticing with the team of builders Ibrahim had raised up while working on the many projects he had undertaken around the country.

What a wonderful way for young people to learn about their country, Dahlia thought. *These young people are gaining the valuable experience of serving and working alongside people who are different than themselves yet who are undergoing the same difficulties of rebuilding lives and communities. It's an opportunity to find common ground, to forge relationships and an understanding of one another.*

Dahlia hoped she had done the right thing in nominating Ibrahim. He was involved in such valuable work, but then perhaps he had already proven himself ready for the job ahead by raising up such a team of like-minded builders who could continue the vital work he had begun. Only time would tell if any of them was really ready for the task ahead. She had to heed her own words—to trust that together they could rebuild this country, that they alone could answer the needs of their neighbor and leaning on one another, move forward.

Al Cazar would be a great nation again one day, she could feel it. Her heart believed it, and she would do all she could to help in the efforts. In the meantime, she would pursue the dream God had given her of providing a home to the lost and weary, those misplaced by the war. And, in the sunny fields, they would work the land and grow strong again—physically and emotionally. They would play on the beach and gather around the large table on the terrace celebrating life's joys together. And, perhaps, some would be baptized in the sparkling surf, embracing a new life of faith and hope, learning to lean back in the healing waters and just let go.

"Dahlia?" Aalim's voice snapped her back to the present.

"Yes?"

"Ghizlan wants to know if she can help you fix supper."

Dahlia smiled at the small, shy girl. "Of course you can." She held out her hand for Ghizlan to take. "I've been looking forward to getting to know you for weeks. Aalim and I spent a good bit of time talking about you while we prepared your room. I hope you'll like it." She squeezed Ghizlan's hand. "And I thought we'd make something special tonight, something a friend taught me how to make not too long ago. Then we'll sit under the stars and tell stories. Would you like that?"

Ghizlan nodded.

"Me, too."

The cares and worries of the future faded away as they discussed the evening's meal. They had a homecoming to celebrate; and, with happiness in her heart, Dahlia knew it was only the first of many.

Then the angel showed me the river of the water of life,
as clear as crystal, flowing from the throne of God and of the
Lamb down the middle of the great street of the city.

On each side of the river stood the tree of life . . .
And the leaves of the tree are for the healing of the nations.

. . . They will not need the light of a lamp or the light of the sun,
for the Lord God will give them light.
(Revelation 22:1-5)

⟶▷ ◁⟵

Thank you for reading *Desert Rose,*
the first book in the *Living Water* series.

We want to hear from you.
Please send your comments about this book
to us in care of sra_chill@yahoo.com
Thank you.

For the next book in the *Living Water* series,
and to learn about other books by Carol Hill,
please visit www.CHillPublications.blogspot.com